REGINALD

Rhonda Smailey

REGINALD

Rhonda Mailey

CHAPTER ONE

REGINALD, RAVENS' WOOD, BRITISH COLUMBIA, PRESENT DAY

R eginald licks his cracked, rust-coloured lips as his red eyes track Leah's naked silhouette. The demon's long, thin body lies flat on its stomach at the edge of the grassy verge, his massive head rising like a gargoyle as he surveys her dimly-lit bedroom. Moonlight reveals his wrinkled, crimson flesh streaked with grey scars that criss-cross his scalp and face. His black, cracked talons twitch in excitement. She has no clue how genuinely insignificant she used to be. But now Reginald needs her.

Leah's "Aunt Shirley" played her hand well, he thinks, separating his lips to reveal a mouthful of rotting teeth. Biting down hard enough to make his black blood flow, his entire body shakes in anticipation. The grass ripples in response, flattening and turning pewter under the full moon. Finally, he growls, his raspy, guttural voice spitting out each word like a gunshot: "I'm coming for you. I'm going to steal your heart." He starts a childlike giggle that mutates into a wild, raucous howl.

CHAPTER TWO

LEAH, RAVENS' WOOD, PRESENT DAY: THE INHERITANCE

I f someone had told me I'd move from Vancouver to a tiny seaside town in a few months, I'd have asked them what they were smoking.

I rewind yesterday in my head. Heights and flights scare the bejesus out of me. I'd gulped back a couple of shots of vodka right after takeoff; the heat of the liquor was calming, and it got me through the forty-minute float plane flight to Einer's Bay.

After a white-knuckling, eyes-squeezed-shut, bouncy landing, the pilot reached for my hand, pulled me out of the plane and pointed me to my cab.

There wasn't much to see on the road to my new home, just tall trees, mountains and the occasional overgrown driveway. Fifteen minutes later, the house's classic widow's walk came into view. While striking, there's no doubt the estate Aunt Shirley left to me had seen better days. A Southern plantation-style home holding court in British Columbia's temperate rainforest. Mint julep meets maple syrup; somehow, it works.

***

Today, I stroll the grounds in the soft, warm light of morning. I realize the past month has been like an out-of-body experience, with all the frantic activities leading up to my arrival here. The pinched, incredulous look on my boss's face as I told her I was quitting; the never-ending sorting and packing; the multiple gatherings at the bar to say goodbye, not to mention the soul-crushing hangovers that followed. They'd kept me from stopping to consider what I was running from. And while I ruminate on it constantly, I'm still not entirely clear on that myself.

There was something weird about yesterday's cab driver. He'd kept his head down and avoided eye contact.

"Ma'am?" he called. "Where do you want this bag?"

He was standing at the top of a big wooden staircase. A large and dusty chandelier swayed slightly above my head as I'd climbed.

"Anywhere will do," I recall saying, and tried not to jump when he dropped the heavy bag. I handed him a wad of bills, which he fisted and then hurried down the stairs like something was snapping at his heels.

I stood in shocked silence before turning to drag my suitcase to the bedroom. What the devil had scared him? Opening the bedroom door, I was surprised to see the windows were closed. What would have caused the door to slam shut from the *inside*?

And then, came a sound that made me jump, BANG, BANG, BANG! The cabbie must have forgotten something, but that was no excuse for hammering at the door! I'd raced down the stairs and yanked open the side door.

By the cloud of dust left in his wake, I could tell the driver was long gone. I'd quickly checked around the side of the house, my stocking feet picking up sharp splinters from the wooden deck, but no one was there.

***

I spend most of today putting away my things. The dimming light outside reminds me I should get settled before it gets too dark. I decide it was probably some mischievous kid who'd almost knocked my door down yesterday. But still, it was unnerving.

***

The stairs to the basement's wine cellar are narrow and uneven stone, but well-lit. Halfway down, I freeze. It sounds like something is sliding along a wall. My hands have the banisters in a death grip and I take a slow, deep breath to calm down. The noise has stopped but I wait a few seconds just in case. Probably a mouse.

***

The sun has almost set by the time I stop to rest. I drop down into the sofa in the living room and sip my Merlot. My hand shakes as I raise my glass and toast Shirley for leaving this remarkable estate to me. I still can't believe she's gone. The grief hits me in waves, and I can go from calm to bawling my eyes out, just like that. It helps to be here. It's comforting to be in her home, surrounded by things she loved.

But the quiet is oppressive. As a city girl, I'm used to the omnipresent, white noise of heavy traffic, blaring horns and airplanes soaring overhead. I'm feeling a bit strung out and missing the grounding routine of my regular life.

Something unpleasant settles in my stomach, and I recognize it at once; I'm already homesick.

***

I secure all the ground-floor doors and windows. Frequent rainstorms have made some windows swollen and hard to shut. The final one is proving to be difficult and as I pull hard to close the latch, I flinch away from a distorted, red face on the other side of the glass. Falling backward, I land hard on the floor, my eyes searching desperately to see who is there, but they're gone. I lurch for the window and jam the bolt home.

Reginald hasn't had such a good laugh in decades. The expression on Leah's face was priceless. His whoops of joy startle the animals in the forest but the nasty snicker trickling out of his nose and mouth now is even more terrifying. It isn't a long walk to his lair at the back of her property, but he opts for a slow stagger home. The nauseating stench of burning sulfur follows in his wake.

***

I'm still quivering as I return to the blue-themed bedroom. It's so cold I can see my breath. I turn up the heat and grab the blue blanket that's draped over the chair.

Sighing, I try to settle on the bed. The house is completely silent for several minutes; I must have seen my reflection. Shaking my head at my frayed nerves, I grab a white pillowcase and pull out a soft, brown cushion, holding onto it like it's a lifeline. Tears soak the sheets, but I don't care. I inhale Mike's essence, click off the light and try to settle deeper into the bed, my entire body wrapped tightly around the pillow. After a crazy replay of the past few days, I finally fall asleep.

SCRITCH, SCRITCH ...

Something wakes me up. The hair on the back of my neck is raised and I'm shivering from the damp, cold air in this room. The dark is thick.

My neck strains as I lift it to hear the sounds that woke me up, but the house's silence mocks me.

Wait. There's something. A scratching noise like a branch scraping a window. *Scritch, scritch.*

It's stopped again—replaced by the steady hammering of my heart. I'm rigid for a good ten minutes before I allow myself to relax. Now comes the worst part; do I get up and explore or try to sleep? My heavy lids close once again. The investigation will have to wait.

The rosy gold of early-morning light blushes on the damp grass outside the kitchen window. I can visualize Shirley in this sun-splashed kitchen. All the little knick-knacks, her puppy-themed tea cozy, the framed photo of Times Square and the curious mix of utensils poking out of an old, wooden apple bucket. Shirley loved to cook.

A flush of emotions washes over me. I miss her. It never mattered that we weren't blood relatives as we were family by choice. She was Mom's best friend from childhood, and while we never met in person, she understood me better than any "real" relative I've ever known. When Mom died, Shirley kept me from falling apart.

Now I find myself in the middle of nowhere, in a tiny town with a huge house and property to take care of.

I head up the stairs for a shower and I hear a muffled sound, like something has fallen.

As I round the corner to enter my room, my hand flies to my mouth. Mike's pillow is now on the floor, on the opposite side of the room. The windows, which were wide open when I left, are now shut tight. I wrap my arms around my body as fear rushes up my spine.

CHAPTER THREE

REGINALD, RAVENS' POND, LOUISIANA, THE PAST

Reginald wasn't born a demon. He came into this world like any other child, with the potential for good and evil. But when his mother died giving him birth, fate carved a darker path.

When Reginald's father, William, received the terrible news, his face twisted in agony and his wails drowned out the cries of his newborn son. In the birthing room, the baby's mother, Helen, was now a waxy shade of ivory.

In the first moments of Reginald's life, there was no one there to delight in those curious, charcoal-coloured eyes. Left alone in a bassinet, his tiny fists punched at an invisible enemy—one that would hound him his entire life.

As Reginald grew, it was clear he had a deep curiosity about life—a trait he shared with his late mother. But they would never have the chance to know their other similarities. Instead, the boy would become a bleak reflection of his damaged father, causing a wound even Reginald's loving older sister, Bridget, couldn't heal.

***

Reginald loved to run away, but no one ever came looking for him. Sprinting through the blistering sun, he'd stop once he hit the shade, bending over to breathe in the swamp's stink and dripping humidity. The swamp was his true home.

He climbed up slippery mangrove trees, scrambling out of the fetid water when he fell, constantly on the lookout for gators. Reginald always filled the pockets of his perpetually muddy pants with stones to chuck at them, and he took great pleasure in squashing bugs and killing small creatures.

No, Reginald wasn't born a demon, but the dark hollow of his youth made him a perfect vessel.

CHAPTER FOUR

SHIRLEY, EINER'S BAY, BRITISH COLUMBIA, THE PAST

F
our mega-trucks moved with purpose, single file, along the road to Einer's Bay. Their presence was a peculiar sight in this place, especially with their Louisiana license plates. It was early August and the voluminous dust cloud the trucks made could be seen from the highest vantage point in town.

The drivers made one stop at the grocery store, lining up their trucks on the side of the road like train cars. After grabbing water and bags of food, they climbed back into their vehicles, then off they went.

Four months later, the dozen workmen finished construction of the most unusual sight in all of Einer's Bay: the bones of a full on Southern plantation-style estate. Some of the locals knew what was coming because Shirley had informed them shortly after her arrival in May. Flying back and forth between her New York City condo and a friend's guest cabin located close to the building site, she'd kept an eye on the project. She'd made it sound somewhat normal, with her subtle Southern accent.

"My great-uncle Reginald is building a replica of our family's Louisiana mansion," she'd said. "Although that place is a ruin, this will be a grand home."

Some of the locals discussed how her eyes had shifted when she said this. The house, while it might be grand, obviously came with some emotional baggage.

The follow-up punch was she was flying up a crew to complete the exterior. The thought that good local builders would lose out on a decent paycheque did not sit well with the community. Shirley had anticipated this reaction and immediately set out to hire the best local designers and landscapers to do the interiors and gardens. She paid them handsomely and no one complained.

The workers set up outhouses and lived onboard their massive trucks. The locals turned up with their cameras to check out the construction of such an unusual house, but the novelty didn't last long.

Unlike other visitors to the town of Einer's Bay, none of the workers sought out cold beers or burgers at the local pub; they had a shopper named Leslie, who filled her rented SUV to the brim once a week. The grocery store was hard-pressed to keep up with her demands for fresh food. There was no alcohol purchased. Ever.

For the most part, Shirley kept her distance from the site, eventually leaving town for one last two-month stay in New York City. Most thought she'd want a daily say in the building of her mansion. Those who claimed to know her well said she refused to discuss it—family business and all that.

The project finished with little ceremony. The only sign of the crew's departure was another thick dust cloud outside the town limits, exactly four months after the first dust cloud had appeared.

Shirley moved into her new home at "Ravens' Wood" and life returned to a semblance of normalcy in Einer's Bay.

Reginald

CHAPTER FIVE

ADRIENNE, EINER'S BAY, PRESENT DAY: A NEW OUTLOOK

Adrienne locks up the front door of her home and hurries to her blue Toyota Rav 4, heels clicking in a steady rhythm as she makes her way to the car.

She flips up the rear-view mirror to check her look. Having just lost forty pounds as she recovered from her heart attack, it seems horribly unfair that she now has an abundance of new wrinkles, stretching out from her eyes when she smiles and making strange pouches at the sides of her mouth. She'd hoped changing her lipstick from her signature bright red to something more subdued might soften her look, but her quick appraisal confirms what she feared: no such luck.

Jim, Adrienne's husband, is thrilled—not by the weight loss itself, but by the health benefits that go along with it. Now a passionate hiker at sixty-two, Adrienne has regained and vastly improved her health. The new wardrobe doesn't hurt either. She smiles, taps the rear-view mirror shut, and heads off.

Adrienne is so eager to meet Leah that it's been keeping her up at night. That in itself is a blessing. The night before, she woke up to find herself sleepwalking down the slippery grass field that led to the marina. Jim would have had a heart attack himself if he'd seen that. He keeps threatening to put a big cow bell around her neck, which she doesn't find funny. But that's just Jim, Adrienne thinks as she cranks up the tunes. Even though she tells him repeatedly that sometimes people don't appreciate his unique perspective on things, he just howls with laughter and adjusts his hat of the day.

She's pretty sure these nocturnal walkabouts are because of Shirley's death and Leah's arrival; she and the other five Guardians of Einer's Bay intend to get in front of things before anything else happens. Their already scheduled get-together will give them a better sense of Leah's character and whether she intends to remain in town, as well as assess any potential threats to the people of Einer's Bay. Lips tight, Adrienne feels a combination of anxiety as well as a sense of pride. There've been protectors of the town for over a century and she takes her role as one of them very seriously.

**

Someone is tapping at the side door of the house.

I open the door to see a woman of medium build, her dark, grey-streaked hair tumbling onto broad shoulders.

She smiles and reaches in to give me a hug, which I return.

"Welcome to Einer's Bay!" She pauses, her nose sniffing. "I hope you found the food I left for you in the fridge, and you obviously found the coffee!"

"I can't thank you enough. I was starving by the time I got settled. Can I pour you a coffee or a cup of tea?" I ask, gesturing to the puppy-themed teapot cozy.

Adrienne's face falls as tears start to tumble. I quickly grab a tissue and place it in her trembling hand.

Turning her back on me, she says, "I'm sorry, Leah. It's just that Shirley's puppy tea cozy brought it all home. No more long chats over a pot of tea."

Adrienne apparently knows her way to the powder room, and she comes back looking refreshed, but her shoulders are bowed and her eyes heavy. Stopping to pour herself a mug of black coffee, we both take a deep breath and sit down at the kitchen table. We share a comfortable silence as we get our thoughts together. She breaks the quiet.

Speaking softly, she says, "We were all shocked when we heard you were accepting the inheritance. We thought, 'What kind of nutcase leaves the city for this piece of nowhere?' The house and grounds are lovely, but do you really understand how boring it is here? From what Shirley told me, you love your career and have an exciting social life in the city."

"You're not the first to question my decision," I respond, slinking down in my chair. "I'd be lying if I said I haven't been asking myself that question every day since I opened the mail and read what Shirley left me." I stare down at the table for a moment, then continue. "I made my decision to accept it relatively quickly. At this point, I'm not sure if I'm running away from something, or toward it."

Adrienne tilts her head to one side. Her big, brown eyes flecked with gold stare intensely at me.

Reaching manicured hands to mine, she says gently, "Just give yourself time, Leah. You've only just arrived."

"Aunt Shirley talked about her group of friends in Einer's Bay and said you all knew how to have a good time," I say, eyebrows raised. As I speak these words, my mind replays the many clips of conversation we had about her friends here. They were important to her.

She pauses, and her smile fades. "Why had you never met Shirley in person? I asked her once, and she just smiled and changed the subject."

A large flock of black starlings darts by, and we both turn to watch.

"I have no suitable answer for that, Adrienne," I mumble. Tears pool in my eyes as she reaches over to pat my hand.

"Don't worry about that now, Leah. We can talk about it when you're ready."

We move on to a less emotionally-charged conversation about the town I now live in. An hour later, I'm up to speed on the goings-on of Einer's Bay. The residents range from hippies to people who are trying to escape the big cities for a more peaceful environment. Many of the families settled in Einer's Bay over a century ago, drawn by the fur trade and employment at the town's then thriving sawmill.

Adrienne sounds like a travel agent as she rambles through a description of my new hometown.

"Now catering to tourists in search of adventure, E.B.—that's what us locals call it—is a town of two thousand. We have a pub called The Sundowner, a grocery store, a library, hardware store, hair salon, pharmacy, bookstore, medical and dental clinic, liquor store and a gas station," she says, pausing to take a deep breath.

"The lone restaurant is a humble greasy spoon, and guests in town have their choice of two bed-and-breakfasts and a boutique hotel. Summer sees more activity with cruise ships, boaters, fishermen and those in search of a true wilderness adventure. Winter is isolating and bloody cold," she says, slapping both hands on the table.

Adrienne checks her watch, pulls the chair back and stands, "I have to get going, but before I do, I need to tell you something," she says, her lips pursed.

"I'm listening," I respond, brows furrowed.

Adrienne pauses to check over her shoulders should someone be listening. "There's been weird things happening in this place for a while now. Carcasses of animals found in the forest," she says, nodding toward the backyard.

"Isn't that kind of normal?" I ask, leaning forward.

Adrienne pauses and shoves the chair back under the table. She walks toward the side door, stops and waits for me to catch up.

"Leah, we're not talking about normal predator-versus-prey killings," she says, turning to look at the thick forest that surrounds the mansion. "These animals were torn to shreds. We're used to coming across dead wildlife in our forests but nothing like this," she says, turning back to face me, her hands clenched tightly. "Our wildlife officers say they've never seen anything so savage," she says, grabbing my forearm.

Recalling the less than normal goings-on in my new home, I feel the tightness in my chest start to twist. All at once, she lets go, smiles and opens the door. Pausing, she turns.

"I'm concerned about you out here by yourself. Shirley spent a lot of her time in New York, and she brought friends to stay when she was spending more than a week here."

Adrienne pauses again.

"She always said she was less than comfortable in this house by herself. I'll text you our contact info. Call me if you run into any trouble; Jim and I are only ten minutes up the road. Oh, and I'd love for you to join us for one of our weekly hikes, once you're settled."

She turns to leave, her heels clicking toward her car.

I watch as her blue SUV speeds up the driveway and disappears over the hill. Stealing a quick glance at the mansion behind me, I'm starting to wonder what fresh hell it contains and why Shirley chose to give it to me. There's no logical explanation for some of the things going on in Ravens' Wood. The vivid memory of Mike's pillow ending up on the other side of the bedroom leaves me with a feeling of dread.

***

Reginald awakens to the gush of black starlings. Their inky wings cover the demon's bloated red body from horns to talons as they swoosh into his lair. One by one, they drop crushed insects into his gaping jaw, some of them still flicking as they tickle down his throat. The beast is temporarily sated.

***

Adrienne kicks off her blue heels and returns them to their little shoe stalls. Jim thought building them for her would be a fun project, and it was handy having the rack right in the entrance closet. But it's taken him about a year to complete, which means he's wasted a ton of time while ignoring more important things like relocating the family of racoons in the garden shed or tracing the source of the nocturnal banging noises that erupt from the decrepit furnace every night.

Sighing, Adrienne bends down to pick up her hiking clothes. Pulling her yellow dress over her head, she replays her chat with Leah. Even though it was brief, she enjoyed their visit. Leah has a way of gripping your attention; you know for sure she's taking in what's being said.

Adrienne pauses for a moment, closes her eyes and allows the tension she's been trying to suppress to come forth. Something bad is going to happen; the Guardians need to get up to speed, and soon.

The first thing she sees when she opens her eyes is a pair of her black hiking slacks with flecks of mud all down one side.

"What the hell?" she says. Holding up her pants for inspection, she sees they're still dirty from her last trek. "This is Jim's fault," she fumes, jamming her feet into her pants and stretching her arms into her bright green thermal hiking top. What's the point of taking turns at laundry if only one of us actually does it?

Socks on, shoes tied, Adrienne grabs her backpack, gives it a quick once-over for supplies, seizes her water bottle, and snaps it onto the side of her pack. She takes hiking seriously, and while it's something she loves to do, she also has great respect at how unforgiving nature can be.

Locking the front door, she pulls her car fob out of her pocket and turns around.

"Oh my god," she whispers, raising a tight fist to her nose.

Her lawn has turned from green to black. There must be over sixty ravens and crows cloaking the grass. This is an anomaly as crows usually gang up on ravens, as long as they outnumber them. Adrienne slowly withdraws her cellphone from her pocket and films a few seconds of this odd comradery. As the gurgles, caws, rattles and clucks grow louder and more intense, she takes a deep breath to steady and finish her shot. Returning her phone to her pocket, she hugs her backpack like a shield as she watches the birds peck at something. Worms? she wonders.

"What the hell is going on here! Shooo!" yells Jim.

The Einer's Bay Marina baseball cap on his head tells Adrienne he's just returning from hours of tinkering on the twenty-foot scow he promises will one day be a fine yacht. When pigs fly, she thinks as she shakes her head. She tosses her backpack into the passenger seat of her car and jumps in as he rushes up the driveway, waving his arms at the crows and ravens, with little effect.

CHAPTER SIX

LEAH, RAVENS' WOOD, PRESENT DAY: THE SHATTERED GLASS

I shrug on my heavy winter sweater. Autumn is transforming to winter and now is as good a time as any to do a full survey of the front yard. Checking out the planters at the front of the house, I notice someone has taken out the remains of the decaying annuals. Raking the soil with my hand, I feel the earth is loose.

Thankfully, I won't have to break out the lawnmower—the inheritance includes a stipend dedicated to the preservation of the home and grounds. Looking up at the house, I'm impressed by its old-world grandeur. It's a classic design, and the windows reflect the greenery before it, giving the illusion of seamlessness.

The sudden quacking of ducks startles me. Chuckling, I forgot I changed my ringtone just before I left Vancouver. It seemed more appropriate for rural Einer's Bay. I haven't heard it quack since I left the city.

"Hello," says a deep male voice. "May I please speak to Leah?"

"This is Leah."

"It's Randall Bertram, one of Shirley's attorneys," he says, clearing his throat with so much force that I pull the phone away for a moment. "I'm checking in to make sure everything is in order at the estate."

"Yes, everything's just fine, thank you. Adrienne came by this morning; thanks so much for arranging that."

"My pleasure. And of course—Adrienne is one of the town's trusted Guardians. I'm so pleased things have worked out. Shirley was very specific in her desire for you to live there. It was the one thing she was adamant about." And with that, he abruptly ends the phone call.

What did he mean by *Guardian*? I ask myself. Just as I touch the disconnect button on my phone, the air splinters into a million pieces with a crash as loud as a hundred cymbals. Holy shit! What the hell was that?

The echo of the crash still reverberates as I turn the corner to the side of the house. I see what's happened: a window from the top floor has come loose. Its frame lies twisted on the cement walkway below, glass shattered into a giant spiderweb. I pluck my feet up and dance quickly out of range.

A strange sound from above draws my attention. As I look up, I see something from the now-gaping hole on the second floor. It's a thick darkness, a grainy, moving shape that vanishes when I blink.

CHAPTER SEVEN

LEAH, RAVENS' WOOD, PRESENT DAY: THE HANDYMAN

Adrienne recommends a local handyman and soon he's knocking on my side door, ready to fix the hole where a window used to be. Josh is a good-looking guy, easily over six feet, with unruly dark-blond curls, warm brown eyes and big hands. He wears a white T-shirt and a worn, dark-brown leather tool belt stuffed with everything from screwdrivers, pencils, a cellphone, industrial file, measuring tape, heavy-duty scissors, gaffer's tape and a most unlikely circle of lollipops. He spins a bright yellow one in his mouth.

Despite his height advantage, he can't seem to resist going up on his toes to check out the inside of the house. One would be curious about such a place, I imagine.

"Come on in. I'm Leah," I say. He hands me a red sucker.

Josh follows me upstairs to the scene of the event. Is it just me, or is it distinctively cooler at this end of the hallway? The window in question is now a hole letting in the soft autumn wind, so I guess that makes sense.

Josh puts his toolbox down and surveys the damage, his thick eyebrows pulling together in a tight stitch.

"This is weird," he says, giving me a curious look.

"Tell me about it. I just about jumped out of my skin when it came crashing to the ground. Thankfully, there was no one under it. Any idea of why it committed windowcide?"

Cracking an enormous smile that reveals perfectly aligned white teeth, Josh steps closer to the open window.

"Windowcide. That's funny!" he says as he slips on work

gloves, cautiously running his hands around the window's frame, checking for glass. His frown returns. "I've never seen anything like this. It's clean around the edges, as if someone cut it free in one stroke. But the good news is, it will be easy to replace. I have something in the truck that should do the trick—be right back."

After noticing Josh looks just as good walking away in his tight, washed-out blue jeans as he did coming toward me, I turn my head and move to the edge of the window, surveying the damage from this angle. I try to block out the disturbing memory of the shifting grainy darkness I saw standing exactly where I am now. My eyes sweep the horizon. Trees and more trees, except for a small pathway that starts around the back of the house. It meanders along a row of purple heather for a short while, then appears to lead to a small building. I definitely have to check that out.

CHAPTER EIGHT

LEAH, RAVENS' WOOD, PRESENT DAY: THE DRIVE

I won't say that sparks are flying by the time Josh has repaired my window, but there's an attraction there, and our banter is easy and comfortable. When he shakes my hand on his way out, he holds it—and my gaze—for just a little longer than is socially acceptable for new acquaintances. Somehow, we've arranged a date for tomorrow. I surprise myself—I probably don't need to get involved with anyone right now, and he's considerably younger than me. Ah well, I tell myself with a shrug, it's just a glass of wine.

I spend the remainder of the morning snooping around the property, and soon discover the woodshed and bring in some dry kindling for the fire. After the unnerving occurrences in the blue guest room, I decide to switch over to the yellow room. Its larger windows let the light flood in far more than the blue room.

Once I've moved, unpacked my clothes and toiletries and gotten Mike's pillow all tucked in safely, I decide it's time to take a ride into town for supplies. I need to stock the kitchen.

Car fob in hand, I follow the small brick pathway to the coach house. Aunt Shirley's champagne-coloured Lexus looks brand new.

I haven't owned a car since my university days because I could always walk or take public transit to any appointments. That was the best part of living downtown. I thought I'd feel stressed by all the noise and constant flow of people—and I was, at first. Weekend getaways to Mom's home on Pender Island always seemed to reset me, but by the time my vacation was done, I began to long for the pulse of the city. In or out of a relationship, I always had my friends and co-workers to fall back on. Now, being way out in the middle of nowhere, the only person I can rely on is myself.

I slip into the Lexus and start it up. Takes me a minute to engage navigations to the town and I'm on my way.

The road to town is two tight lanes, bordered by farms. I think I see a fat pink pig trotting along the opposite side of the road, but I could be mistaken.

For every farm that appears to be thriving with tables of produce for sale and cars coming and going, there's a boarded-up house and long-dead grass. It's an interesting contradiction.

After about twenty minutes, the town reveals itself in clustered buildings—some tall, some short, some brick, some panelled. A quick tour helps me locate a small strip mall with a hair salon, shoe store, bookstore, pharmacy, coffee shop and, just up to the right of the strip mall, a pub. The weathered and cracked Sundowner sign hangs precariously, creaking loudly as it moves back and forth in the breeze. A single car putters through the parking lot but it appears to be full. The Tudor-style pub looks quaint if a little worse for wear with its faded black-and-white arches. I'll check the pub out another time, I tell myself. But for now, I need supplies.

***

The Lexus is now loaded with liquor and groceries from Willie's Market. I start the car, exit the small parking lot and turn on the car radio. Fumbling around and keeping my eye on the road, I'm not having success tuning in anything.

I give up and turn off the radio. Expecting silence except for the sound of passing cars, I'm surprised to hear a hissing sound coming from the radio. I know I turned it off. I shake my head in confusion as the noise grows louder. When I push the power button hard, something snakes out of the side of the radio and grabs my hand! I slam the brake and pull over to the skinny dirt path on the side of the road. I shriek in terror at the sight of a large red spider encasing my right hand.

I open the driver's door with my left hand and fall hard to the asphalt below. The spider is now squeezing my fingers so viciously that I scream in pain. The creature has wiry legs and a large head. The bulbous ugly face is pinched, and as it opens its scarlet mouth to bite, I scream and smash it again and again on the ground. It doesn't budge. I hear the sound of a car door slamming just behind where I've fallen.

"Are you ok?" asks the young man standing on the ground beside me. "Do I look ok to you?" I screech in his face, raising my right hand so he can see for himself. He frowns and tilts his head.

"I'm not sure what I should be looking at, ma'am. There's nothing on your hand."

CHAPTER NINE

LEAH, SHIRLEY'S STUDY, RAVENS' WOOD, PRESENT DAY: THE SCRITCHING

My hands are still shaking from the spider event. The little monster must have scuttled away right before my rescuer arrived. I've just filled up my second large glass of Merlot and it's helping me calm down.

I'm finally ready to enter Shirley's study. Memories of the countless times she'd call or video chat from there are at once calming and sad. I know it will be hard to sit in her chair; even the thought of checking out her books and desk drawers feels like an invasion of her privacy. But I also know she'd want me to get comfortable in what she used to call her haven.

From the time I was a child, I've always longed for a study like Shirley's. Cherry-coloured bookshelves, deep tobacco-coloured leather chairs and the black walnut desk with intricate pulls that desperately need some brass cleaner. As I search through her library for just the right title, my hand strokes the spine of each book, and I revel in their uniqueness. Some are new and others are weathered and antique.

My hand stops at a burgundy, leather-bound book with gold lettering that says dollhouse: The Sad Story of a Missing Child. I gently release it from its place on the shelf and settle back in my chair. The brass lamp sets the pages alight.

The book was published in 1945 and the author is Winnifred MacLean. There's a hand-drawn sketch on the cover that looks to be an outbuilding converted into a playhouse. Toys litter the foreground outside the window, and the pale silhouette of a little girl holding a lantern in one hand and a toy in the other appears inside the house.

I'm getting a bad feeling about this particular book, though I can't put my finger on why. As I close it, a slip of paper slides out to my knees. It's some kind of receipt; a delivery slip for a building labelled as the "dollhouse" shipped from Louisiana to Ravens' Wood in 2013. Aunt Shirley had mentioned the arrival of a new outbuilding to her property, and she wasn't thrilled about it. Something about this building upset her.

I tried my best to press her as to why this addition made her uncomfortable, but the closest I got was she associated it with some terrible memories. Chewing hard on the inside of my cheek, I replace the receipt and put the book aside, click off the table lamp and slowly sip my wine by the light of the fire in Shirley's office. Before I realize what's happening, I start to doze.

Scritch, scritch...

With a start, I jerk up to find I'm still in the study. What's that sound? How long have I been here? It's almost pitch-dark outside and there's no light inside since the fire died out long ago. I reach my hand up toward the lamp on the desk, only to collide with cold brass. The switch turns, but there's no light. Great.

Candles! I remember seeing a supply of emergency candles in the pantry. I slip down the hallway toward the back of the house, assisted by the light of the full moon streaming through the downstairs windows.

SCRITCH, SCRITCH, SCRITCH ...

This time it's louder—so loud I freeze as a scream rips from my throat. What the hell is going on? I'm about to bolt out the side door when lights flood the house. Since the electricity is back on, now everything seems back to normal.

Shaken, I wait to see what will happen next. I almost want the noise to occur again so I can locate the source. I need it to be something normal. Something natural. Something Josh can fix.

CHAPTER TEN

LEAH, RAVENS' WOOD, PRESENT DAY: THE WATER DREAMS

My night is long and filled with dreams. Painful, disjointed, heart-wrenching, disturbing dreams. The Salvador Dalí night of dreams. No big mystery considering the abrupt change of scenery and the weird sounds in the night.

I saw a therapist once, years ago. She lived in an older Tudor-style mansion in a place called Shaughnessy—old Vancouver money. I was fighting occasional depression, still grieving over the loss of my dad.

Rashinda, the therapist, was in her seventies at the time; she wore her long, grey hair swept up in a bun, skewered with a lacquered chopstick. She unwound me like a coil of string that had become hopelessly tangled. We discussed dream therapy, and she told me I would know the state of my subconscious mind by the condition of the water in my dreams.

And so my water dreams began. The water was a roiling, black frightening force in the beginning. Then it transformed to a frozen curl that I walked along, like an arctic balance beam. As our time together progressed, the water became calmer and clearer.

Rashinda thought my progress had been tremendous—from a terrifying brown tidal wave to a sweet stream in about eight weeks. Then, a while later, came the setback. Since I had already concluded my sessions with her, Rashinda seemed slightly surprised to hear my voice on the phone asking for another appointment. I can still remember her soft voice, brushed with the hint of an accent, as she promised to clear her calendar for the next morning. Another terrible and suppressed memory had clawed its way to my consciousness. It would seem my time with Rashinda was not over yet.

**

It was a typical grey morning in Vancouver as I arrived the next day by bus. I took a deep breath and knocked softly on Rashinda's massive, wooden front door. She let me in and ushered me to her office. She was wearing a beautiful indigo sari with a shiny trim that trailed as she walked, polishing the floor and leaving little bits of silver sparkle in her wake.

The next couple of hours are vague in my memory. Rashinda told me after the session she had unveiled some dreadful memories and permanently erased them from my consciousness. The parts I remember are gruesome enough. Now, the memories that remain are like watching a scary movie instead of a vivid and personal replay of what he did to me.

In this movie of the mind, I'm attending university. The scene begins with me walking along the rose garden path to the school building, my mind busy with thoughts of unfinished homework and what ferry I would catch to Pender Island that Friday. Back then, I had made an effort to visit my family home in the Gulf Islands weekly, whenever possible.

It was still daylight, but not for long. The rest of the scene is now a blur, but certain details remain: his height, his strength, his hairy forearm going around my neck, his putrid breath, his filthy hand slapped hard over my mouth, his knee as he pushed me face-first to the rough ground below.

Kneeling hard in the small of my back, I felt his hand struggling to open my backpack. He punched my right side hard and I moaned in agony. Finally, I felt my laptop pop free. I lay still, waiting to hear his footsteps as he took off. I was about to turn my head when he kicked me with his sharp, pointy shoe. I was breathless and couldn't call out for help. The filthy, cowardly little shit got away with it.

Years later, in the house in Einer's Bay, I'll have a setback even Rashinda would have proclaimed as extraordinary. Tonight, I'll dream I'm drowning in thick, hot, oozing black sludge. There's no water in sight.

***

When morning comes, it's a relief. I'm comforted by the normalcy of waking up with nothing to hear but birdsong. I give Mike's pillow a big hug, then luxuriate in a big, cat-like stretch. I fill my lungs with the fresh air flowing through the open window; it carries a note of winter in its crisp scent.

CHAPTER ELEVEN

AN ENTRY FROM SHIRLEY'S JOURNAL, NEW YORK CITY, THE PAST: REGINALD'S LETTER

Mom passed away six months before I began my studies at NYU. She'd been ill for such a long time. While I missed her and mourned for her, I couldn't be selfish. She was at peace. She left me enough money to attend one of New York's finest schools and a small amount to keep me from starving.

I loved living in the dorm and made lifelong friends there. Having lunch in Central Park, throwing my head back and inhaling all the scents, listening to the different accents from around the globe. It was an exciting time. The theatre, parks, libraries, architecture, dining and shopping; I filled my days with discoveries. I always felt at home there. I wasn't in touch much with my family. Mom's death devastated my relatives, and I reminded them of her so much I had to leave for their sake.

My friends at school had become my new family. I hardly ever thought about Ravens' Pond. Except at night, in my dreams—mixed up stories of Mom, Dad, Grandma Bridget, and Great-Uncle Reginald. I had one repeating dream where I was in the pond looking for Aunt Ruby.

It was always dark as I dove under the surface of the turbid water and found nothing. These dreams were so vivid, I'd wake up with goosebumps all over my body. I didn't find Aunt Ruby, but in one nightmare, I found Great-Uncle Reginald. He was at the bottom of the pond, but he wasn't dead. He was bloated, wearing a black suit and smiling at me as worms gushed from his mouth. I screamed so loudly that I woke up the entire dorm. My nightgown soaked in sweat, my half-asleep roommate handed me a damp towel and dug out a fresh nightie so I could change and try to go back to sleep.

***

I graduated with a master-of-psychology degree, found a place of my own and was setting up my practise when my world ground to a halt.

I'll never forget that day. It was October 13, and rain was bouncing off the streets of New York City. Yellow leaves whirled around, caught in updrafts of wind that made me shiver as I ran. I was soaked to the skin despite my calf-length, bright-blue raincoat, and my umbrella was doing more harm than good, pushing me one way, then almost pulling me off my feet in powerful gusts of wind.

Grabbing the edge of the umbrella with one hand to keep it from launching out of the other, I caught my reflection in a store window. Not a pretty sight. Mascara zigzagged down my cheeks. Dark chunks of wet hair had long since escaped my hood, dripping cold rivulets of water between my breasts.

The flickering light outside the aging walk-up I called home was a relief to see. Stomping my boots on the doormat, I did my best to shake the water from my umbrella. I remember grabbing my mail, thundering up the stairs to the second floor and with a shivering hand, opening the door.

My small apartment was freezing that night. Worried the landlord had shut off my heat again for being an hour late in delivering my rent, I hurried to the thermostat, which registered seventy-two degrees. I could see my breath it was so cold. Something was obviously wrong with the thermostat.

A hot shower later, I remember how good it felt to pull my soft, blue flannel nightgown over my head and step into fluffy, white slippers. While the temperature in the apartment hadn't warmed up much, at least I was dry.

The other clear memory I have is opening the mail. As soon as I saw his handwriting, I froze. I had carefully avoided Great-Uncle Reginald for my entire life and even the thought of opening the letter was repugnant. At twenty-five, I could graduate as a psychologist largely due to the inheritance left to me by my mother. But Great-Uncle Reginald had also contributed.

My hands were trembling as I opened the envelope. The message on the single buff-coloured card was simple: "You must come home to Ravens' Pond. There's a problem with your mother's inheritance. Inside the envelope you will find an airline ticket for a 9 a.m. flight tomorrow. Use it. I will have someone pick you up in New Orleans and drive you to Ravens' Pond. Fondly, Great-Uncle Reginald."

***

The plane ride was uneventful. I didn't recognize the strange man at the airport in New Orleans hoisting up a sign with my name on it. The ride to Ravens' Pond was unsettling, as I relived some terrible memories from my childhood.

***

I didn't see or hear from Great-Uncle Reginald for several days. My basic needs were attended to by a soft-spoken servant named Jenny. I stayed in my room, reading or sleeping, and had very little interest in food.

Jenny tried her best to get me up and out of the house. I took to wandering the grounds after breakfast every morning. The place was a mess. The once-lush gardens were overgrown with weeds, and the pond I once looked forward to seeing every day as a child was now like a swamp. It took me a little while until I could find the courage to go over and see Ruby's statue. Taking a deep breath, I lifted my shoulders and walked slowly to where she had been for decades.

The once-pearly white alabaster was faded to a dull grey. Her eyes looked dim and sad. I reached down and yanked up a chunk of damp moss to clean up the black rivulets of dirt flowing down her head. The sick sensation I had when I first saw the statue all those years ago returned and I quickly stepped away, turned and ran back into the house.

***

Several days went by before Great-Uncle Reginald summoned me downstairs to what had become his office. My palms were sweaty from fear. I had grown considerably in the years away. At twenty-five, I had shed the bonds of childhood and returned as a woman, but the dread of seeing my sinister relative reduced me to a quivering little girl. As I reached the bottom of the stairs, I remember taking a deep breath to calm down.

He, however, had not changed. I had drawn back in disbelief at his unwrinkled skin and those strange, dead, black eyes. He smiled at me and my insides turned to liquid. It was all I could do to not turn and run.

"Shirley," he whispered in a way that chilled my blood. "It's so good to see you again. Why don't you have a seat and we can talk through the problems with the estate?" he gestured with a hideous red hand, his long nails like claws.

I shook my head. There was no way I was going to sit with this monster.

"Please tell me what I need to sign so I can get on with my life," I said, arms crossed.

For the longest time, he just sat there and stared at me with a lopsided grin, drool leaking from the right side of his mouth. I waited a minute or two for his response, then turned and went back to my room.

I waited and waited for him to call for me. My entire life was on hold until I could get this nonsense straightened out and get back to my career in New York. If it wasn't for the money, I would have left on the first day.

***

I grew increasingly impatient for Reginald to give me some answers and decided to move ahead with some of the plans for my clinic. I made a deal to rent space in a New York heritage building, right in The Village. I was excited and eager to get home and set up my practise.

Finally, Jenny said Reginald would come to see me after dinner that night. She said he'd figured everything out about the estate and all he needed was my signature. I paced the floor of my room for hours, it seemed, before giving up and going to bed. It was dark—the moon blanked out by ragged black clouds. The silence—ominous. Where were the night birds? I remember hearing a creak on the stairs, followed by another, then another. Drawing the covers up to my chin—I froze. No breath to give me away.

Something was scratching at the doorknob. I could hear breathing like he was on his knees, polishing the doorknob with his breath. I wanted to scream, but Jenny was gone. Then the breathing stopped—my heart pounding, tiny streams of cold sweat pooling in my belly button—was he there?

CHAPTER TWELVE

SHIRLEY, RAVENS' WOOD, LAST YEAR: THE MANSION

Shirley's trip to and from New York had gone smoothly. Back in Einer's Bay, she paid her driver, got out of the car, retrieved her carry-on luggage and walked to the side door of the house. Before entering, she paused, then pivoted to walk along the deck to the backyard. Sighing, she brought her hand up and shaded her face from the bright sunset.

"Home, sweet home," she said dryly. She dropped to sit on the top of the steps that led to the expansive lawn.

She rested her chin in her right hand and adjusted her dark, gold-rimmed glasses with the left. As a well-known psychologist and author of many books, she recognized the irony of the situation: she needed a shrink, and fast. She closed her heavy-lidded, dark-green eyes and took a deep breath, luxuriating in the pure, cleansing scent of cedar.

At seventy years of age she was in good shape, thanks to her passion for pickleball. When she was home, she played weekly games with her Einer's Bay friends—Patty, Giselle and Adrienne. She smiled at the thought of another rousing game booked for later in the week. In the meantime, she'd be up at first light every morning, driving the fifteen minutes to Einer's Bay Marina, where her little, yellow, wooden runabout awaited her. Nothing calmed her like the hours she spent motoring up the coast in search of quiet bays where she could cut the engine and just drift.

She checked her freshly-dyed strawberry-blond hair in her pocket mirror and then glanced at her watch. The sun would be down soon. She needed to get inside where it was safe.

CHAPTER THIRTEEN

LEAH, RAVENS' WOOD,
PRESENT DAY: THE ATTIC

Morning segues to afternoon, and I busy myself with a deeper inspection of Aunt Shirley's antique desk. I sit in her cracked, faded, dark-brown leather chair, roll it up to the desktop and breathe in. The scent of the leather is mixed with a faint lingering of Chanel perfume. I know it was Shirley's fragrance of choice, but I am still unprepared for the wash of emotion knowing this is the closest I'll ever get to Aunt Shirley in a physical sense. I'll never get to wrap my arms around her, know the texture of her hair or feel the warmth of her hand in mine. As my eyes drop down, I notice several circular water stains on the large tobacco-coloured blotter and consider what was going through Shirley's mind as she sipped her nightly gin and tonic.

There's a framed photograph of Aunt Shirley hanging on the wall beside the window. It's crooked and I take a moment to straighten it. Shirley has her right arm around the shoulders of a young boy. He's trying to smile, but his tightly-stretched, pale lips appear more like a grimace. Shoulders raised, hands clenched, his arms seem pinned by tension at his side. Shirley's head is tilted toward him, her warm-reddish hair flowing over one shoulder. Shirley had told me what an anomaly in her family she was with her copper tresses; a gift from her mom's side of Cajun and Celtic ancestry. This picture appeared to be taken in a professional setting, perhaps in Shirley's clinic based on the office furniture and generic art on the walls.

Although I'm somewhat enjoying the spooky overtones of my new abode, in all reality, I need to find out what's causing the noise. My logical mind tells me it's something mechanical, not supernatural. I'll don overalls and cover every inch of this house. This is my mission for the day. Then, I'll clean up as best as I can and look forward to my date with Josh.

I begin with the attic—though it isn't easy to locate. After several false starts, I find access in the closet of the blue-themed bedroom. It even has a retractable ladder.

I shove the trap door over to one side and climb up so I can stick my head into the hole. A quick click of the flashlight reveals the attic is huge. As expansive as the level beneath it, it appears to be one large space with limited headroom, even for a shorty like me.

Everything in it seems to be in good shape and well-organized. Rubbermaid containers line the walls along with wardrobe racks and stacks of cardboard boxes. Taking a closer look, I see carefully written labels for items like winter clothing, boots and camping gear.

What is that? There's something moving, disturbing the silence of the room. It doesn't sound like a mouse. This is something big shifting around. I gulp and hold my flashlight to my chest like a weapon. I move the beam around the room's perimeter, eyes wide and adrenalin pumping. I'm ready to make a quick dash down the ladder if need be.

There's a form at the periphery of my vision. It's a shroud of fabric, soft in shape and shifting slowly back and forth. Am I hallucinating? Is there a draft? I'm scared, and my hands are shaking, but I need to know. I move one sluggish step at a time, my flashlight fixed on the figure. It continues to move, then suddenly stops.

Reaching out, I tug the faded fabric away from the shape: it's a statue of a child holding a bunch of wildflowers; the style of her dress is from another time. But why did she move? Or am I seeing things? I can't logically answer that question. Her base is wide and even, and there's dry earth around the circle she stands upon. The weathered, red-coloured clay and bits of dead moss cling to the folds. Her hair is long and wavy, much like mine.

Sculpted beautifully, the hair falls gently to slender shoulders. Her eyes, while downcast, are heavy lidded and appear sad. The shape of her eyes, nose and lips is remarkably similar to mine— even her tapered fingers holding the flowers could be my own. Strange, I think, as a chill runs up my spine.

All at once, I understand who this statue represents: Ruby. While my logical mind suggests there must have been other works of art and statues around the property, I somehow know, without a doubt this one is of Ruby. Shirley and I had many conversations of her aunt's mysterious disappearance and the sudden arrival of her statue by the pond. No one ever took credit for the sculpture.

I leave the figure uncovered and pile the cloth to the side. She belongs outside in the garden, but I remember Aunt Shirley clearly stated her wishes in the will: "She cannot leave her place in the attic. Ever."

I leave the attic and make my way to the kitchen for coffee.

***

Later, cup in hand, I open the back door to behold a beautiful sight. The sun is still high in the sky, waning in its warmth but with the brightness of a summer sun.

Off in the distance, toward the line of trees, a man in a red cap is riding a lawnmower. I watch as he turns carefully, creating perfect alleys of cut grass.

An hour later, I hear the clanging of the garage door closing. Even though I'm expecting it, the rapping on the side door startles me.

I hustle to the door, seeing a foggy outline of my gardener through the glass panel. He's shifting his weight from side to side, holding his red cap with both hands. He's much shorter than he appeared on the lawnmower, and countless years in the sun have etched his face.

He avoids eye contact and doesn't bother with small talk.

"This is my last cutting until spring," he says as he shoots a quick look over his right shoulder. "Lawn dies around this time of year."

Slapping his cap back on over sweaty, short, grey hair, he turns his head around for one more look to the side, then heads quickly up the driveway where a black scooter awaits. As the tinny sound of his engine fades away, my shoulders rise, and I'm filled with unease.

CHAPTER FOURTEEN

SHIRLEY, RAVENS' WOOD, SEVEN YEARS AGO: THE DOLLHOUSE

The Louisiana dollhouse was sent from parts unknown and delivered to Shirley's plantation-style house while she was still in New York City. She arrived home shortly after, just as the light was fading.

As she turned the corner leading to the backyard, she stopped abruptly. A nightmare had come to life: the dollhouse stood there in all its foul darkness.

There was something on the door of the dollhouse; Shirley thought it must be packing material as she stepped closer to remove it. But it was an envelope taped to the handle, and it had her name on it. Tentatively, she pulled it off and backed away, the envelope shaking in her hand. She shuddered and hurried back to the safety of the house.

After grabbing her suitcase off the front step, she could barely open the door, her hand was shaking so much. But eventually she heard the click of the lock as it turned. Once inside, she flicked on the lights in the pantry and then ripped open the envelope. All colour drained from her face as she read the message scrawled in red ink:

> *A little welcome home gift, Shirley. I know you'll take good care of her, until I come for you.*
> *—R*

CHAPTER FIFTEEN

LEAH, RAVENS' WOOD, PRESENT DAY: THE DOLLHOUSE

I 've come no closer to discovering the source of the noise. I've had my head down listening attentively to the water heater, furnace, fridge and virtually every other appliance with a plug. Everything is running smoothly and quietly. I've raked through the backs of closets in the basement, ignoring the chills that run along my shoulder blades, and I have again visited the attic. The statue doesn't appear to have moved. I cover her up.

Lunch is a quick tuna sandwich I'd picked up from Willie's Market washed down with iced tea with an extra teaspoon of sugar. Then it's back to the hunt.

Nothing. This leaves me with one other possibility; the source of the noise is outside, not inside the house. Time to walk the perimeter. The outbuilding, which I've decided has to be the "dollhouse" as it's the only other building on the property, is my destination.

The crunch of my shoes on the gravel path echoes through the silent estate. Even the birds sound subdued.

The first thing that strikes me is the age of the dollhouse. The wooden house appears silver, the boards weathered and full of slivers, no doubt. There's no doorknob, and the door hinges squeal open as I push. A blast of frosty air hits my face and I can see my breath. The house has a single, medium-sized window at the front; the faded yellow light of winter illuminates the thick dust on the wooden floor.

There's one room, and it's sparsely equipped with a few pieces of child-sized furniture: a rocking chair, painted red at one time, now faded and peeling badly and a large fabric-covered oblong box on wheels, which seems out of place even for this oddity. A yellow hand-painted sign has fallen to the floor; black, poorly-painted letters spell out DOLLHOUSE.

The walls are bare, with one exception: a painting over the rocking chair. It's a faded scene of a house, much like the one depicted in Aunt Shirley's canvas, but in this painting there's a large pond in front of the house. Puffy clouds dot the sky.

My blood freezes. There, in the far-right corner of the picture, is a dollhouse—*this* dollhouse! Someone has scrawled a faded signature on the bottom of the canvas in the stick-form printing of a child: RUBY.

My knee slams into something unyielding as I turn to escape. Whatever it is, it's draped by a stained, white sheet. I've seen enough. I turn up the path and walk briskly. It's all I can do to stop myself from running.

CHAPTER SIXTEEN

LEAH, RAVENS' WOOD, PRESENT DAY: THE SECOND THOUGHTS

L ater that afternoon, while soaking in the bathtub, I picture myself back in the dollhouse. Suddenly I feel dirty and gritty. I shiver, despite the warm water. There is something unnatural about that place—there's no reason for the dollhouse to be that frigid. Despite my fears, I know I must go back. Though I can't explain why, I know there's someone or something I must confront in there, but I won't go alone.

I get out of the bath, dry off and wrap myself in a bathrobe. Glass of water in hand, I exhale and settle in a high-backed chair in the living room. The reality of my situation is coming into focus now that I'm settled and have a moment to pause. I realize I have acted a little irrationally and out of character.

The months following Mom's death two years ago were excruciating. My boss was incredibly understanding and patient, giving me as much time as I needed to grieve. That last trip to Pender almost undid me. As the ferry doors opened, I breathed in the wash of fresh sea air that normally would have exhilarated me. I couldn't help but see the ghostly figure of my mom, standing right at the top of the hill, waving like crazy, but I knew she wasn't real and would never be there again.

Packing up her things had been agonizing, especially when I discovered the box marked for leah. Perched on the side of her wooden sleigh bed, I struggled to find the strength to open it. Tears tumbled down my face. Mom had her way of organizing little bundles of memories, each tied up in a different coloured ribbon.

I made it through just one before I resealed the box, tucked it under one arm and left. This single box of memories would never listen to my fears, laugh at my terrible jokes or offer words of wisdom. I'd lost my best friend.

When I finally returned to work, I was aware of the stares. I was no longer the confident, driven professional my colleagues once knew.

The inheritance Shirley left me allowed me to run from the grief, thinking somehow I'd find peace in this small rural town. Mike's passing no doubt contributed to my need to flee. I'm finally off the meds, but the stabbing pain of loss is never far away.

***

Standing at the living room window, waiting for Josh to pick me up, I feel like a captain's wife who longs for her man to return from the sea. I realize the pain of losing precious loved ones isn't something you can alleviate by running away. Catching my gaze in a glass picture frame, I see my eyes reflected back—puffy and bloodshot from one glass too many last night. I'm tired... so tired. I realize I'm probably not going to be the best companion for Josh this evening.

Scritch, scritch ...

"You've got to be kidding," I mutter when I hear that weird sound again. My hands shake, spilling water out of the glass I'm holding and onto the hardwood floor. Now I hear a car approaching. Perfect—I'll have a witness!

I place the glass on the table and hurry to the front door as headlights advance. Josh looks at me through the windshield, puzzled by my rapid approach. He hurries to get out of the car.

"What's the matter, Leah?" he says, grabbing my arms which are hugging myself tightly as my shoulders crunch up.

"There's a noise! You have to hear it!" Yanking open the front door, I pull him in behind me and put my finger to my lips to indicate we need to stay silent.

At first, there's nothing. My mind races. He'll think I'm crazy, I think. Then the sound comes back.

Scritch, scritch ....

"What the heck is that?" he asks, brown eyes wide, brows pinched.

"No clue," I answer. "But it's been frightening me since I arrived and I need it to stop."

And it does. Just like that.

Josh moves quickly through the house. "It definitely came from the upper level," he yells. "Where's the access to the attic?"

It doesn't surprise me that we end up there.

"Up through the first bedroom at the top of the stairs," I say, trying to catch up to him.

By the time I do, he's already in the closet, up the ladder, penlight in hand.

"Don't you have any electricity up here?" he asks.

"I couldn't find a switch when I was up here earlier."

We both scramble up into the attic. The light is minimal as twilight falls. We can see shapes and the floor, but the shadows are deepening by the moment; it's getting dark.

Josh cocks his head to listen.

"That scritching sound," I whisper. "It's gone."

"Wait, what's that?" he asks, heading for the statue of the girl. I walk behind him, our footsteps soft and shuffling on the bare wood floor.

"Wow," he breathes. "She's haunting."

What an odd choice of words, I think. Josh moves closer, using his penlight to illuminate the entire length of the figure.

"Where did this come from and what's it doing in here?"

"I don't know for certain, but I'm pretty sure this is the statue of Ruby, Shirley's aunt who went missing as a child. There is earth beneath her, so she must have been in a garden at one time."

Josh stoops to examine the soil.

"This is old dirt. Kind of red, nothing like what we have around here."

Brushing a rogue strand of black hair out of my eyes, I slowly back away from the sculpture. Josh continues to explore it with his hands.

"If I had to guess," he says, "I would say this piece is several decades old."

All this from a handyman? Josh must have read the surprise in my eyes; he smiles somewhat sheepishly and says, "Art history major."

"I look forward to hearing all about it," I say. "Speaking of which, I wouldn't mind getting out of here for a while."

Josh looks away from the girl with the sad, haunted eyes and steers me gently by the elbow to the ladder, where we silently make our way down and to the front entrance.

CHAPTER SEVENTEEN

LEAH, EINER'S BAY, PRESENT DAY: SHIRLEY'S DEATH

C ustomers pack The Sundowner—it is, after all, a Saturday night. Josh puts his hand on my elbow and directs me to a small booth at the back of the pub. It has a reserved sign on it.

"Friends in high places?" I ask, my eyes sweeping the busy pub.

"My family owns The Sundowner," he says, gesturing to me to sit.

The seats are comfy and deep. A little too deep. I struggle forward to perch at the top, elbows on the table to secure myself.

Josh mimics me, and we're two feet from each other, eye to eye. The music is country light, the lighting amber and soft.

After a few seconds of silence, Josh rests his chin on his hand and looks at me.

"Must be weird, huh?" he says.

"Yeah, a little," I respond, not entirely clear of what he means.

Just as he begins to speak, the server arrives to take our drink orders.

I realize I have someone special on my hands. Josh does not push or prod. He leans back, lips in a soft smile. His eyes are shining, and his lips look kissable. I reflexively touch my own lips; they feel dry. I wonder if I should reapply my lipstick.

Our drinks arrive, and soon the Merlot does a wonderful job of calming my nerves.

"What's good on the menu?" I ask, welcoming a release from the tension of our conversation.

Josh relaxes a little and smiles. "Pretty much everything.

Burgers are popular."

I take a moment to scan the menu. "The salmon burger looks good," I say with a smile and take a sip of wine.

After the waitress has left with our food order, Josh kinks his head to the left. "Why are you here? What made you come?"

"Tough question," I sigh. "It has a great deal to do with how I was living, the pressure I was under as head of public relations for a big investment firm. There was a point where I needed to get out. My mother's death devastated me. Aunt Shirley's passing came at a pivotal time in my life, I guess."

I avert my eyes; I can't even consider mentioning Mike right now. I'll fall apart on the spot.

After what seems like a long pause, Josh runs his hands through his thick, curly hair and says, "Tell me about your relationship with your aunt."

"She wasn't my aunt by blood. I mean, we weren't related in any way. In fact, I never met the woman in person."

Josh almost drops his beer at that one.

"What are you saying? A woman leaves her entire estate to someone she's never even met? That sounds crazy."

"Aunt Shirley was my mom, Laurena's, best friend from childhood. They met at a camp one summer in Oregon; they were like sisters. Shirley's family was from Louisiana. It's a sad tale. Her father died by suicide, and her mother packed up the family home and headed to Canada. Shirley was their only child."

"Go on," he says, eyes crinkling in concentration.

I take a breath and move into a comfier position as the waitress serves our food.

"Mom stayed close to Aunt Shirley all those years, even though they lived miles apart. My mom lived on Pender Island until she died. Aunt Shirley went to school and lived in New York City before she moved up here and built her own little piece of the South. We were in each other's lives for decades; in some ways, after Mom died, she became my rock, always giving me advice or just being the best listener ... but we never met."

Heads bowed, we finish our meals in comfortable silence, stopping only for a sip of wine or beer.

"Aunt Shirley was a haunted woman," I say, staring down into my wine. "Her father's suicide was difficult for her to accept."

"How old was she at the time?"

"Ten."

"Tough age."

"Her family has a tragic past. Shirley told me her aunt Ruby had gone missing as a child. She went out for a walk by the lake one day and never returned; she was only eight years old. Shirley said her father, Robert, felt guilty about it all his life. He was meant to be fishing at the lake that morning and was the reason his little sister went out in the first place. They drained the lake but didn't find a body. The townspeople searched for weeks but no trace of Ruby was ever found. It was like she vanished into thin air."

"Who's responsible for the statue in your house?" he asks.

"Aunt Shirley said they never did find out; it just showed up by the pond one day," I say, taking a sip of wine. "But she believed the statue was of Ruby."

"Did you know Shirley?" I ask.

"Shirley? Of course. It's a small town. She came in for a drink once in a while, but she travelled a lot, so there were big stretches of time before we'd see her again. She was nice. And smart. And rich."

"Do you know much about how she died?" It's the question I've been dreading to ask.

"You mean, you don't know?"

"Her attorney told me she had a nasty fall somewhere on the estate and her heart stopped," I say.

There's a lengthy pause where Josh says nothing. The music and the noise of the crowd seem to have dimmed. Something important is happening here; the hair on the back of my neck is tingling.

"What? Do you know something about her death that I should know?"

He sits back a little and sighs and clamps his hand over his mouth. His eyes scan the pub for a minute. Then he picks up his beer and takes a long drink.

"They found Shirley outside by the dollhouse. She suffered a painful death," he says, reaching a hand across the table to grab mine. "I'm sorry. This is going to be upsetting for you to hear."

"No, please. I need to know." His hand feels soft and strong, all at once.

"The coroner said she appeared to be in tremendous pain or shock when she died. The official cause of death was a severe heart attack. She was also in her nightgown and the time of death showed she was out there in the middle of the night. They could find no reason for her to be at the dollhouse then."

I'm shivering a little now.

***

I would love to stay for another glass of wine after we finish our burgers, but Josh seems agitated as he fumbles and drops his keys twice before opening the door for me.

Turning out of The Sundowner parking lot, he clears his throat and says, "I just got an annulment."

Josh checks my reaction with a quick glance.

After an awkward moment, I ask the inevitable question: "Josh, how old are you?"

The oncoming traffic is sparse as the yellow streetlights struggle and flicker.

"I'm twenty-eight," he says.

"Well, I've got a decade on you, if you haven't already figured that out," I say with a chuckle. He nods and shoots me a flirty smile.

"Adrienne had told me you were married briefly," I say in a

soft voice.

He takes a while to reply.

"I was married to Finola for two days," he mumbles. "I met her at art school in Edinburgh. She's Irish and a talented sculptor," Josh pauses as he turns up the road to my property. "I can hardly remember our wedding night; we were both hammered on scotch whiskey and champagne," the slight smile on his face falls to a deep frown. "Two days later, I woke up to find divorce papers on the bedside table. Oh, and somewhere along the way, she forgot to tell me she was already married to some guy in Cork."

I reach over and squeeze his right shoulder as he pulls his truck in front of my house. Josh turns off the car and we sit in silence. He finally turns to face me, eyes filled with unshed tears.

"She said I would never be an art historian because I didn't have an artistic bone in my body."

We sit quietly for a moment or two, listening to the engine click and wheeze as it cools down. Josh slowly exhales his tension, his dark-blond curls flowing over the headrest.

"What kind of goofy name is Finola, anyway?" I laugh softly. I am happy to get a small chuckle from him.

"I think it all worked out for the best, actually," Josh says. "She was a total slob."

Without too much more discussion, we both agree it's time to call it a night and we get out of the truck. The porch light is on, but the rest of the house is in complete darkness. The night air has a proper bite to it, and I can tell it won't be long before snow falls.

Josh is a total gentleman—walking me in, turning on the lights, checking around for anything suspicious. He senses my fatigue and settles for a short but sweet first kiss.

Soon his tail lights fade over the top of the drive and I'm once again alone with my big, silent, spooky house. Heading straight for bed, I turn off all the lights except for the one at the base of the stairs. Just in case.

CHAPTER EIGHTEEN

LEAH, RAVENS' WOOD, PRESENT DAY: THE LIGHTS COME ON

I'm dreaming of the sun. It's bright, but not particularly warm. A strange sensation drags me out of slumber and into a moment of total terror. I turned off all the lights last night but now they're back on. My heart pounds like crazy and my mouth is dry.

There is no sound, and for that I'm grateful. I try to get up, but my body isn't cooperating. Move, I tell myself. Soon I'm up and at the door to the hall; it's dimly lit, like a prison at night.

I move more quickly now as I feel an overwhelming sense of panic. Every light in the entire house is on! Even the dusty chandelier is lit and swinging ever so slightly, cobwebs and all.

I feel a scream building at the back of my throat, but the thought of it ripping through the silence frightens me beyond description. I will not scream. I will call 911. Rushing back to the bedroom to retrieve my cellphone, I stop and consider how foolish I'll sound making an emergency call because my lights are on. Sliding into a chair, I remind myself to take a breath. Breathe. Just continue to breathe. Think this through.

It could be an electrical anomaly. A mouse might have chewed the wrong wire. The thought of his stiff little body with curled claws sticking up isn't a pleasant one, but better than any number of alternatives. I sigh. That must be it.

I take a pill. No dreams to plague me, no lights on or off to notice, I sleep the sleep of the near dead. Blank, black and perfectly uneventful.

CHAPTER NINETEEN

JOSH, EINER'S BAY, PRESENT DAY: THE FUR TRAPPER

Afterescorting Leah inside her house and checking to make sure all is well, Josh heads home to his cabin—the ramshackle relic his father Jack offered him when he returned from Edinburgh. It has taken Josh almost a year to make the eighty-year-old cabin livable, and he couldn't have done it without the help of his dad and friends.

The road in begins at the entrance to his dad's acreage; even in the dark, Josh knows the land well. Headlights bounce up and down as he drives up the slight incline to the cabin. Josh puts the vehicle in park and shuts off the lights, plunging him into total darkness.

As is his habit, Josh stands in front of the bumper and waits for his eyes to adjust. While checking for potential wildlife threats, he walks carefully up the three wooden steps, pulls his cabin key from his right front pocket and opens the door.

Until the fire starts, or the heat is on, the cabin is like walking into a freezer. Josh leans back on the front door, exhaling little clouds of vapour. Resting his chin on his chest, he thinks about Leah.

Such an unusual person, he thinks, shaking his head and picking up a pack of matches en route to the fireplace, where he's already set up wood and kindling. The first strike illuminates his furrowed brow as he reaches in to light the wood. In minutes, the fire fills the cabin with light and warmth.

Josh kicks off his boots and empties a bag of potato chips into a small white bowl, then snaps open a cold beer from the fridge. He's about to settle in front of the fire when he hears footsteps coming up the stairs to his cabin.

He freezes and waits. Cocking his head, he hears the unmistakable sound of metal clanging.

"What the hell?" he mutters.

He tosses the bowl of chips onto the counter, moving swiftly to the front door, which is already opening. His jaw drops in shock at the sight.

A man dressed like a fur trapper bursts into the cabin, all grizzled and weathered by the outdoors. Wearing a long, amber-coloured suede coat with red trim, his pants flare out of the top of knee-high, dark-brown boots caked in mud. The clanging he makes is loud, and the source appears to be from what he carries: leg-hold traps and pots and pans.

The man has a quiver loaded with small arrows, which no doubt are the cause of death for the half-dozen black squirrels he has slung over his shoulder. Their thick, inky fur shines in the firelight as their little bodies sway back and forth. The rank smell oozing from his person is a combination of sweat, blood, urine and a whiff of campfire smoke.

Josh gags on the foul stink. He has seen enough and he grabs his rifle from behind the kitchen door.

"Whoa, mister!" Josh shouts. "What the hell do you think you're doing?"

He stands square, gun raised and ready to fire.

The trapper, who doesn't appear to be aware of Josh, carries on, removing all of his burden onto the floor with a loud crash, then pulls up in front of the fire to warm his hands.

Josh is wide-eyed, in shock at this behaviour. Stepping forward, he places the muzzle of the rifle to the back of the trapper's head; no response.

Whirling around to face him, Josh, his face reddened with anger, shouts, "Get the hell out of my house!"

Unresponsive to Josh, the old coot starts to whistle. Josh

lowers the gun and thinks this guy is either on drugs or deranged.

Suddenly, the intruder jumps to his feet, knocking the rifle out of Josh's hands and thrusting one gnarled hand around his throat. Josh tries to remove his grip, but it's like a vise.

They face off eyeball to eyeball. Josh feels a palpable hatred emanating from the man. Struggling even harder to escape, Josh kicks his right leg out and behind his attacker to sweep him to the floor. The man doesn't budge.

With his right hand, Josh grabs a piece of burning wood from the fire and smashes it into the attacker's face. He screams and releases Josh, who proceeds to roundhouse kick and punch until the bloodied man is on the floor, writhing and tangled up in his pots and pans, leg-hold traps and dead squirrels.

Josh stands over him, his breathing fast and deep. "Get the hell out of my cabin, you freak!"

But the trapper starts to slowly dissolve into the wooden floor. Josh shakes his head, thinking he's oxygen deprived from the choking. He can't tear his eyes from the sight in front of him. As all the tension seeps out of his body, the violent intruder smiles widely with his yellow teeth and eyes. Licking his lips, he lifts his head so quickly that Josh raises his weapon in response.

The old man chuckles. Just a chuckle. Like one you might share around a campfire. But this is a nasty noise that sounds almost like a hiccup.

Staring Josh in the eyes, the trapper whispers, "Reginald says hi."

And at that, he melts into the floor until there's nothing left. No crazy old coot, no clothes, no pots and pans, no arrows and no dead squirrels.

Josh sits down hard on his coffee table, sweat running down his entire body.

Shaking his head, he mumbles, "Holy shit," then rises and slams the door shut.

CHAPTER TWENTY

LEAH & ADRIENNE, EINER'S BAY, PRESENT DAY: AN OFFER

The morning after my date with Josh, Adrienne and I walk along Einer's Bay Beach. There's a marina at the end of the sandy bay. Even at this time of the year, it appears to be busy. Large, gleaming super-yachts are scarce in the fall, so I speculate that the majority of these smaller boats with laundry drying on the railings are full-time residents. A fuel dock on the other side of the marina rocks back and forth with the tide, and the float plane dock is unoccupied for the moment.

The sun attempts to warm us, but it's still brisk. The salty air is sweet and I take deep, cleansing breaths.

"I can't believe what you're telling me," says Adrienne as she buttons up the top of her dark-green wool sweater.

"No one finds this harder to believe than me," I drag my feet in the sand, head bowed, sunglasses firmly in place.

Adrienne stops to face me, lines of worry etched on her face.

"Leah, I don't know you well, but I know people, and you're not the type to see witches in the wardrobe." This comment has me truly puzzled. "And Josh heard the noise—there's obviously something going on in that house."

I nod in response.

"The thing is ... the thing is I don't believe someone is trying to scare me. I think they're trying to get my attention, and they certainly have that," I say.

"Why don't you come stay with us?" she offers. "We have a guest cottage. Safer that way, and it's all yours." She flashes a big, warm grin. "Though, be warned: Jim might drive you crazy! He's a bit of a goofball."

The loud screech of a seagull above has us both looking up, shielding our heads with our handbags. It wouldn't be the first time I got pooped on.

"Thanks so much for the offer, but I need to stay—at least for now," I tell her.

After half an hour of shopping and grilled cheese sandwiches for lunch at the café, we go our separate ways.

When I get home, I sit in the driveway for a few minutes and ponder how the house looks so benign in the light of day. After stepping out of the Lexus, I stand for some time looking for signs of intruders. Birds tweet, the trees sway in the light breeze and the house stares back at me in total silence. I'm the first to blink.

CHAPTER TWENTY-ONE

LEAH, EINER'S BAY, PRESENT DAY: THE RAVEN'S ATTACK

The next morning, I decide it's time for another visit to town. I'm beginning to suspect there's something behind my newfound desire to flee my estate, but I'll explore that more later. The sky is a damp, leaden blanket this morning, and I wonder how soon the first snowfall will be. I shiver in my black cotton sweater and plan on trading style for functionality, right after this excursion.

As I drive into town, I see there are no roadside pigs this morning to greet me, only a few wayward leaves bouncing across the road. They're hypnotic in their own way. I sit up straight and give my head a quick shake.

The sky has darkened over the town of Einer's Bay, and it casts a dramatic pallor to its usual warm aura; it's more like a scene from a Stephen King novel. The store rooftops cut a hard edge against the grey, and for a moment, the place looks like a ghost town.

Pulling up in front of Willie's Market, I notice the windows are dark and there's no sign of shoppers inside. Strange. Shouldn't be closed this morning. In a useless gesture, I tug on the front door. Nope. Peering in the window confirms the obvious: Willie's is closed.

Have I missed a local holiday?

The slightly nauseating feeling of dread grows stronger within me. I realize things are not what they seem. The sky has turned a dark, gloomy grey by the time I head back home. The road ahead looks slick—there's no good reason for that. I accelerate and feel my car sliding into the oncoming lane.

Fighting for control of the wheel, something dark hits my windshield! It smacks and bursts into blood and feathers. I scream and wrench the wheel in the opposite direction, trying hard to not look at the raven's beady, dead, angry red eyes that stare back at me. My heart is pounding, and I scream even louder when the raven blinks. I'm transfixed as the life finally fades from his eyes.

Stomping on the brakes with all I have, the car swings in a half-circle and stops. As I stare through the shredded body of the raven, I realize I must be hallucinating; there's a red-earth desert in front of me. That can't be possible.

All I can do is remove the carcass myself. There are no gloves in the car, so I have little choice but to use my bare hands to grab the raven by its crooked, broken wings and tear it off.

I see the earth has returned to its regular brown colour, but the raven is still there. The bloodied corvid is, apparently, not a hallucination. The weight surprises me as toss it on the ground, where it lands with a terrible wet thump.

Wiping my hands on my jeans, I remove most of the blood. With a wingspan of at least three feet, it was a large predator. British Columbia is known for its ravens, but why this one chose this moment to dive-bomb my car, I will never know. I feel equal parts fear, revulsion and pity.

The drive home is a blur. My body is vibrating with anxiety, my hands shaking on the wheel.

When I finally drive up to the gates of my estate, it's like I'm seeing it with fresh eyes. The black paint on the fence is flaking like a scab on a wound. The hinges are rusting, and the gate is improperly hung. The white columns look dingy and dull. As I look up to the widow's walk, a shadow slinks across it. I feel the blood rush to my head, but there's nowhere else to go. I'm home.

I stop at the laundry room and quickly shed myself of my bloodied jeans. I should throw them out. I'm not sure I could ever wear them without the memory of this terrible event.

My nerves are frayed, and I wander aimlessly from room to room. I realize I need to find a housekeeper as my finger doodles on the dusty mantle of the living room. Ironically, a dirty house seems to be the least of my worries here.

There is such loneliness here. I can't help but think of what I have left behind. A noisy, chaotic, stressful life, but one that was so alive. I'm missing the adrenalin rush of the corporate PR world, the thrill of the kill. The celebrations after the win, even the stress of having to start the process all over again. I was good at what I did.

As the fading light outside draws me closer to the window, I reach out to stroke the burgundy curtains. As I touch the fabric, what I assumed would be velvet feels rough. I recoil as something jabs my fingers. Wide-eyed with fear, I cringe; the burgundy curtains have somehow transformed into the bloodied wings of a bird. I back away from the window and as I turn to run, the curtain rod crashes to the hardwood so hard, the floor beneath my feet rumbles.

***

Several glasses of red wine in the kitchen later and heading for bed, I'm relieved to see that whatever twisted dark magic is at work here has cleaned up after itself—the curtains are, once again, back up and made of burgundy fabric. Bone weary from the nightmare that was my day, my sleep is surprisingly undisturbed.

CHAPTER TWENTY-TWO

LEAH, EINER'S BAY, PRESENT DAY: COLD RIVULETS OF FEAR

Morning arrives with the soft patter of rain against the window. I cuddle Mike's pillow, snuggle deeper into the covers and try to go back to sleep. In my half-awake state, I picture the statue in my attic. There's something wrong with this figure, and it's somehow linked to everything going on in this house.

***

My eyes fly open as I remember Josh will be at my door just before 8 a.m. to weatherstrip my new window; I have little time to get ready. Throwing back the covers, I stumble out of bed, brush my teeth, catch up my hair in a clip and slip into a pair of blue jeans and a black sweatshirt. I'm halfway out of the room when I return to the bathroom to apply two quick swipes of mascara and my favourite coral-coloured lipstick.

Before long, he's sitting in front of me, his hands cupping a mug of steaming coffee. Our conversation drifts to the statue and I tell him how uneasy I am about it.

"I think you need to get her out of the house and into the garden," Josh pronounces. "That's where she belongs."

"No!" I yell, a little louder than intended. Josh's head jerks back in surprise.

"It was part of Shirley's will," I whisper. "It specifically said, 'The statue located in the attic must never be moved.'"

"That's weird, don't you think?" he asks.

I nod in agreement.

"So, what's the deal with the town closing down yesterday?" I ask, wanting to change the subject.

Josh tilts his head. "What are you talking about?"

"I drove into town yesterday morning to get some supplies and everything was closed. I guess I missed that update in the *Einer's Bay Gazette*."

"Leah," he plants his hands on my shoulders and speaks slowly like I'm a little kid. "The town wasn't closed yesterday. I was there all day, repairing a deli case at Willie's. I think I'd know if it were closed."

Cold rivulets of fear course through my body, and I start to tremble. Josh gets up from his chair, stands in front of me and pulls me to my feet.

"What's going on with you?" he asks, one hand tilting my chin up. He draws me forward and my hair tumbles out of its clip. I can feel the tears leaking from my eyes, but there's no stopping them.

Clutching him like a life preserver, I start weeping—deep, wracking sobs pour out of me like a geyser. He holds me until I gain control.

"Kleenex," I mumble.

Grabbing a big handful of tissue from the counter, Josh holds a wad to my nose and commands me to blow. I'm touched, embarrassed and relieved all at once. I needed to blow.

Taking custody of the balance of the Kleenex to remove my streaky mascara, I walk over to the sink and stare out at the trees. They sway back and forth in the breeze, branches conducting an invisible orchestra.

"I think I'm losing my mind," I say. It seems a foregone conclusion at this point.

Josh smiles. "No, Leah, you're not cracking up. Remember, I've also witnessed some weird shit around this place. I think we should call somebody."

"Who might that be, Josh? Anyone around here know anything about suicidal ravens?" I snarl, left hand clutching his wrist.

Josh takes a good, lengthy pause before responding.

"What the hell are you talking about?"

Spinning on my heel, I take a quick moment to dump the wet tissue and lead him to the laundry room.

Josh shakes his head in confusion, and as soon as I pop open the washing machine, his head jerks back from the rancid stench of blood. I was too upset to turn on the washer yesterday—and I pull out a pair of blood-streaked jeans. I feel a bit silly, like I've just completed a magic trick. Josh, on the other hand, backs away.

"Holy hell, Leah! What attacked you?" he says, his face tight with concern.

"It dive-bombed me while I was driving. The earth turned red, I lost control of the car, and then this giant raven smashed onto my windshield. I had to use my hands to pull it off, and I didn't have anything to wipe my hands on except for my jeans. It's sickening," I say shakily.

Josh paces back and forth for a few minutes, then says, "We need help. And we need it now."

"Who? Ghostbusters?" The thought of Dan Aykroyd and his buddies wrestling with the pale-faced angel upstairs cracks me up, and I even manage a smile.

Seeing my smile has returned, Josh walks toward the door. "I'll be back," he says. "The weatherstripping can wait."

Within seconds I hear the engine start, and the tires bite into gravel. I turn to the unpleasant task of washing the blood and gore from my jeans.

Once the washing machine is running, I go in search of clues to the strange things going on. Aunt Shirley's study must have some answers.

The light in the study is even dimmer than in the kitchen, so I turn on the desk lamp and take a seat in the padded leather chair. Sitting back, I survey the room with fresh eyes and spend an hour going through the drawers again. Where would Shirley put something of importance? And what would that thing be?

My eyes fall on three paintings: a creepy one with the doll-house, a lovely seascape and a landscape. This last one looks old, with its paint cracked and shiny in places.

Getting up for a closer look, I feel as though I'm walking into the scene. Dark-green imposing trees frame a small wooden cabin; there's a slight glow to suggest a light on inside. Snow has fallen, and it covers the walkway with a light dusting of white. A face! I jump back and catch my breath, hand covering my mouth.

There's an image in the woods. It's an old man, and the artist has blended his subject's leathery face in a way that connects the flesh to bark. One hand thrusts forward in a gesture of warning, as if pushing me back and away from the painting.

I slowly step back from the disturbing painting and make a quick exit down the stairs to the front door, where someone is knocking.

CHAPTER TWENTY-THREE

LEAH, JOSH & ADRIENNE, RAVENS' WOOD, PRESENT DAY: THE INTERVENTION

J osh's quick departure earlier makes sense when I see Adrienne's unmistakable curvy silhouette through the frosted glass panel. Josh taps again and opens the door; Adrienne walks past him, and if I'm not mistaken, she's assumed a little of the persona of that short, scary woman from the Poltergeist movies. She has arrived.

"Psychic investigator on the side?"

"It doesn't take a psychic to see how stressed out you are," she says, shifting slowly into the light.

"Good to have you on my side," I whisper, wrapping her in a warm hug.

Adrienne pulls back to get a better look at me. One hand reaches up and pushes my rebellious fringe off my face.

"You. A bath followed by a nap—now," she says, spinning me around and giving me a little shove.

***

Josh follows Adrienne to the den, where they sit in silence. Adrienne is the first to break the quiet with a deep sigh.

"Josh, we knew this day would come. I'm shocked beyond description that he has made his move so quickly. Nothing good will come of this."

Josh drums his fingers on his knee. "I don't know how much time we have. We thought she'd make it through the winter. We could easily explain a few minor incidents, but nothing this dramatic. If this goes on much longer, there'll be another dead body on the estate."

The fire cracks like a shotgun, and both of them jump. He reaches over to give Adrienne a protective pat on her left hand. Josh and Adrienne's son Sam have been good friends since grade one, and with his mother living and working in Victoria, Josh and Adrienne are close. Josh and his mom are way too much alike and argue all the time. Adrienne has become like a surrogate mom to him, and it's her who he seeks out for advice.

***

I can hear the murmur of voices below as I click off the light in the bedroom. After my bath and five minutes lying on the bed with my eyes wide open, I dress in a pair of fresh jeans and a comfortable sweatshirt. I feel somewhat refreshed as I make my way downstairs.

The fire casts jerky silhouettes on the wood panels as I enter the room, and soon, three glasses of red wine glow like rubies on the table before us as we sit in silence; me on the sofa, Josh and Adrienne on chairs across from me. Reaching for another sip of liquid courage, I touch Josh's arm.

He raises his head, eyebrows tight. Adrienne glances briefly at Josh, then settles deeper into her chair.

"I need to know what I'm up against here," I say, crossing my legs and straightening my back against the sofa.

Josh sighs and turns his head to the side. "I'm not sure where to start."

"Start with the statue. She's the problem." I say, nodding my head toward the attic.

"Actually, she's not the problem," he replies. "She's somehow at the heart of all that's happening, but both Adrienne and I agree: she is an innocent spirit—if, in fact, that is what she is."

The fire crackles away as I twist a lock of my dark hair around my index finger. Taking a deep breath, I ask them the question that's been on my mind.

"Can you please tell me, what the heck is a Guardian? And how do you get to be one?" I note Adrienne's almost-guilty expression and the somewhat guarded one on Josh's face.

Josh and Adrienne move closer to each another, both slouching down in unison, with concern etched across their faces. Josh is the first to speak.

"There have always been six Guardians of this town," he says in a soft, low voice. "The fur traders and sawmill families who settled the town in the mid-1800s felt safe until one day they found the body of a farmer's wife torn to pieces, left in the middle of the main road into town."

"That's terrible!" I say, drawing my knees up under my chin.

Josh gives an almost imperceptible nod in Adrienne's direction. She begins to speak.

"Of course people panicked. The locals stayed home or travelled in groups. Then suddenly, they were talking about the big animals they saw in the woods. Nobody could really pin it down; one guy thought it was a big man. Others saw everything from elephants to horses walking on their back legs." Her voice softens, as her eyes flash around the study. "The consensus was that it was a large cougar that walked on two legs."

Josh gives me a few seconds to respond. When I don't, he carries on.

"Livestock and dogs were killed. Food started getting scarce, so people began fishing more, getting out at first light to be safe." Josh pauses as the fire crackles in the background. "Then a little girl was butchered." Josh tents his hands and avoids my eyes.

All at once, a loud bang hits the side of the house and we all jump.

"Just a gust of wind," mumbles Josh. We're all a little tightly wound.

Before we can catch our breath, a strong draft blasts down the chimney to the hearth. Chunks of burning wood shoot through the fireplace screen, followed by bright orange embers.

The fringe of the carpet closest to the fireplace catches on fire, and Josh quickly stomps it out with his shoes. I grab the tongs and get the burning chunks of wood back into the fireplace. Adrienne secures the screen and we collapse back in our seats. We all reach for our wine, and after a couple of big gulps, refill our glasses.

Adrienne picks up where Josh left off. Smoothing back her hair, she sighs. "After that, fear turned to rage."

"The community decided to form a group of town defenders," Josh says, sliding closer to the edge of his chair. "The mayor believed in the power of numbers, and he chose the number six."

"And just like that," Adrienne says, snapping her fingers, "the killings ended. Of course, no one understood exactly why they stopped, but the town felt safer with the six Guardians."

"Since then, there have always been Guardians; as they leave or die off, newcomers are assessed as candidates, watched for six months before being approached and then asked to join," says Josh. He stands and walks over to the window overlooking the backyard.

"Who are the current Guardians?" I query. Josh nods his head and Adrienne begins to speak.

"Josh and his father Jack, Giselle, Willie, who owns the market, Patty from Happy Hair and me."

As I let this sink in, I hear the wind unsettling the trees once more. I wonder when it started up, as it was calm when we first sat down. "Just one more question—for now," I say. "Can the Guardians help me?"

CHAPTER TWENTY-FOUR

LEAH, RAVENS' WOOD, PRESENT DAY: THE BLOOD & GORE

After Josh and Adrienne leave, I retire for the night, but I struggle to sleep; my mind is filled with so many questions. Night birds whisper softly on the brisk wind that continues to rustle against the side of the house.

Soon I drift into an unsettled slumber, though I'm still aware of my surroundings ... but things seem brighter, more colourful, as if a black-and-white photograph has been hand-painted to a greater vibrancy.

The sheets curl around my body like water. I dream of early-rising sun sheening on a metal-grey lake. The water is warm and tickling as it surrounds my body like a cloak. This isn't right. This isn't real. I settle into the comfort of knowing this is a dream.

Soon the water seems viscous, and it's warmer. Not right. Not right. The smell of rust fills my nostrils. I wrench my eyes open to look down upon myself ... and I discover I'm lying in a pool of blood.

Heart pounding, I hurl myself out of the blood-soaked sheets onto the floor below. A hot, red waterfall cascades as I turn. I choke on the blood as it reaches deep into my stomach, and I vomit onto the carpet.

CHAPTER TWENTY-FIVE

JOSH, RAVENS' WOOD, PRESENT DAY: A STENCH

J osh ponders the weak, watery presence of the sun in the early-morning sky, rubs his hands together and walks toward the side door of Leah's house. The house itself appears to be sleeping as waves of vapour blow off the roof in occasional gusts. It's so quiet that the thought of ringing the bell seems intrusive. A soft knock is all he can bring himself to do.

Moments later, concerned she's not answering, Josh uses the key Leah gave him in case of an emergency.

"Leah?" he calls out. His voice echoes in the damp hallways.

The silence confirms his gut feeling something's not right. He races up the stairs to Leah's bedroom, and as soon as he reaches his destination, he draws back in shock. Her bedroom is a scene of horror. Sheets are twisted like bloody snakes on the floor. Red rivulets run from the headboard to the end of the bed, where they drip to the carpet below. Her pillow has been flung against the wall, a sodden, bloody lump. The room has a stench like an animal has been freshly killed. It's rusty and putrid, and it makes Josh gag.

"Leah!" he screams.

He sees, with a moment of relief, there's no body in the midst of the gory scene. He lurches toward the bathroom, following a trail of blood. Moving warily, he catches sight of a shiny, black tuft of hair. Propped up against the bathroom wall, Leah is drawn into herself like a nautilus shell; her hands are tangled up in her bloodied hair. Her eyes are wide, and she looks like she's about to scream, but her lips are tightly closed and pale.

Wrapping Leah in a large towel, Josh cradles her firmly in his arms and places her gently on the shower floor. Once the water is warm, he puts the shower head on its softest setting and tilts it slightly, so the water bathes her like rain.

Closing the bathroom door behind him, he backtracks to her room and rummages through her dresser to find underthings, sweatpants and a bulky sweater. He taps softly as he opens the door and gently deposits the clothing on the counter.

CHAPTER TWENTY-SIX

LEAH, RAVENS' WOOD, PRESENT DAY: THE SAFE

Josh tucked me back into the blue bedroom last night. The horrible shaking stopped after I drank half a glass of vodka. The smell of blood still lingers in the hallway. Josh called a good friend who runs a cleaning company; she's promised everything will be squeaky clean in the yellow guestroom by the time she's finished. He found a trail of blood that led from the backyard, in through the side door and up the stairs to where I was sleeping. We know how they got in, but why would someone do such a terrible thing?

***

Perched on the bottom of the staircase, I sense the house has taken on a distinct personality—dark, sneering, leering. Looking up, I can see spiderwebs in every corner of the entranceway. I hadn't noticed them before today.

I listen to Josh rattling around the house, turning down the heat, shutting off lights, closing doors. My head is pounding in time with his purposeful footsteps. He's already packed me two overnight bags filled with clothes and toiletries, as it's clear I can't spend another night in this house. They sit waiting at the front door.

Standing up, I shuffle slowly down the steps, pick up both bags in one hand and open the door. It pulls back. I give it a little tug, and it slams shut, my hand vibrating with the force of it. I scream in frustration and fear.

Reginald

"What the hell?" Josh shouts, flying down the stairs, shaking his head in disbelief.

"The door just blasted shut while I was holding the knob!" Sliding down to the marble floor, I hold my head in a vise grip and chew on the inside of my cheek so hard I can taste blood.

"This is insane," I whisper.

Josh wrenches on the door handle, but it's immovable, like someone has nailed it shut. We're trapped. I pull out my cell to call then text Adrienne. There are annoying beeping sounds on both attempts and not the slightest hint of a connection. Josh runs to the pantry entrance, and his curses tell me we're staying for a while. I hear what I believe to be the sound of a chair being thrown against a window and bouncing back to strike; Josh is now yelling and cussing, feet pounding from room to room. It seems like he has a bad temper, but who can blame him at this point?

This manic running from door to door continues for several minutes. Josh's heavy breathing reaches me before his physical self. Sweat runs down his forehead as he drops to the floor beside me. We are prisoners in a madhouse.

An hour later, we've exhausted all attempts at leaving the house or communicating with the outside world. There is an entity in this house, and it has tampered with the electricity and cellphone service.

***

Later that day, resigned to the fact we're not going anywhere until the entity releases us, Josh and I sit at the kitchen table, with the light of a flickering candle casting dramatic shadows on him as he slumps forward.

"We need to know what this spirit wants with us," he says. "Perhaps we could try automatic writing?" He gives me a slight smile as he makes this suggestion.

"What's that?" I query, picturing a pen spinning around on a piece of paper.

Standing up, Josh paces a little, then squats down to my level.

"Automatic writing is as simple as it sounds," he tells me. "We get a piece of paper and a pen or pencil, and leave it alone in a room. If the spirit wishes to communicate with us, it will write what it wants."

I shake my head. It seems so unreal. After a few moments of dead silence, I've come up with an idea.

"We need to find Aunt Shirley's journal. I know she kept one. Let's check out her study."

After inspecting the study for a few moments, Josh asks, "Where's her computer?" He eases himself to the floor in front of the fireplace.

"Well, that's an interesting question. I have not seen a computer—and I know she had one because that's how we communicated."

While I speak, I find myself drawn to that unsettling painting of the cabin and the leather-faced man. Walking over to it, I grasp both sides of the picture frame and lift up. It's astonishingly heavy, and I'm happy to set it down on the floor. What is revealed behind the picture frame surprises me.

I grasp the safe's handle and discover it's not locked—in fact, it opens easily. Josh gets up from his spot in front of the fireplace and stands beside me. We both peer in and see several items inside the safe—including a MacBook laptop, a small wooden box and a leather-bound book.

As soon as my hand touches the book, the lights go on, and at the sight of the power going back on, Josh sprints out of the room. I can hear his hurried footsteps bounding toward the front door. His cry of freedom rips through the halls.

I need a moment to get my bearings—my head is pounding so hard I can barely think. As tempted as I am to get out of here once and for all, I know there's something going on that defies logic.

It's probably the reason for Aunt Shirley's premature departure from this world. It's a dreadful mystery, and for whatever reason, I know I'm the one chosen to unravel it. I need to stay.

***

An hour later, dishes lie in a heap in the sink, and we feel better for having eaten. Josh, slunk back in a kitchen chair, slowly flips the pages of the leather book, which turns out to be Aunt Shirley's journal. He doesn't speak; he only gives an occasional grunt, grimace or sigh. After my blood-soaking ordeal last night, I decide to let Josh read the book first.

"Okay, the anticipation is killing me," I say. "Sooner or later you're going to have to share."

He looks up at me with tears in his eyes. Since I haven't read the journal myself, I wasn't expecting it would have that effect on him.

***

We make our way to the living room. As much as I want to read the journal tonight, I can't even keep my eyes open. I need to rest, undisturbed by maniacs pouring hot blood over me while I sleep. The moment I lay my head down, I'm out like a light.

CHAPTER TWENTY-SEVEN

LEAH, RAVENS' WOOD, PRESENT DAY: THE MORNING AFTER

My eyes open slowly. The grey tones of early morning softly illuminate the room. There is no sense of sunlight breaking through, just a dull beginning of the day. We've both fallen asleep in the living room, with me on the sofa and Josh curled up in an awkward position on a chair.

Shirley's journal lies face down before me on the coffee table. Sitting up, hand shaking, I reach out, and before my courage leaves me high and dry, I carefully open the front cover.

Something slinks onto my shoulder and not realizing its Josh's hand, I rise up, drop the journal and accidently smack him hard in the chin with my head.

"Ouch!" he says, his hand clutching his chin. "What made you do that?"

"I'm sorry," I say, handing him a tissue, which comes back clean; thankfully, the skin isn't broken. "I think my nerves are shot."

"We need to discover the root of the evil that exists here," I say with determination. "And to do that, we have to leave this house—and Einer's Bay."

We make our decision to fly south with relative ease. I immediately call Adrienne and invite her to join us, but her son Sam is coming into town; of course she wants to spend time with him. Worst-case scenario: we're on a nice brief tour of Southern plantations and nothing more. Best-case scenario: we uncover the source of the unbearable supernatural activity happening in what's supposed to be my new, peaceful home.

CHAPTER TWENTY-EIGHT

ADRIENNE, EINER'S BAY, PRESENT DAY: THE HIKE

Adrienne is about to do something she rarely does: go hiking alone. It troubles her to break the very rule she makes everyone else adhere to upon pain of being tossed out of the hiking group. There were usually six of them; five, now that Shirley is dead. Alice, Joy, Senise and their "token" guy, Ali.

But on this overcast, chilly morning, she has no one to play with, and with the stress of all the haunting and demon drama going on, she desperately needs to find some peace in the woods.

The breath of early-morning fog is damp and frigid. Adrienne pauses to zip up her coat to her chin and snug her toque down. A quick shift of her backpack and she's back on the trail. The sound like small rocks cascading has her stopping, right ear cocked. After a few seconds, she recognizes it as one of the strange sounds ravens make. Kind of like if you have a glass full of pebbles and you shake it hard.

Adrienne resumes her hike. Following an old creek bed, the going is challenging with rocks whose only reason for existing seems to be to make sure you get your foot stuck. On either side of the creek bed, the trees sway with a light wind. The scent of cedar refreshes Adrienne as she stumbles up a gravelly part of the trail.

A wan winter sun is doing its best to cut through the fog and warm the air, but it's too feeble to make a difference. Adrienne takes a quick look to drink in the view where the mountain slopes down to a choppy sea. Just as she turns her head back to the trail, something very large and black flies in front of her face, its ink-black feathers stroking across her cheeks. She could feel the strong pulse of air emanating from its powerful wings. Adrienne stands in shock, her hand on her mouth. Why would a raven come that close? She's shaking from the cold and the fear of what happened.

She's noticed the increasingly large numbers of ravens in Einer's Bay. Not only are there more of them, but they're enormous, their hooked beaks rounded and sharp. There's something weird going on here. She turns around and heads back down the trail; she has some research to do.

***

Still shivering after her chilly hike, Adrienne pulls a warm blanket around her as she reaches for her field guide on birds of the Pacific Northwest. Her hand shakes as she attempts to sip hot green tea without soaking herself in it.

CHAPTER TWENTY-NINE

LEAH & JOSH, EN ROUTE TO LOUSIANA, PRESENT DAY: THE QUESTIONS

We're strapped in for another float plane ride to Vancouver, and I can't get the flask open fast enough. Josh is looking at me sideways, lips pursed. His eyes follow my trembling hand as I return the vodka to my front pocket. Josh reaches over and places his big hand on mine, and the shaking starts to settle down.

"Fear of flying?" he questions. After a couple of deep breaths, I nod, "And heights."

Once we land at the seaplane terminal, Josh and I take a taxi to the Vancouver International Airport. Soon, we're checked in and waiting to board our flight to Louisiana. Armed with little more than determination to find the original plantation house, we're desperate to uncover the origins of the haunting of Aunt Shirley's house ... now *my* house.

Before too long, we're somewhere over the midlands of the United States; I sneak quick glimpses from my aisle seat. Josh is napping on my shoulder, and I've ordered my third tiny plastic cup of red wine. It occurs to me I'm drinking more than usual, but it's not surprising considering the stress I'm under plus the two flights in a row.

Our plane lands ten minutes early at Louis Armstrong New Orleans International Airport, thanks to a strong tailwind. Carry-on bags in hand, we jump into an Uber and head for our hotel. The air is hot and humid, as expected.

"Okay, so it's not the Ritz, but it's not that bad!" Josh says when we pull up at our hotel.

Retrieving our suitcases from the driver, we both look up at the dated building we have chosen to stay in. I take the lead, pulling the dull brass-trimmed door open.

"At least it's got air conditioning." I say over my shoulder as the cold air blasts me.

I sigh, resigned to eight days in this dive. The reception furniture is worn, mismatched and lumpy. The dull gold fabric on the sofa is stained with god knows what. The uniformed doorman is elderly and snores loudly, his head slumping down as he sits in an ancient wooden chair. Trying its best to channel *Gone with the Wind,* this place is overblown. Four-star? Not even close.

With only one other person in front of us, it still takes almost an hour to get checked in. I take a quick look at my room, knowing that only copious amounts of alcohol will put me to sleep in the thin and narrow bed. I drop my suitcase and head for Josh's room a few doors down the hall—I'm starving and in need of booze.

His door is open, and Josh stands by the bed, a shaft of light streaking his dark-blond hair with a paintbrush stroke of gold. His dark-blue jeans, faded at the knees, fit perfectly over sculpted, muscular legs.

"Okay, Leah," he says tilting his head to one side and licking his lips, "let's find us some Southern comfort."

"Oh yes, I seriously need a drink and some food, but we don't have a lot of time to find the right plantation before the land registry office closes. So, let's spend an hour doing some research," I say.

***

Our quest to find the exact plantation takes much longer than we thought it would. Antebellum mansions permeate the South, but scores of them have fallen to ruin or have been burned to the ground. I only hope Aunt Shirley's original version is still standing.

Our search leads us to the registry of plantation era properties in the area. There we find out the estate called Ravens' Pond is still in the name of Shirley's family—and so, legally, the place now belongs to me. I call Frank, the current property manager, to introduce myself and make an appointment to visit him at the house in the morning.

Our search over, we follow the hotel clerk's recommendation and settle into the corner booth of a local bar for some homegrown Southern cuisine.

"I seriously hope we find some answers," says Josh, looking up at the server who's arriving with two Hurricanes—a rum drink popular with visitors.

"How y'all doing?" the waiter queries with a warm Southern drawl. "Ready to try some authentic Cajun cuisine?" He gestures to the menu in front of Josh.

I nod and smile up at him, taking in the sweat stains under his arms and his flushed face. The air conditioning isn't strong enough to overcome the heat outside.

"We'll order a couple of po' boy sandwiches," Josh replies, scanning the menu one more time.

I've already decided on the fried shrimp po' boy but am startled when Josh orders the grilled alligator sausage.

Handing the menu back to our server, Josh grins and says, "When in Rome!"

I can't help but put my hand to my mouth.

Looking for something to distract my mind from gator in a bun, I check out the amazing historical photographs in this bar. Plantations with Spanish moss draping like giant cobwebs from massive oak trees; slaves standing unsmiling for the camera; little children trying hard to remain still for the photograph, clearly itching to take flight.

Finishing our meal, we walk back to our hotel serenaded by the noisy cicadas; the heat is still oppressive, the air is heavy with humidity and the rum is making my head buzz.

Josh walks me to my hotel door. The sexual tension between us is getting stronger, and it's all I can do to not grab him by the hand and lead him to my bed. Pulling me in, he nuzzles the top of my head with his chin. Reaching up, I run my hands through his soft curls and explore the contours of his head. Our lips find each other. His soft tongue in my mouth feels so natural. As he pushes in closer, I feel his arousal and softly place my hand on his chest.

He smiles, kisses my hand on both sides, drops his chin, his eyes undressing me from head to toe in a way that makes my knees week ... and then he leaves for his own room, calling it a night.

Climbing into a soft white cotton nightgown, the exhaustion of the day catches up to me. With thoughts of Josh's soft lips on mine, I drift off to an easy sleep.

Reginald

CHAPTER THIRTY

LEAH & JOSH, RAVENS' POND, PRESENT DAY: THE ANSWERS

The morning air is scorching hot and humid—and it's only eight. I'm covered with insect repellent and wearing a loose blue cotton dress to stay as cool as possible. Josh looks like he's heading out on safari in his khaki shorts, white cotton T-shirt and a stained, well-worn brown leather hat.

"Is that your *Out of Africa* look?" I tease.

Josh shoots me a quick smile as he navigates the road in our rented jeep.

We had a brief chat this morning over breakfast about what happened last night. We've agreed to view our relationship as fellow investigators rather than lovers—at least for now.

The sky is bright blue with a few wisps of clouds. Tall oak trees line up on either side of the boulevard like giant soldiers. I think there's a river running to my right, but I can't see it for the high bank of red earth.

"How long?" I ask, shielding the rising sun from my eyes.

"About an hour," replies Josh. He shifts around in his seat to avoid getting stuck to the hot vinyl upholstery.

An hour passes slowly and allows me time to gather my thoughts. We're making a monumental mistake coming here, I think. I should abandon Shirley's house and go back to the city where I belong. I'm not an exorcist, and the cold hard truth is that I may be putting my life in danger—and Josh's too.

The dirt road leading up to Ravens' Pond is, not surprisingly, red, just like the horrible red soil now spreading on the grounds of Ravens' Wood. The notable contrast of the earth with the dark-brown bark of the trees and the huge green branches looks surreal.

I sense Josh leaning forward in anticipation. I'm doing the opposite, leaning back in my seat and wishing I were anywhere but here. My cotton dress sticks to my back like a second skin.

The scene before us unfolds: a body of water with the house sitting—more like slouching—at the back of the pond. The red road slopes to the left and as we approach, I get a better look at the house. What must have been a once-welcoming patio now sags dangerously to one side. The supports below are bent and missing, and the paint—once blue, as I recall from Aunt Shirley's painting—has faded to parched grey.

"What was that?" asks Josh, sounding alarmed.

"What, where?" I can't see anything except house, water and sky.

Josh exhales and leans back. "Nothing, I guess. I thought I saw somebody move around the side of the house to the back."

It may be a hundred degrees, but I'm now freezing. I hate this place already.

Josh pulls the jeep up to the parking area on the side, and soon we're out, making our way to the front door. I raise my hand to knock. Josh pulls his hat down a notch and takes my elbow.

The door creaks open. Dust motes dance in the sliver of light cutting its way inside. There is no furniture, only a wide, curving staircase with worn and stained carpet. We tiptoe in, afraid of waking somebody or something. The house has a presence, and I'm twenty seconds away from bolting back to the jeep.

I put one foot forward, shuffling to stand in the entranceway. I'm frozen in place and feel an unpleasant puff of air at my chin. Josh walks to the left and stops. He raises one hand up as if greeting someone, and I feel his tension.

All at once, I hear footsteps—thundering footsteps—accompanied by a deep-throated growl. My feet feel like they're encased in cement, and I can't move. The scream builds deep within me but releases quickly; the screeching sound is as loud as a siren.

Josh has my arm and is attempting to pull me out of the house, but I can't move. In fact, I don't want to move. I need and want to see whatever is causing this sound. I feel a fiery breath before I see its source: a massive dog that bounds toward me, ears plastered down, lips pulled back, teeth revealed. He doesn't seem to notice Josh.

He moves toward me, lunging for my neck. For a moment, I truly believe the dog will rip out my throat and I'll look down from the angels in the plaster ceiling above me as my blood stains the honey-coloured floor.

"Anubis! Down!" comes the harried cry of a man in pursuit of the dog.

My knees give out and I stare into the canine's enormous caramel-coloured eyes. He's still sizing me up. I feel sick to my stomach.

"Miss, I'm so sorry if my dog frightened you," says the man in a soft Southern accent. "I'm Frank. You must be Leah." He extends his hand. "Please, let me help you up."

Frank leads Josh and me to the kitchen as if everything is normal, offering us iced tea—probably laced with god knows what, I think. Even though I'm suspicious, the refreshment goes a long way toward calming us down. Josh drops his shoulders and gives Frank a smile. Anubis—named for the jackal-headed Egyptian god—apparently thinks he's a lap dog. After several unsuccessful tries at climbing onto my knees, he's parked himself on the floor beside me and soaks up as many pats as I can offer.

Frank shares stories of the property's history and its tenants. Not surprisingly, most of the previous renters had sought out a *Gone with the Wind* experience. What they found instead was a worn-out old shack with termites. Its day has come and gone.

Frank sits back slowly in a worn-out chair across from me and slides one knee over the other.

"So, you're the last member of the Everett family?"

Sighing, I reply, "I'm not a relative; my mother and Shirley, who was the last in the line, were best friends. She left the estate to me."

"Huh," Frank replies, standing up with considerable effort. "Well, then, I'll leave you while you take a tour of the grounds."

Josh borrows a cloth from Frank and is doing his best to mop the never-ending stream of sweat flowing from his golden crown. His complexion is flushed.

As we move toward the back of the property, we see what appears to be abandoned homes. I take a few steps closer to view doors ripped off of their hinges and broken windows, and to hear the wind moving through empty rooms. Turning, I see Josh moving back to the front of the house, and I hurry to catch up.

The crystal-clear pond depicted in paintings of Ravens' Pond in Shirley's house is now more like a swamp, with clouds of bugs wafting up from a grungy, muddy surface.

"This is where Ruby came looking for her big brother," I whisper to Josh.

Josh nods. "Where was he?"

Strolling over to the mucky edge, I lay a hand on his arm and quietly say, "Robert was at his friend's house. They were getting ready to go fishing."

Josh knits his brow. "But didn't little brothers and sisters talk about stuff like that? Why did she think to look here?"

"We'll never know for sure because they never saw her again," I say, tears filling my eyes. I find this story terribly sad. Clearing my throat, I wrap my hand around Josh's arm and head back to the house. "Maybe Frank and Anubis might have something to share," I say.

When we return to the house, Anubis shoots past Frank to greet me like I'm the last dog lover on earth, putting his enormous paws on my shoulder. I stand my ground, however, in a somewhat feeble effort to show him I'm the boss. I've put it off loo long. We need to see the house—or what's left of it.

I signal Frank with a nod; he turns and shuffles to the staircase, Anubis by his side.

"The Everett family history is interesting," he says. "William, who built the house, was an Egyptologist. He came back with a bunch of mummies and stuff and built this strange plantation house."

We move to follow him up the staircase.

Frank continues, "The servants here felt the evil from the artifacts he brought into the house and it freaked them out."

We reach the top of the stairs, and Frank leads us left, toward the bedrooms.

"The family lived in these rooms," he whispers as his bony hand reaches out to open what would have been Aunt Shirley's room, in my Einer's Bay version of the plantation. We glance in. Chunks of shredded faded wallpaper hang down. One cot remains, with no bedding—just twisted white metal.

Moving along the corridor, we see more of the same. No paintings remain on the wall, only their outlines on the faded paint. My heart thuds as we approach the access to the attic.

Frank waves a gnarled nicotine-stained hand and says, "Attic is up there. Nothing in it."

As I sigh in relief, I realize I need to see it for myself. "Frank, could I have a quick look?" I ask.

"Sure," he says. "Just be careful on the stairs. They're barely hanging on."

Josh takes the lead and holds my hand as I climb up three rickety steps. The attic is as described: empty. Cobwebs lace the windows, and on the floor is a dusty sheet. No sign of red earth up here.

Frank leads us back down the rotting staircase and stops at the bottom. Anubis lies down on the floor beside his master.

"There's nothing left of the basement. They say there used to be an exact replica of an Egyptian tomb down there," Franks says.

"When William returned to Egypt, there was a fire here, which destroyed the tomb and everything, except the sarcophagus and the death mask of a pharaoh. Inside, they found what they thought were the charred remains of William's son Reginald." Frank turns around as he crosses himself. "That turned out to be wrong, however, as Reginald Everett sightings have been going on for decades."

Two hours later, we have learned all there is to know about Ravens' Pond. Aunt Shirley's great-grandfather William built the house in the early nineteenth century. The remaining family members lived there until the 1970s, when it seems they abandoned the property. It has a long and disturbing history of terrible people.

I have another question for our host but unless there's more than one dollhouse, I already know the answer: "What happened to the dollhouse?"

Frank slowly turns his head to look at an empty patch of dirt.

"They shipped that cursed thing to some small town in British Columbia, Canada. Some woman wrote a book about the damned thing. Had people talking about it, but once it was gone ...."

"Ok, one more question, before we go," I say. "Why is the property called Ravens' Pond? I haven't seen a crow or a raven since we arrived."

Frank's eyes narrow as he brings his fist up under his chin.

"Well, now, that's an interesting question. You see, Master William brought home several ravens from Egypt and they bred. They were everywhere on the estate. Great big flapping things that, frankly, freaked everybody out. Everyone except William and Reginald, it was told."

"Why was that?" asks Josh.

"It had something to do with their obsession with Egypt and the afterlife. Some fairy tale of these birds having the ability to help you cross over," says Frank, shifting from foot to foot. "Those damned things were everywhere, apparently, and noisy as hell. Someone said when William left on his last trip to Egypt—a trip he never returned from—the ravens flew north and were not ever seen again."

The crumbling plantation house is the only building left standing on the once-stunning estate showcased in Aunt Shirley's painting. They have razed all outer buildings to the ground. There's nothing more to see here.

CHAPTER THIRTY-ONE

WILLIAM EVERETT, LUXOR, EGYPT, THE PAST: THE TREASURE HUNT

Ravens' Pond was custom-built for Shirley's great-grand-father, William Everett. The Egyptologist and thief had made many returns trips once he had located the best tombs to pilfer from and, most importantly, the best buyers to make the deals happen. He came back from that country with pockets full of gold and containers of antiquities bound for countries like Germany and England. He'd created a fortune selling key treasures to the British Museum, but now it was time to go home and finish building his mansion.

William was a handsome man. Blessed with fine features, large blue eyes and a head of thick, dark-blond hair, he had no problems attracting women. He and his African-American man-servant, Louis, stood out in the desert city of Luxor; the staff of the Old Winter Palace Hotel took excellent care of Mr. Everett, even when they dreaded his arrival.

***

It had been a long, sweltering day under the excruciating Egyptian sun. William shot back his first cold mint julep and thumped his empty glass on the table in front of him. Louis scooped it up, refilled it and popped in a fresh mint leaf before he handed it back to his boss.

William surveyed their surroundings. Booked into one of the most luxurious suites at the Old Winter Palace Hotel , William cast a critical eye at the fading wallpaper and cracked paint. The

Egyptian sun was cruel to any surface. He stepped onto the enormous deck overlooking the gardens. The stillness in the searing air—even though the sun had almost set—entranced him.

Louis had retreated to his quarters, and William did not expect to see him again until first light. This was William's favourite time of day, when he could enjoy his much-loved activity: cataloguing. Finally alone, he could sip his drink and fondle the winnings of the day. While most of his antiquities were small, they were also precious. The stones were all cut with incredible skill, and the designs were the most unusual he'd seen in a lifetime of searching for the best.

William held up the women's ring he had won at this evening's poker game. The gold was rose-hued; its stone was lapis and exquisitely carved in the shape of the dung beetle. The scarab was one of Egypt's most powerful symbols, inspired by the humble insect that existed on its own excrement. For William, the scarab was the perfect example of self-sufficiency. He paused and lifted a beautifully painted Shabti doll.

Another inexperienced player he'd beaten had given him a dozen of the dolls in exchange for something rather worthless. The man obviously didn't understand their value. William liked the little funerary dolls, and these were exceptional. Next, he selected a lemony yellow one with long, silky black hair. William decided to hang on to her. For some reason, she reminded him of the part crocodile, part lion, part hippo demon, Ammit, and that is what he named her.

He filled his glass with a healthy splash of bourbon and glanced up to the wall beside his bed. After years of swindling, lying, cheating—even thieving and eventually murdering—he had his treasure, his key to immortality. There she lay, rolled up carefully in a sheet of blue silk: the priceless Papyrus of Ani, the crowning jewel to his collection.

Carved on an alabaster stand in the tomb of Mycerinus, the

letters had a lapis lazuli inlay. But it wasn't its exceptional beauty William lusted over—in fact, killed for. It was for sheer and enormous power. With that single piece of dark-lettered papyrus, he could move in and out of this world at a whim.

But the first and no doubt the most critical step was into the great unknown. William shook with excitement at his latest discovery: the time portal. He knew how to obtain that powerful tool. He just needed to get his hands around Einer's neck to make it so.

CHAPTER THIRTY-TWO

LOUIS BARDIN, OLD WINTER PALACE HOTEL, LUXOR, EGYPT, THE PAST: THE MANSERVANT

Louis always seemed to be exhausted while William seemed to possess endless energy: to bed at 2 a.m., dressed and ready for breakfast at 5 a.m. Maybe it was the slight difference in their age or the heat. Either way, it was annoying. Removing his cummerbund, Louis took a deep and cleansing breath, and then flung it across the room.

"I hate that damn thing," he growled, pants and jacket tossed to a heap on the chair, and then squeezed his shoulders to relax them.

While not all people would agree, Louis found his boss to be a mostly fair man, if occasionally cruel and capable of holding a grudge that could only be measured by decades. Shaking his head, Louis turned on the water in his bathtub, waited for the right temperature and stepped in. Breathing in a sigh of satisfaction, he took a long swallow of the white wine he'd preordered.

Louis was aching to know what his boss was up to. Something significant, he believed, and something ominous. William would normally have filled Louis in by now. Theirs was a relationship of respect.

Louis's family had worked as slaves at the Lewison plantation that would someday become known as Ravens' Pond. When the slaves were freed in 1865, the Lewison family—who owned both the mansion and adjacent slave houses—offered employment to those who chose to stay. The Bardin and Lewison families became very close, celebrating birthdays and special events.

Frank Lewison actually renovated then deeded the previous

slave quarter town to the Bardin Family. Together, they worked tirelessly in the sugar cane industry, right until the plantation house was burned to the ground.

Louis felt his nails biting into his palms as he recalled the time his father told him about the savagery of the group of men, covered head to toe in black, and how they had murdered every living soul in the house by sealing them in and lighting it on fire. His voice had cracked with rage and sorrow as he spoke about women jumping from the rooftops, landing with their limbs cracked and twisted. The bizarre sight of Mr. Lewison running, his burned skin falling behind him like he had casually shrugged off a sweater.

They spared the livestock, and the now free slaves, living in their own community at the back of the land. These were hateful, evil men who didn't approve of white people sitting at the same table as the help.

Later, Louis's father had the remains of the plantation house cleared, and the property sat bare and held in trust until one day, when a dapper Englishman came knocking on Louis's front door, hat in hand, and an idea to purchase the land and build his own mansion.

Louis smiled as he recalled that encounter. Times were tough. The sugar cane business was hard and the days long, but they were slowly getting back on their feet. William's offer came at the right time.

While Louis knew he occupied a different class than his boss, William had never treated him as such, and the two of them had spent countless hours going over the building plans for Ravens' Pond. William appreciated Louis's broad depth of knowledge, and they formed a friendship that would end up being a lifetime one. William so valued his wisdom that he offered him the permanent position of his manservant as well as that of his business partner, which Louis accepted with gratitude. Times were changing for the better, but what William offered his friend was security for life.

CHAPTER THIRTY-THREE

WILLIAM, IN THE DESERT, 40 MILES WEST OF THE VALLEY OF THE KINGS, THE PAST: THE GOD FORSAKEN HEAT

The following morning, the sun was scalding hot as William adjusted his pith helmet, mopping the ceaseless sweat cascading down his face, neck and back. Even his forearms were sweating.

Turning to a fellow dealer to his side, he said, "How do you stand this god forsaken heat?!"

The man next to him laughed and said, "You get used to it after a few seasons." William shook his head, pulled up his rucksack from the hot sand and made his way over to a wisp of shade.

Dropping to the ground, he scrunched up as far as possible to the skinny palm tree responsible for a bit of shade no wider than his fist and removed his water flask from his pocket. Glugging back mouthfuls of warm water, William wiped his brow once again and exhaled, his shoulders sagging in fatigue.

Trading had been disappointing today. That was how it went. Significant discoveries by the archaeologists, followed by a precision raid of the relics. The most nefarious and dangerous gangs in Egypt did these activities in the black of night. Once they loaded the goods, they transported them to a little-known spot in the desert where top traders would try to outbid each other for the cream of the crop.

William had staked an early claim with these thieves who were taken in by his smooth style, impeccable English accent and generous tips. It was still kill, or be killed, thought William, raising the corner of his mouth in a smirk. All a part of the game.

The sound of the traders chatting about their treasures was suddenly broken by a familiar sound; the easy, floating wingbeats of a pair of the local ravens. They made the oddest sound, thought William. A cross between someone choking and gurgling.

These ravens fascinated William. Bonded for life—as a friend informed him—they were extremely intelligent and marvellously talented at scooping up treasures and flying off to bury them where they would never be seen again. At first, William thought it was daft they weren't shot on sight. Why would the raiders allow this pillage? He was soon to know there was much more to the glossy black birds with their big, hooked noses and penetrating eyes.

CHAPTER THIRTY-FOUR

EINER & SLAITH, DUBLIN, THE PAST: THE TOMB RAIDERS

W alk into any bar and you'll find a lonely-looking guy sitting all by himself on the furthest stool to the right. He's slumped over, swaying back and forth, giving a clear indication he's about to fall flat on either his face or backside. Either way, it's going to hurt.

Einer Magnusson was parked on that lonely chair. Despite his troll-like looks, he could scan any bar anywhere, and with the laser-like focus of his bleary blue eyes, reel in the most attractive woman in the place. Her eyes would light up not because of his toad-like face, or his paunchy stomach or his rank breath—she saw just one thing—money. Lots and lots of money.

Einer came from a dirt-poor family. Living like gypsies all the way from Norway to Ireland, they settled on the outskirts of Dublin, where they scavenged daily for a hunk of bread to break amongst the family of five. The mother passed shortly after her youngest son died at five, leaving Einer to cope with his drunkard father and two snot-nosed and useless sisters. Einer left them one dark night and never looked back.

While Einer wasn't even what you could remotely call home schooled, he had a way with numbers. Math came easy to him, and he quickly settled into the gambling world in Dublin.

***

Einer was bored. He'd been hearing about valuable treasure being hauled out of tombs in Egypt. He had the money to go to Luxor now, but he'd met a friend recently who had some very powerful knowledge that might result in greater success, so Einer decided it was worth a slight delay to find out more.

Slaith was a good gambler, and the ladies loved him. Tall with a solid build, he had a habit of constantly slicking back his jet-black hair and pulling deeply from a diamond-studded, ivory cigarette holder that was never far from his hand.

He was a cruel man and didn't hesitate to whack you with the black leather crop he kept by his side. Still, men and women flocked to him for what others couldn't offer: insight into the power of portals that could transport you to other worlds.

Slaith had been seeking a partner in his business of robbing other countries of their valuable treasures. Portals would make the game so easy! Locating the damned portals had not been easy at all.

So far, he'd located one in here in Ireland called Brun a Boinne, the Palace of the Boyne in Newgrange, Ireland. "Thin spots" is what Celts called places where the line between the living and the dead, the ordinary and the mystical, might be penetrable.

Recently he'd heard rumours about one in Egypt, but the other traders didn't know or trust him, so he was having trouble breaking in. That's where ugly little Einer came in. Slaith slicked back his hair while envisioning what it would be like when it was all over and he could slit the little shit's throat. He laughed as he envisioned the shock in those beady little eyes as fiery blood spurted from his scrawny neck.

***

A month later, Einer and Slaith were on a boat destined for Cairo. From there, they would take a train to Luxor, home of the Valley of the Kings and nearby Valley of the Queens. While the world focused on the tombs of kings and queens, the robbers were making a fortune selling everything from priceless gems to mummies as star attractions for parties hosted by the European elite. Mummies were also ground into powder as a medicinal treatment. Many fortunes were made during the time of "mummy mania."

The tomb raiders were a fiercely competitive and nasty group. Einer and Slaith knew it wouldn't be easy edging their way in, but the big bags of money they'd earned gambling would definitely open a few doors.

CHAPTER THIRTY-FIVE

EINER & SLAITH, LUXOR, THE PAST: THE TOMB RAIDERS

Comfortably settled in two suites at the Old Winter Palace Hotel in Luxor, Einer and Slaith agreed to meet downstairs at eight for dinner. Einer was already seated when Slaith slithered in. Dressed in his usual uniform of a shiny black suit with a stiff, starched white shirt, he swept the room with his heavy-lidded dark-green eyes. Einer had received a good whack on the backside for suggesting Slaith looked and moved like a snake.

"Einer," Slaith said as the waiter snapped a thickly starched white napkin before placing it softly on his lap. "What have you learned about the portal?"

Nervously sniffing three times before he spoke, Einer gestured to the waiter to refill his glass of red wine.

"Not too much, my friend. There is some talk about a secret passageway that connects Egypt to Morocco, but nothing else."

Slaith tapped his fingers as he drilled a hole into Einer's forehead with the intensity of his stare.

"That's it?" he hissed.

Einer sniffed three times again, swallowed deeply and paused before responding.

"I have, however, made great inroads with the local tomb raiders. It would seem they have too much treasure to cope with and could use more traders to move the artifacts."

Slaith cracked his knuckles and picked up a piece of bread from the table. Staring at Einer until he started to sweat, Slaith nodded once.

"Fine. You deal with the nasty little thieves, and I'll find the portal. The real portal, not some mythical passageway to Morocco."

And that's how the partnership began. Einer was masterful with his fellow traders. He had all the charm in the world for men who could make him rich. He became quite comfortable living in Egypt and really saw little of Slaith, who was gone most of the time in search of the portal. Einer knew he also spent a great deal of time in the whorehouses; they shared a love of sex for hire.

***

Slaith was growing impatient with Einer. He'd been missing for three days, and while he'd been known to linger for two days at the local whorehouses, this was unusual, even for him. Standing in front of his bathroom mirror, Slaith dipped his fingers into his hair oil. While Macassar oil was usually quite aromatic with ingredients of coconut oil, ylang-ylang and other fragrant oils, Slaith added whale oil to his concoction. The ladies—drawn by his good looks and sharp style—would instantly recoil when they got within sniffing distance. Slaith was oblivious to their reaction.

"Damn his eyes!" he shouted at his mirror image, picking up a bar of soap and turning to hurl it over his shoulder where it smashed into a lampshade.

CHAPTER THIRTY-SIX

EINER, ABU GHURAB, EYGPT, THE PAST: THE GATEWAY TO CANADA

E iner had, in fact, already discovered the Egyptian portal, located just south of Cairo. During the time he spent with the tomb raiders, he befriended a man called Bakari. Bakari was one of the oldest of the tomb raiders and had been making a living stealing treasure for decades. His family ran an extensive business in Egypt, and while generous and easy to work with, they'd behead anyone who stole from them.

Bakari was slowing down, which meant he wasn't able to move the goods as fast as he should. He needed help and a new part of the world to ship them to. Einer fit the bill. Over many days, working side by side, Bakari began to trust the strange little man from Dublin. Their plan was solid; Einer would load up his rucksack with as many antiquities as it could hold, step onto the portal and transport himself to the west coast of Canada. Bakari had made the journey once but was so freaked out about the experience, he refused to return.

Einer agreed to take the chance. For two days they filled the rucksack with priceless gold and silver jewellery for melting, precious stones and small ancient statues. In addition to these treasures, they bundled up valuable relics of mummified fingers, toes, noses and penises, which would command enormous sums of money in the New World.

***

Einer's first trip to British Columbia's wilderness went smoothly. After the initial terror of stepping onto the platform at Abu

Ghurab, he lost consciousness for a few seconds and woke to find himself lying in wet grass.

Having no idea where he was—he decided to declare the large wooded acreage he landed on as his own. Walking to the end of the property, he had no clue where the closest civilization might be. Trudging across Europe as a child had taught him much, though— he knew he was close to the sea by the salty breeze, so he followed the scent to see where it might lead. Where there was ocean, there were often fishermen he could use to ship his goods.

After several minutes of walking, Einer cupped his ear; he could hear people laughing. Following the voices, he reached the top of a hill and smiled at the sight of fishing boats. Looking west of the marina, he could see shops and shacks. He had successfully landed in a place where he could do business. Einer sniffed three times then spit on the ground; he'd found his new home.

***

Einer connected with a gold digger in town who helped him move the artifacts and precious stones to Canadian or American collectors and have the gold and silver melted down and exchanged for goods, services or cash. He paid very little for the deed to his new property and with money in pocket, he quickly returned to Egypt. He had to deal with Slaith.

CHAPTER THIRTY-SEVEN

SLAITH & EINER, LUXOR, THE PAST: A STRAINED PARTNERSHIP

Slaith's anger had built to a terrifying rage by the time Einer returned from Canada. The head concierge at the Old Winter Palace Hotel advised Slaith of Einer's return, and a meeting in the hotel bar was arranged for 7 p.m. Slaith was already at the table by the time Einer wandered in. Einer strutted across the floor, dressed in a blue suit, white shirt and colourful paisley tie. Slaith did not stand or shake his hand. His lips were tight, his eyes blazing with outrage.

Einer ignored him and sat down at the table. A waiter appeared from behind a red curtain, his hands shaking as he approached. Einer ordered a gin fizz, while Slaith gave an almost imperceptible nod to his glass of scotch. The server practically ran back to the curtain, clearly rattled by Slaith.

Slaith slicked back his hair with one hand, while the other came from beneath the table holding a small but deadly looking knife. Einer instinctively backed his chair away from the table and held up both hands in defence.

"Wait, Slaith!" he cried. "Don't you want to see what I've brought you?"

Slaith's knife hand was shaking in anger. Taking a few deep breaths to calm himself, he gave Einer a quick nod of his head. Einer stood up, reached down into the front pocket of his pants and pulled out a large wad of dollar bills.

"How much?" growled Slaith.

Einer slowly sat down, pulled his pants up at the knees and grinned.

"Two thousand dollars."

Slaith paused to consider this large amount, then extended his hand, palm up. Einer quickly handed the money over to his partner, who snatched it so hard, Einer's hand bled.

Wrapping his napkin over the scratches, Einer smiled and said, "Happy now, partner?"

Slaith laughed. Just a quiet chuckle at first that built into a roar as he tossed his head back. Einer joined him as other patrons looked on in disgust at this boorish behaviour.

***

Slaith went missing that night. There were many theories tossed about by the tomb robbers which went on for several weeks. Then, it was like he was never there.

Einer knew where he was. He'd drugged Slaith's scotch that night at the bar, reclaimed his money, packed Slaith into a cheap wooden coffin and shipped him back to Dublin. Einer, of course, assumed Slaith would die en route, but on that count, he'd be wrong.

Einer went back and forth to the town in Canada that eventually became known as "Einer's Bay" thanks to the largesse of the exporter who called it home. While he came and went like the wind, Einer could always be counted on to make huge donations to the town, and it grew and prospered for many years. Then one day, he simply stopped coming back.

CHAPTER THIRTY-EIGHT

LOUIS, WILLIAM & EINER, ABU GHURAB, THE PAST: THE TIME PORTAL

William had detested Einer from the moment he laid eyes on him. There was an unspoken respect the tomb raiders had for one another. It was important to establish at least somewhat of a rapport with them. They all had one thing in common: they plundered the antiquities of Egypt and made a lot of money doing it. Trades were essential to long-term success.

Short, fat and smelling like rancid oil, Einer wasn't a team player. William loved to stand back and watch him work the room, trying to impress everyone with his false compliments delivered with beady eyes and a phony, plastered-on smile. William could hardly wait to wipe that look off his face, but first he had to figure out how Einer was able to sell off his antiquities with such speed and be back at the poker table with a seemingly endless supply of money. William tasked Louis with the job of following him until they figured out his game.

Exhausted after the train trip to Cairo and countless late nights following Einer from one whorehouse to another, Louis thought this evening seemed different. The crickets were dead quiet, and the normally serene palm trees rustled in the blustering wind. The sand was blowing around, and the air was thick with it, so it was a challenge to keep watching that short little frog man. Louis carefully rubbed sand from his eyes, replaced his glasses and dropped down in case he was too close.

After several days of trekking through the desert, he now realized where he was: Abu Ghurab itself. Close to the Great Pyramid of Giza, and known as "The Raven's Nest," the belief was Nyuserre Ini, a Fifth Dynasty pharaoh, built the temple to worship the sun god, Ra. It was said that its alabaster platform was used to connect to other portals or gateways around the planet and to the stars.

Louis pulled off his outer sweater, gave it a good shake and put it back in his rucksack. Now that he was better positioned with his binoculars, he leaned back on a palm tree to wait. Einer wasted not a moment strutting up to the large circle at the top of the platform. Lightning split the sky; for a moment, Louis thought Einer might scamper off like a rabbit, but he stayed. A couple of minutes later, a second bolt of lightning lit up the dark so bright that Louis had to close his eyes. When he opened them moments later, there was no sign of Einer.

CHAPTER THIRTY-NINE

WILLIAM, ABU GHURAB, THE PAST: THE TIME PORTAL

William waited several days for Louis to return. He finally received a telegram from him and packed a small bag and made the trip to Abu Ghurab. Louis had indicated in his note that he intended to step onto the platform on the heels of Einer. William wasted no time getting to Abu Ghurab, and under a luminous moon, he hefted his heavy pack over his right shoulder and ran as fast as he could to the platform circle. Sweat poured down his face, and his knees shook with fear.

Could this be real? If the time portal truly existed, where would he end up? William panicked and was about to jump off the platform when, seconds later, a great bolt of lightning streaked through the sky. The vibrations inside his body were so strong, he thought he was about to be blown apart. The acrid stench of burning hair filled his nostrils and he blacked out.

In what seemed like mere seconds, he was prone, face-first in a pile of cow dung, at the foot of a large boulder. He wiped his face as best he could by smearing it on the grass and mopping with his handkerchief, and soon he felt human again. Back on his feet, he snapped open the front pocket of his pack and pulled out his binoculars. Einer had bragged to pretty much everyone about his property in British Columbia, Canada, describing it as a large chunk of land, surrounded by giant trees and mountains so big they reached the sky. What William and Louis didn't know was anything about the time portal.

Einer really did have a nice piece of property here, he thought. It was shaped like a big horseshoe, with some of the most spectacular trees he'd ever seen, surrounding a large patch of wild grass. Off in the distance, he saw a building, but how far away was hard to calculate. He opted to set up where he was against the trees for the night.

***

William spent the better part of the next day looking for Louis. If he had made it to this site during the current time period, there would have been some signs. There were none, so William returned to the boulder and waited two long days before the sky darkened, the lightening flashed and he was once again transported, this time back to Abu Ghurab. He returned to Egypt with a heavy heart, knowing he'd probably never see his friend again.

CHAPTER FORTY

RAVENS' POND, GRAND OPENING, THE PAST: THE CLOUD OF CORVIDS

William exhaled and tilted his head back in the hot sun. He was excited about the grand opening of his new and impressive Southern mansion, especially since the ravens had arrived. It had cost him considerable money to smuggle the male and female ravens out of Egypt, but they would soon prove themselves most useful.

He'd spent hours with fellow tomb traders, talking about the remarkable abilities of these impressive corvids. He'd seen a pair at a local dig, and their level of intelligence mesmerized him. How they communicated with each other through a strange series of low honks, deep, guttural croaking and a hollow wonk-wonk. William learned about the important role ravens played as guides to the afterlife, and with that, he knew he had to have them.

***

Preparing for the plantation's grand opening had exhausted the staff. They had scrubbed, washed, polished, swept, trimmed and raked for weeks. When they weren't doing manual labour, they were on their hands and knees praying for a miracle to keep the weather calm and dry for the next few days.

After the terrible death of the lady of the house who died giving birth to her son Reginald, Shelly had advanced from personal maid to head housekeeper. While the staff worked tirelessly to make the house and grounds perfect, Shelly planned every detail of the grand opening. She'd done a wonderful job of organizing it all. At least three times a day, long white sheets of paper covered with meticulous handwriting would come flying out from beneath her office door; her orders were to be followed to the letter.

Shelly had taken excellent care of Mistress Helen during her second pregnancy. The two of them were together a great deal. When the staff walked past the mistress's closed door, they had to clap a hand over their mouths to not laugh out loud when Mistress Helen barked out a belly laugh as deep and robust as any man they'd ever met. Then there were interminable days when Shelly would slide silently from that room, softly squeezing the rose-painted ceramic door handle shut; the pregnancy wasn't going well.

Everyone knew William had married Helen for her bloodline and her beauty. Tall for her era, she had hair the colour of a raven's wing, creamy skin and heavy-lidded dark-brown eyes. Helen was a gentle soul who never felt at home in America. She missed everything about London. She also despised her husband and wished him dead with every breath she took.

Toward the end and bedridden, Helen's face was thin and pale, her once-glorious hair hung like black strings. She wasn't showing as much as she should in her third trimester and could barely eat. The local doctor had done his best, but in the end, Helen's fate was sealed. She died in childbirth and would never meet her son.

William was inconsolable, and after several weeks of listening to the baby crying, screaming and hammering the walls with his fists, the house went dead quiet. William had left for Egypt.

Four years later, he had finally come to terms with the loss of his beautiful Helen. Now it was time for the grand opening of Ravens' Pond.

***

While the house itself was majestic, with its pristine white columns standing guard in front of buttercup-painted walls and creamy trim, those who attended the party left soon after William had cut the large red satin ribbon. There was something sickening about how the ribbon snapped, like a frayed, taut wire.

If the intent was to welcome guests up the gleaming oak stairs to the wide-open double front doors and the immense tables of food and wine, the grand opening had failed miserably. Not long after the ribbon-cutting ceremony, dark clouds surrounded Ravens' Pond, and the handful of remaining guests scurried like slick dark rats to their coaches while the rain poured down.

An unkindness of ravens suddenly appeared as a black cloud, causing guests to panic— pushing, screaming, flailing in the mud before launching their sodden bodies into their coaches. People were terrified by the unusual and shockingly vast number of huge black birds raining down from the sky.

The front doors of Ravens' Pond swung shut, the locks shot like bullets into their chambers and the grand opening was like it had never happened.

CHAPTER FORTY-ONE

REGINALD AS A CHILD, RAVENS' POND, THE PAST: THE DEMON'S BIRTH

*It is a frightening thought that man also has a
shadow side to him, consisting not just of little
weaknesses and foibles, but of a positively demonic
dynamism. The individual seldom knows anything of
this; to him, as an individual, it is incredible that he
should ever in any circumstances go beyond himself.
But let these harmless creatures form a mass, and
there emerges a raging monster.*
—**Carl Jung**, *Psychology of the Unconscious*

W illiam and Helen had two children: a daughter named
Bridget, and a son, Reginald, born two years apart.
The two children couldn't have been more different.
Bridget had a sweet nature and curly, golden-red hair. Her eyes
were blue, like her father's; her soul soft, like her mother's.

Reginald, on the other hand, was strange from the time he
squirmed purple-faced into the world, the cord wrapped around
his neck as his mother fought for both of them to live. The doctor
spanked Reginald soundly into existence, and the child spent the
rest of his life seeking revenge for losing his mother—and, it would
appear, his soul.

His father blamed his son for the death of his beautiful wife
and could barely look at him, let alone show any affection.

Reginald's hair was raven black like his dead mother's, dark
eyes like hers, but where his mother's eyes were brown with flecks

of warm honey, his were black pits of pure charcoal.

Ravens' Pond had always had a negative energy. The interior of the house was curiously more Egyptian in decor than one would ever see in the South. Funerary items and tomb mosaics with their strange paintings adorned the walls.

Bridget would spend hours running her fingers over the figures, trying to understand them. Reginald also enjoyed the unique decor, but his favourite place was in his father's office and the chamber located directly below it. It was there, in the blood-red chamber, that Reginald first encountered the sarcophagus.

If Reginald had died during childbirth it would have been a blessing, for even as a youngster he was a pariah. Children of the servants would run screaming and laughing if he tried to move into their well-guarded circles. His sister, Bridget, tried everything to make him feel included, but his jealousy was suffocating; he loved to sketch pictures of the many ways his sister could die.

He had one friend named Rufus, the African-American son of his father's manservant, Louis. Although Rufus was several years younger than Reginald, both boys loved to pretend to be gods or demons of Egypt, sneaking down into William's tomb, trying, without success, to lift the heavy lid of the stone sarcophagus. Then Ammit entered Reginald's life, and nothing was ever the same.

One of the little games Reginald played with William was to sit on the floor in front of his dad's huge, black, wooden desk and chuck a rubber ball against the wall. He knew it made his father crazy. With each toss, Reginald threw the ball harder, making the glass window above vibrate, with delicate crystal trinkets moving precariously closer to the edge of the windowsill with each toss. To his credit, William barely blinked an eye.

"Reginald," he said after two or three ball slams. "I might have something for you."

The boy got up from the floor at once, his black eyes large and hungry. "What is it, Father?" he asked, hands clasped in front of him.

His dad reached down to open a drawer, and he pulled out something wrapped in old, crumpled paper. "I found something in Luxor I thought you might like. Do you want to see it?"

Reginald couldn't believe his ears! His father had a gift for him. He took a deep breath to calm himself as he walked over to the side of the black walnut desk. His father handed him a small package and advised him to be extremely gentle when he opened it. Reginald's heart was beating wildly as he nervously reached for the gift.

With delicate hands, he slowly unwrapped what at first glance appeared to be a statue. It was a wooden carving of a woman.

"Father," Reginald asked, his voice trembling, "is this a *doll?*"

William did something he almost never did in front of his son: he smiled.

"Why yes, son. It is a Shabti doll; she's named for Ammit. Do you like her?"

William reached forward as if to take it away.

Reginald pulled it beyond his dad's reach and continued to unwrap the Shabti.

"I think she's a fine example of a New Kingdom funerary figure, Father," he said, straightening his posture but afraid to make eye contact with his dad. He was sure there was some kind of cruel joke being played on him; there always was.

After a few seconds of silence, William sighed.

Reginald looked up in surprise to see his father smiling at him again.

William rose and came around to Reginald's side of the desk, planting an arm around his son's slender shoulder.

"I'm glad you like it, son," he said.

Reginald didn't move or breathe until he was certain his dad was out of range. He couldn't bear the thought of his dad watching as the gush of tears of gratitude flowed down his face. His father would think him weak and despise him even more.

From that day on, Ammit—the demon spirit inhabiting the Shabti doll— would keep her eye on the boy who would soon be a powerful demon. She would become the eyes of Ma'at, the all-powerful Egyptian goddess of truth, justice and morality. Reginald's fate was in her hands, There may have been hundreds more Shabti dolls in the dollhouse chest shipped last month from Luxor, but there was only one Ammit, and she was a mighty beast.

CHAPTER FORTY-TWO

THE DEMON NAMED AMMIT, EGYPT, THE PAST: THE TRANSFORMATION

Before her supernatural transformation from human to demon, one of Ammit's earliest memories was that she was small for her age, except for her feet. She hated her big, grimy toes, and despite daily scrubs with the yellow sand she walked on, they were never clean. Ammit collected little wooden sticks, and with these she would pull the chunks of dirty skin and sand from between her toes. Following a hurried rinse, she'd tumble quickly into the shallow part of the water, washing her body as fast as she could before returning to the River of the Night's edge.

Her friend had not been as lucky last week; the sound of his youthful body cracking and snapping as a hippo killed him had terrified her. Afterwards, she woke her family with her night terrors so many times that her father threw her out of the tent to sleep with the animals.

Grabbing another one of her wooden sticks, she quickly brushed her teeth and then stuck her head in the cool water, scrubbing hard with her fingernails to remove the sand and bugs.

As the water drained from her ears, she heard another sound—

boom, boom, followed by a hiss that turned into a terrifying low growl. Ammit knew that noise. She grabbed her clothes and shoes and risked one last look over her shoulder. The ferocious grey beast steamed toward her, his nostrils shooting great geysers of water, his giant feet digging deep pits into the earth as a backdraft of sand filled the sky. Ammit had no chance to escape.

***

The next phase of Ammit's transformation was just as painful. Encumbered by her now enormous hippo feet, she could not out-run the lion who pinned its claws into the backs of her legs as she ran, stripping them down to the bone. Her blood gushed and left a strange blotted pattern in the sand.

Her final conversion was comparatively simple but no less painful. As Ammit immersed her bloodied head into the cool waters of the Nile, she thought she caught the reflection of a crocodile standing close by her at the water's edge. She had no time to flee. As she turned to run, the beast pushed her down into the hot sand. Ammit could feel his hot breath as his sharp teeth sunk down into the base of her skull. As the blood puddled down around her chin, she lost consciousness, mercifully.

***

She woke up with the cool water lapping at her chin. This time, she did catch a reflection of a yellow-eyed crocodile standing at the water—but it was her own image she saw. She would now be known as Ammit, Devourer of Bones. With the legs and feet of a hippo, the body and arms of a lion and the head of a crocodile, there wasn't much left of the girl with the big grimy toes. She was tall, lethal and steadfastly loyal to her master, Ma'at. The goddess had given Ammit an important assignment, and Ammit wouldn't take it lightly.

Reginald

CHAPTER FORTY-THREE

REGINALD AS A CHILD, RAVENS' POND, THE PAST: THE INITIATION

People in strange costumes filled the tomb at Ravens' Pond. When Reginald first arrived, he thought it was a fun party. At nine years of age, he felt special because his father had included him in what he described as a "very rare ceremony." Now, he wove his way amongst the partygoers.

Being little was a clear advantage: He could scoot around, grab people's drinks from the tables and drain them, then watch what the guest's hands were doing below the waist. The partygoers looked like someone had peeled them off the walls of an ancient Egyptian tomb. Reginald saw the goddess Isis with her beautiful gossamer wings; he spotted the cow-headed Hathor, who smiled at him beneath her Colombina half-mask. His heart skipped a beat when Horus swept down to his level and brushed the top of his head with his right wing. It startled Reginald to feel blood run down his right cheek.

All of the adults were drunk. Reginald knew his father liked to drink amber-coloured alcohol, always served in his special crystal glass. He loved to sneak in when his dad was away and pick the glass up, twirl it in the window and watch the rainbows dance around the room.

This night was different, though. The women shrieked with laughter, twirling around, their hands pulling down the necks of their outfits to reveal heavily powdered breasts. The men were even worse—they shoved their hands down the front of the dresses, sometimes two hands at a time.

Reginald wanted to leave, but first he needed to find his father.

After some time, he finally spotted William across the room and walked over to greet him. He smiled as he realized his dad would see him safely removed from these crazy people. William stopped so close to him that Reginald thought he'd fall backwards. He bent down, and in a voice low and sinister, he whispered something that caused Reginald to fear he would wet himself with terror:

"Come with me, son. It is time."

***

Reginald lost track of time and realized he must have had lost consciousness. His father had put something in his drink, bound his eyes tightly and put a gag on his mouth. People were chanting in a language he couldn't understand. But he knew where he was—the tomb had an indescribable odour of must, metal and blood. It was here that his father had enjoyed embalming the bodies of animals he killed. But why was Reginald here now?

He was on his hands and knees, and his limbs were tied down to something. What was happening? Suddenly, the room fell silent. Reginald struggled to remove the mask from his face. He used his right shoulder to push it up, and he could see shapes moving closer. The chanting was getting louder. Candles were lit along the wall that displayed the papyrus.

Someone was close to him. He could smell sweat and a foul stench.

Reginald dipped his chin to his right shoulder. He could just make out the shape of a masked man. As the form moved into the candlelight, Reginald screamed under his gag. A man was behind him now, and they were both on top of the sarcophagus. But that wasn't his father's face. It was the face of Anubis! Reginald screamed again, and this time he could feel the warm trickle of urine dripping down his legs.

Reginald pulled to get away from the sarcophagus, but it was no use. They had his hands and feet tied tight to the top of the box. Through the left screen of his face mask, he saw a tall man standing in the shadows who looked like his father.

"Dad!" he cried, hot tears spewing from his eyes.

The tall man in a black, hooded cloak turned once in the direction of the boy's cry. Tears fell silently down his aged, furrowed cheeks; with his head bowed forward, the cape covered William's face as he turned and walked slowly away. Reginald knew then his father was leaving him for dead.

Anubis kept approaching, unrepelled by the urine. He pulled down Reginald's pants, and then the boy felt a horrible, burning, piercing pain when the demon plunged into him. Just before losing consciousness, Reginald heard Anubis grunt with lust and breathe out the words: "I'm so sorry, son. Your father lost the bet."

The last sound Reginald heard was the thunderous applause of the crowd. Then the world went black.

***

Reginald awoke to find himself in the sarcophagus. He'd tried kicking and screaming, but no one came to his rescue. There was little air, and he figured out fast he'd better calm down or he'd suffocate to death. His hands read the stories on the side of the stone grave to keep him calm.

In the gloomy, creepy silence of the sarcophagus, Reginald heard a quiet voice. Someone or something was calling his name.

"Reggie, boy! Are you here, lad?"

Reginald tried to scoot over to the far side of the box, as far away as possible from the voice that couldn't possibly be in here with him.

"Who are you? *Where* are you?" Reginald whispered. He had planted himself to the wall of the sarcophagus and was clinging tightly to the edge.

"Why lad, you need not fear me. I'm the answer to all of your prayers," cooed a feminine voice.

Reginald jumped as he felt claws prickling up and down his back.

"Come on, little man. What have you always wanted to be?"

The creature's disgusting breath and the sharp claws tracing up and down his body immobilized him. All at once, the soft voice became a loud, high-pitched scream—a scream merged with Reginald's own screeching.

"Come on, you lousy piece of crap!" she cackled loudly. "You know what you are! You're like him, but you're so much stronger than him! He might be evil ... but *you* are a demon. Or should I say, you'll soon be one!"

***

Reginald awoke to the sound of servants cleaning up the mess after the party. The terrible creature was gone, and he shuddered at the thought of the unearthly strength it took for her to lift the lid of the sarcophagus. Hooking his right leg to drop over the side of the coffin, he almost passed out from the pain. He somehow made it to his bedroom closet before blacking out.

CHAPTER FORTY-FOUR

WILLIAM, RAVENS' POND, THE PAST: THE PARTY IS OVER

By the time William returned to Ravens' Pond, the party was long since over. The house reeked of cigars, booze, sickeningly sweet perfume and sex. Furniture was tossed about, and ladies' undergarments fluttered from lampshades. Tossing his overcoat to the floor, his head fell forward to his chest. It was some time before he found the strength to lift his head and look at the nightmarish scene he had created. His hand flew to his mouth in shock. Someone had removed the heavy stone lid of the sarcophagus! But how? There was nobody there.

***

William searched for hours for his son; the shame of what he had done to his own child sickened him. He slammed his hand against his forehead again and again, sobbing and choking on his disgust.

CHAPTER FORTY-FIVE

REGINALD AS A CHILD, RAVENS' POND, THE PAST: THE ARRIVAL OF AMMIT

I t took weeks for Reginald's body to mend, but his soul was beyond repair.

Finally, he was well enough to leave the house and go to the bayou, where he felt safe. His dad returned to Egypt soon after he discovered his son alive, and for that, Reginald was grateful. He would have been happy to slit his father's throat in the night as he slept, had he stayed.

Now, he ran as fast as he could through the burning sun, shot his arms up and screamed in joy once he hit the shade. He was in his true home, once again.

He scrambled up mangroves, squashed bugs with stones and, when his own stink was too much to bear, dove into the dark-green waters behind Ravens' Pond. He now felt fearless after his ordeal, and he dared the alligators to come near him. His encounter with the demon had transformed him, and while he didn't know what he was becoming, he knew he'd never be the same as he had been before that night.

When he came up for air, he found himself eye to eye with a crocodile—but the face was somehow ... different. The creature appeared to smile at him with razor-sharp teeth. Reginald pulled away, scrambled up the bank of the river and waited. The beast turned its scaly head in his direction and glided forward. Reginald took several steps back and was prepared to climb the nearest tree when something unbelievable happened. The creature climbed out of the water, pulled itself onto two feet and grinned.

"Hello, Reginald," she hissed out of her reptilian mouth. "It's your friend, Ammit. Nice to see you again." She waddled closer.

Reginald kept blinking, hoping she'd disappear. Ammit's head was in the form of a crocodile; her legs and hindquarters appeared to be those of a hippopotamus; her torso and arms were like a large cat's.

Reginald stood his ground and watched in fascination as she began to transform; a woman now stood before him, her scaly hands hooked into a ripped and grimy dress that was as muddy-brown as her hippopotamus skin had been. Her face was long and scaly, her yellow eyes sparkling under heavy lids. When her lips drew back in an awful grin, Reginald couldn't help but take a step back from the dead fish stench of her breath.

"We will start your studies today, my little man. Come, let's find us a cozy piece of shade that we'll use for our classroom. There is much to learn!"

And so the lessons began. They sang praises to Ra when the silky, soft, yellow light appeared in the sky and bid farewell to Goddess Nut at night. They chewed on dung beetles when they got hungry, and a servant from the plantation hauled two big buckets of cold water to drink and splash on their faces.

Ammit taught Reginald much about ancient Egypt, and for the first time in his life, he understood the obsession that drove his father year after year. It was hard for him to understand Ammit at first—her long, grey, braided hair fell in front of her face when she spoke. She'd use one of those whip-like braids to whack him across the face if he leaned in, straining to hear. But mostly she was kind and soft-spoken.

One boiling hot afternoon, they decided to seek shade on some rocks above the river.

"Ammit?" he asked.

She nodded once in response.

"If I become a full-fledged Egyptian demon, will I be able to cross over to eternal life?"

Another nod.

"So, I know I need a heart which will weigh lighter than Ma'at's feather, revealing me as worthy of eternal life; my name must be written on papyrus to show how many good deeds I have done, and someone who knows me well must speak about the good things I have achieved." He paused, then slowly turned his head to face her.

Ammit cleared her throat, but it sounded more like a growl.

"Reginald, you are fortunate to have me as your teacher. What you swear to now will be much harder to actually accomplish," she said, pulling her coarse braids over her left shoulder to face him. "Just remember: it is much easier to speak of good intentions than to live them."

"Ammit?" he asked once more.

One flickering yellow eye in his direction was all he needed to continue.

"Why do you hate my father so much? He's the reason you're here, right? He brought you here for me, to keep me company."

She went so quiet that Reginald thought she'd gone to sleep. He waited.

All at once, the old witch was on her feet and he was in the water—and not just any pool of water. It was the deadly, frothing, practically-boiling-with-gators part of the river. Reginald felt the cold, slimy teeth of the creatures that ripped at his legs, while others used his body to ascend to the top, where they tried to chew his head off.

He heard himself screaming for help, but the only sound he received in response was Ammit's ear-splitting cackle.

He didn't see her again, although he came to believe she had somehow saved him from the gators. He'd lost part of his scalp and carried deep, dark-red claw marks from the top of his thighs to his ankles. The local doctor did his best to stitch him up, but from that day forward, Reginald wore black pants, black shirts, black shoes and a dark-green hat to cover the scars. Ammit had left her mark on him.

He checked for signs of her many times over the years, but it was like she didn't exist except in letters. Every six months, a large envelope would arrive from Cairo, and Reginald's hands would shake so hard with excitement he could barely get it open. There they were—six months' worth of instructions on everything to do with ancient Egypt, including its gods and goddesses and demons. As always, her directives were the same: find ways to do good and evil.

***

As the years passed, Reginald continued his studies of the dark arts. He also had a tutor who did his best to teach Reginald about science, geography, the written language and history. Reginald tolerated Mr. Marrits because he knew that with knowledge came power and it would only make him a stronger demon. But at night, when everyone else had gone to bed, Reginald would slither down the stairs to his father's work chamber and practise skills only a true demon would need to know. Skills like blood-letting, embalming, teleportation, shapeshifting and making people bleed internally, just to name a few.

CHAPTER FORTY-SIX

RUBY AS A CHILD, RAVENS' POND, THE PAST: RUBY'S LAST DAY

Ruby woke up to a day packed with promises. The promise of sunshine, as morning's subtle hues of light had already filled her room, and the promise of fun. Her brother Robert had left the house at the crack of dawn to fish, and her plan was to surprise him with her presence at the pond. It would make for a grand day.

And then there would be the most special part of her day, when her uncle Reginald would sketch her picture. He was a talented artist, and she felt lucky to be the subject for his next piece. She imagined the look of surprise and delight that would beam from her mother's face when she saw the picture.

Ruby tiptoed through the mansion, careful to not disturb anyone. Her parents were strict about her whereabouts—especially when it came to the pond. But she wasn't afraid; Robert would keep her safe.

The birds sang their dawn chorus, as her grandmother used to say. The song was sweet. Ruby's bare feet felt cool on the dewy lawn as she made her way to the water's edge. She heard whistling and knew Robert was close. She smiled, twisted her hair back off one shoulder and stopped to consider the best approach. Ruby wasn't known to be an early riser, so she understood her arrival would shock Robert. That was what she was hoping for.

The smile on her face turned to a frown of confusion—someone else was at the pond. Turning around, she smiled to greet him. Then she walked toward him, reached out and placed her small, warm hand in his. The day would turn out differently after all.

The sun was rising. Reginald sensed the shift from dark to light. Black eyes opened, then grew wide as he remembered the importance of the day. Today—in honour of his sixteenth birthday, he would pay homage to the gods as they so deserved. Months of planning had finally come to fruition. Ruby would become immortal. After all the years of research, he was finally ready. He loved his niece. This was an act of love, giving them eternal life and happiness together.

It had all gone smoothly. His original plan to lure her out of her sleep was unnecessary since she bolted from her room in search of Robert. The rest was easy.

She loved him and trusted him. Admittedly, taking the life from her small body had been hard. At first, she thought it was a game when he pushed her to the floor of the dollhouse.

"Why did you push me?" she asked, her eyes wide in confusion.

Reginald had a vise grip on her small arm and held her down. His other hand clamped on her neck as she scrambled to get her feet under her. He watched her struggle to escape from his tight hold around her small throat. He closed his eyes but couldn't shut out the screams, gurgles and final gasps as her body went still. She did not suffer for long.

CHAPTER FORTY-SEVEN

REGINALD, AGE SIXTEEN, RAVENS' POND, THE PAST: THE EMBALMING

While the family attempted to come to terms with the disappearance of their beloved Ruby, Reginald, using inconsolable grief as an excuse, packed his bag and slunk out of the house in the dark of night. He stopped only to pick up the stiff and bloodless body of his niece concealed under a sheet in the dollhouse and headed for the pirogue he had hidden.

It took him some time to locate the boat; he'd done an excellent job of camouflaging it, and that brought a smile to his face. Once he'd cleared the branches off the boat, he gently placed her body at the bow. Under the cover of a pale slice of moon, he paddled quietly to his destination.

An abandoned house, half a mile to the west of Ravens' Pond, was the perfect place for Reginald to complete the embalming. He'd set up in the dining room.

With lanterns lit, he began the procedure. He washed her small body with the utmost care, closed her sweet eyes shut with glue, stitched her lips together and made a small incision in her abdomen. Once he removed all organs (except for her heart), he took great pleasure in applying the finishing touches. When it was over, Reginald stood back, pleased with his work.

Once he completed the embalming and the plaster was hot and bubbling, Reginald completed the statue he had worked on for weeks. With gentle hands, he wrapped Ruby in papyrus and wrote his name in black ink on her chest. He was creating a soulmate for his endless journey to come. He was finally ready to seal the statue.

***

Seven days later, Reginald paddled back to Ravens' Pond, this time under a full moon. Ruby's statue was safely secured to the small raft he towed. Eyes popped up from the surface of the green water as something bumped up from below. The shotgun by his side comforted him. Once docked, he hauled the statue up to her new home beside the pond.

Early the next morning, hunkered down deep in the foliage, he watched as the family crept forward to see his handiwork. Their sobs echoed across the lake in waves of indescribable grief. The corners of his mouth crept up in a smile that was more like a grimace; he was oblivious to the odd-shaped yellow eyes which watched his every move.

CHAPTER FORTY-EIGHT

LEAH & JOSH, THE FLIGHT BACK TO BRITISH COLUMBIA FROM RAVENS' POND, PRESENT DAY: THE DREAD

With our flight booked for 9 p.m., we have nothing better to do than sit and wait at an airport bar. Josh's lids are heavy, his normally ramrod posture slumped. Stirring a red swizzle stick, his eyes downcast, it's a sure sign he's working up to asking me a tough question.

"Leah," he asks. "Why are you so afraid of heights?"

I knew this would come up eventually. Settling in my chair, I sip my Merlot and begin the story of the loss of my big brother.

CHAPTER FORTY-NINE

LEAH AS A CHILD, PENDER ISLAND, BRITISH COLUMBIA, THE PAST: BROTHER DANNY

Danny was always reckless. My big brother woke up every morning with a new adventure, all planned and ready to go. My cherished brother was thirteen; I was ten. It was my goal to keep up with him and stay alive. Our parents were mostly ignorant of the danger of our time together, which was a good thing.

Pender Island, while beautiful, was also pretty dull for kids. We sought our amusement by hunting for hidden coves and high cliffs, and uncovering some of the island's mysteries. A good day would be when we came home needing a bandage or two; a bad day meant a sprain or a broken toe. Danny was my hero, but he almost cost me my life.

The mist rolled in off the seas that day; I assumed he'd cancelled our adventure. I tiptoed down the hallway and gently pushed the door open to Danny's bedroom. Wincing at the squeak it made, I looked in to see his room was empty. I ran back to my room, yanked my nightie over my head and pushed my feet into jeans before grabbing a sweater and tying my sneakers. Running fast for the front door, I was relieved to know both parents were still sleeping,

I checked my watch. Danny couldn't be that far ahead of me; it was 6:25. Shaking my head as I ran, I realized he'd ditched me. The question was, why? Sweat ran down my back; I cursed myself because I knew better. Danny taught me to always layer, so if you got hot, you could peel away one or two.

Our destination that morning was a high cliff with a tempting beach at the bottom. We'd been there by boat with Dad, but Danny wanted desperately to reach it from the top. As I approached the path leading down, the fresh sea air washed over me, refreshing and cool. Tentatively, I approached the edge where Danny would most likely have descended. To my shock, he was already on the beach, waving his arm like a flag and yelling at me to come down.

I remember that it felt as if I stopped breathing for a few minutes, feeling the rush of blood to my head in utter terror. I couldn't do this. One wrong move and I'd be dead. I shook my head back and forth, but Danny wouldn't let up. I had to at least try.

Ok, take the first step, I told myself, scanning for trees or shrubs I could hold on to. Danny was telling me to take my time. I had no problem with that suggestion. Gingerly, I turned around to face the cliff and slowly lowered myself to the first ledge.

My heart was pounding so hard, like a steady, heavy drum beat. I let go a small sigh of relief when my left foot made contact with the ledge, followed by my right foot. I grabbed on tightly to the small chunk of wizened vegetation, looked over my shoulder and froze. The waves were pounding the beach, Danny running back and forth into the water, screaming with delight. The rocks seemed to tumble down to the sea with no visible place to step.

Looking up, I realized there was no way to climb back up. My hands were shaking in fear as I held onto the shrub like a lifeline. Danny continued to yell at me to come down. I closed my eyes and took a few deep breaths. I only hoped Danny could make it back up safely to haul me up. Time passed slowly as I waited to be rescued. I was getting cold, my body shivering even more.

I remember thinking if I couldn't stop shaking, my feet would slip off of the edge, when I heard a voice above me. I looked up to see a neighbour of ours and his dog.

"Leah!" he cried out. "Don't move! I'll be back with a rope to get you to safety."

It seemed like hours before Mr. Crawford returned. I hadn't

moved a muscle, and my body was aching from the effort. He lowered a looped rope down and told me to put it around me and hang on to both sides while he hauled me up. I tried to steady my hands and wrapped them around the rope.

"What about Danny?" I cried.

"Your dad is taking the boat around to pick him up," he said. I reluctantly let go of the shrub as I felt the rope's pressure on my back. "That's it, Leah! Just take it slow," he said.

Finally, I was in the loop, my hands clutching the rope.

"Leah, we're going to bring you up now. I need you to use your feet against the cliff. Can you do that?" he said.

What choice did I have? As soon as I felt the pressure on my back, I held on even tighter to the rope as I was being pulled up. Using my legs, I straightened my back, head up high as I climbed. Several voices from the top called out to encourage me; even Mr. Crawford's dog was barking. Within seconds, I was on the top, Mom's arms around me as her tears spilled onto my neck. Mr. Crawford's two teenage sons raised their hands to greet me; they had provided their dad with additional strength to get me to safety.

I won't forget that horrific time on the lip of the cliff, and it scarred me with a fear of heights I could never overcome.

Two years later, our lives took a terrible turn.

***

That winter was a harsh one. It was a rare occasion for our lakes to freeze over, but that year the smaller ones did. There was an ice-skating party one evening. The night sky blazed with bright stars against the obsidian-coloured sky. The burning tar from the barrels smelled awful, but they kept us warm.

Mom and Dad were cozied up on a bench, something hot and spicy in their mugs and a glow on their cheeks.

Mom cocked her head and said, "Where's your brother, Leah?"

I did a quick twirl around hoping to spot his red toque but no luck.

"I'll skate around a little and ask if anyone's seen him."

Pushing off with the pick on my right boot, I made way to the group of older kids huddled near one of the barrels. Joey, Danny's best friend, turned to me and asked me if I'd seen him.

I shook my head, my face flushed with worry. Joey was shorter than my brother by a few inches but had a strong build. Curls of his red hair peaked out from his black toque as he scanned the rink. Then, the sound of someone shouting for help.

We all scattered in different directions, chunks of ice flying like shattered glass. Mom and Dad were on their feet, trying not to fall on the hard ice. I was just behind Danny's group of friends when I heard another yell. The older kids were on their knees, trying to pull something out of a hole in the ice.

"Danny!" I shrieked, pushing the people in front of me.

"Stay back, Leah!" someone shouted. "You'll break the ice!"

The adults had formed a human chain to pull whoever had fallen through the ice. But I knew who it was. He'd been trying to kill himself all his life. As it hit me that I was losing Danny, I fell to my knees and in the clear ice below, I saw the terrified ghostly white face of my brother glide away in the frigid water.

***

Josh holds me tight on our flight back home. As the tears flow down my cheeks, I feel something inside me settle. I'd walled up the pain for so long. Now I could think of Danny's life, not his death. His impish smile, his crazy energy and his love for his little sister.

***

Once the tears stop falling, I feel like someone has sucked all the air out of me. I'm not sure if Josh and I are contemplative, disappointed or just tired. Either way, I need to crawl inside my mind and meditate. Pulling the thin, small, blue airline blanket up to my chin, I order my second glass of red wine and try to relax. So much has happened in eight days, and I have no clue what to do next. At the top of my list is to sell my property. I don't need this horror show.

Or maybe I should tear down the walls, crush it into the earth and leave it to fester on its own. I'm already pining for the hustle and bustle of the city. Happy hours with my girlfriends, movies, concerts, walks in the park and of course, retail therapy.

***

Our float plane from Vancouver Harbour back to Einer's Bay departs on time. After we land, Josh yawns widely in the car as we approach the gates to hell. The sky is an odd shade, somewhere between slate and pearl. I cannot seem to look directly at the house as it pulls at me. It's all I can do to stop myself from jumping out of the car and running.

Saying goodbye to Josh is harder than I thought it would be. Part of me wants to grab him by his hoodie, pull him in and insist he stay with me.

"I'll come back later this afternoon to make sure you're okay," he says, hugging me into his warm and slightly woodsy smell.

I can't speak for fear of crying, so I just nod and release him. The sound of his motor starting up, fading away from me, leaving me alone in this dark place drops me to my knees and I let go of the ocean of tears that has been welling up.

CHAPTER FIFTY

LEAH, RAVENS' WOOD, PRESENT DAY: THE LIGHT IN THE ATTIC

Tonight, dinner is an apple and cheese; my appetite is pretty much nonexistent. Josh has called to say he can't make it over after all. Turns out Willie, the owner of the grocery store, has had a flood in our absence and is adamant Josh stay at the store to help clean up the worst of it.

I don't feel comfortable in any room, but the kitchen seems to feel the most normal, so it's there I nurse a cup of peppermint tea. The wind has picked up, and the leaves on the trees outside the kitchen are tapping and scratching. And now the scritching is getting louder. It's definitely not the trees making that noise.

The table lurches up by the force of my knees as I scramble away from the kitchen up to the stairwell. As the volume of the scraping rises, the sound becomes ear-splitting, like a metallic saw hacking into sheets of steel. The noise halts as I reach the bottom of the attic stairs. It's replaced by the sound of a child screaming. Blood rushes to my head, and I black out.

When I come to, I have no clue how long I was out. My head hurts from cracking it on the edge of the stairs. The screaming has morphed into sobs—keening, wailing cries that destroy my soul. The child's sobs catch as if she's listening for someone; I realize that someone must be me.

The light in the attic is fading. Her shroud has fallen to the floor, and I can see the statue is beautiful, like one you might see in Versailles or an art gallery in Florence.

And yet, somehow, the figure has changed. She's now rose-hued, and she turns her face away from me. One hand reaches up like she's shading her eyes from the sun. She's looking for something. Or someone. Her small marble shoulders are raised in tension. What used to look like a dress is now a nightgown. It floats mid-shin, a ruffle of marble fabric.

"What do you want, Ruby?" I say in a soft voice.

There is no response; she utters no words from her cold lips.

I need to touch her. My hand stretches out to feel her arm. She feels smooth and cold, like ice. Her soft cries fade away until they sound like they're in another room. Then they're gone.

***

I decide an early bedtime is in order. Slipping into soft sheets, I snuggle Mike's pillow, and it doesn't take long for my eyes to close. The wind is up tonight, buffeting the house and shaking the trees in the forest. The last image in my mind before I drift off is the painting of the scary old man in the woods. What is he trying to say?

What seems like only seconds later, I hear a voice. A woman is screaming and wailing, crying out my name.

"Help me, Leah! He's killing me! Help me, please!"

I bolt upright in bed, and my hand is at my throat as if it could stop the word erupting from my mouth: "Mom?"

In seconds, I'm out of bed, pulling on sweatpants and a jacket, hopping into rubber boots and bolting out the back door into the bitter winter night.

I have a flashlight in my right pocket and I pull it out, testing it a couple of times.

"Leah!" The scream is so close, maybe forty feet away.

"Mom!" I yell, crying as I run. "I'm coming! I'm here! Who is trying to hurt you?" How is this even possible? Mom is dead. I buried her ashes on Pender Island.

My flashlight slashes across the darkness, revealing nothing but trees as they rock in the wind.

"Mom!" I cry, stumbling over roots, pushing off from the massive trees that now seem to grow closer together.

A face! Over to my right, there's a man coming toward me. My light makes his leathery skin look silver, but he's the same man—the one in the painting. The one who is trying to warn me or push me away. He comes toward me in jerky motions. Head to the right. Head to the left.

His mouth is open, his hands reaching toward me. I can't hear what he's saying because the wind is too loud. I'm terrified but unable to turn and run. Then, somehow, he is at my side, icy lips pressed up against my right ear. Impossible.

I feel his cold breath as he screams, "Get out!"

Then he's gone and I'm lying on the forest floor, staring up as branches whip back and forth in a frenzied dance. Terror fills me, and I'm up and running as fast as I can to safety. But there's no safety. There is only the house.

Reginald

CHAPTER FIFTY-ONE

SHIRLEY, RAVENS' WOOD, LAST YEAR: THE HEART ATTACK

S hirley shot up straight in her bed. It was the middle of the night, and something had shattered the silence. She panted in fear and strained to listen. Someone—or something—was in trouble. When she heard it a second time, Shirley hit the floor, and without thought or fear for her personal safety, ran barefoot into the night toward that terrible sound.

She'd been a dog lover all her life. While she'd never had one of her own, her best friend growing up did. Zeus was an adorable little terrier who made up for his size with his bigger-than-life personality. He'd carved a special place in Shirley's soul.

Her heart pounding furiously, she flew down the stairs, grabbing the shotgun she kept by the back door. Someone was torturing a dog, and she was more than happy to kill the bastard. As she ran, a murder of crows appeared overhead, seeming to be leading her to the dog's screams.

But there was, in fact, no dog—and as Shirley turned the corner, there he was: Reginald, waiting in the dark by the dollhouse. Shirley gasped, heart pounding. She turned to run back into the house but he was on her. Picking her up with one arm, he spat in her face and threw her to the ground. As her head hit the earth with a thud, Shirley felt like someone had their hand around her heart and was squeezing it hard.

The massive heart attack was mercifully swift. Reginald's blood-red eyes widened in disbelief. He had waited decades for this moment, to cut out her heart while it was healthy and still beating. This stupid woman might have cost him his ascension to eternal life. Dropping his head back, he shook his big bony fists at the black sky and screamed. The heavy thumping wings of the crows slowed, finally coming to an end when they landed in the trees.

CHAPTER FIFTY-TWO

LEAH, RAVENS' WOOD, PRESENT DAY: THE VANCOUVER VISIT

After that terrible night in the woods, I return to the house, pack a bag, wait for the sun to rise and take the first float plane out of Einer's Bay. Following a smooth flight that requires only one shot of the good stuff, I settle into a room at a downtown Vancouver hotel. The traffic, sirens, laughter and shouting are like a forgotten lullaby. Josh and I speak on the phone for half an hour; he understands my need to flee. He is, in fact, relieved. I choose not to tell him what transpired in the woods; I know he'd never let me come back.

The next morning, I ask the hotel valet to hail a cab and I'm off to visit one of Aunt Shirley's lawyers in Vancouver. He might have some of the answers I so desperately need.

The office of Moir & Tait—a small firm specializing in family estates—is upscale and contemporary. Roger Moir is a nice-looking man in his early sixties. Silver-haired with piercing blue eyes and a big smile, he rises somewhat stiffly and takes my hand.

I spend the next hour explaining everything that has happened since I first laid eyes on that place of horror, watching his eyes grow wider. His posture wilts until his hands twist together on his knees.

When I'm done, we both fall back into our chairs as if our muscles have turned to jelly. He exhales.

"I take it you want to sell," he says.

That takes me by surprise a little. But now I'm here, now that I'm faced with the choice, I can't. I cannot abandon her.

***

I'm not entirely sure why I choose not to call Josh when I return to Einer's Bay. I think I just need time. Time to re-establish myself here. Time to listen to every little creak, of which there are so many.

I also switch bedrooms. My next choice is the biggest one and I'm fairly certain it's the former bedroom of Aunt Shirley herself. I feel a need to be closer to her.

Walking down the hallway, I glance at the many works of art that line the walls. They remind me of the old man and the haunted cabin scene, and I wonder if they're by the same artist.

I haven't opened the door to Aunt Shirley's bedroom since the day I arrived. The brass doorknob is cold to the touch, and the door seems to push back when I open it. Everything in here is dark polished wood and burgundy. This is a chilly room, and it gives me a terrible feeling to even think of sleeping in her bed. It is from this bed that something awakened her and led her down the stairs, out into the gloom and to the dollhouse, located directly below her window. As creeped out as I am, I have a strong feeling I might understand what happened to Shirley if I stay in this room.

My things for the night put away, I pour myself a cold glass of water in the bathroom and yank open the drapes and the window. The birdsong calms me as I take a few minutes to breathe in the fresh air and sip my water.

Falling on the king-sized bed, I look up to the burgundy ceiling, which is painted with gold and blue cherubs who stare back at me with evil, little grins. Shutting my eyes, I imagine them turning into sweet white unicorns with gold and silver horns. My ears pick up on a strange sound, but I'm unsure of where it's coming from.

The bird-like chatter of little children grows louder. I sit upright with eyes wide open; the laughter has now transformed to the drunken cackle of a cocktail party. Impossible! Looking up, I'm horrified to see the cherubs are now people dressed in strange costumes, and they're clearly drunk.

One leering male turns away from the crush to stare directly at me on the bed. He holds a glass of amber liquor in his hand, raises a toast to me, then pours the liquid in my face and eyes.

"This isn't real!" I scream, rushing to the bathroom. My eyes are burning as I stumble in the dark to find the light switch. Once I do, I turn on the water and grab a washcloth.

The pain in my eyes abates slowly with repeated applications of icy water. Fearful of what I'll see when I go back to the bedroom, I'm somewhat relieved but also repulsed to see the return of the grinning and evil cherubs. I need to get out of here.

I leave the lights on in the hallways and entranceway. No way am I coming back here in the dark.

CHAPTER FIFTY-THREE

LEAH, RAVENS' WOOD, PRESENT DAY: THE TWILIGHT ZONE

Aunt Shirley's car is freezing cold, even in the garage. Shivering, I push the ignition button, press my foot on the brake and cross my fingers. Cars don't like it when we take them for granted.

I turn up the music and head for The Sundowner. I need a glass or more of wine after that shit show. The roads are quiet tonight; there are only a few cars heading down the marina road and a young guy riding a bike along the dirt side of the road.

When I push open the big double doors of The Sundowner, I'm a little surprised to see Josh cozied up beside a woman with spectacular long, curly, strawberry-blond hair that she seems obsessed with, constantly twirling, twisting and fluffing.

I do my best to scuttle along the side of the restaurant, but they see me. Josh yells my name as he stands quickly and waves somewhat manically to catch my attention. Damn. I don't need this right now. I wave, indicate I'm heading to the takeout counter and nod to him so he knows I'm coming back. This will at least get me out of here as fast as possible.

Meal ordered, I saunter to their table, pushing my hair back theatrically. I wish I'd fussed with my makeup a little more, but that's life.

Josh stands, but the woman at the table stays seated. Kind of rude, but okay.

"Leah, I'd like to introduce you to Finola. We studied arts together in Edinburgh. She's just making a quick stop here before visiting my mom in Victoria." Josh looks pleased with himself, rocking on his black high tops, both arms behind his back.

The words that claw and scratch their way in desperation to my vocal cords are, "Oh you! You little red-haired fairy sculptor who dropped this fine young man on his head, put on your high-heeled green dancing shoes and jumped up and down on top of him until he passed out from the pain? Little Miss Messy, if I'm not mistaken?" But of course, I don't do that. I drop my hip, extend my right hand limply, so she can kiss it, shake it lightly or ignore it.

"Hi," I say, then turn my back on her to face Josh.

Finally picking up on the murder in my eyes, he takes a step back and says, "Aren't you supposed to be in Vancouver?" I almost feel like I'm dreaming. The colours are too bright, the voices loud and the music is out of tune.

"Yes, I was. Now I'm back." And with that I pivot toward the takeout stand, wave over the top of my right shoulder and say, "Nice to meet you, Canola!" and I'm out the door, dinner in hand.

Josh calls my name and threads his way through the busy dinner crowd, but I'm too fast for him tonight. I leave him in a cloud of dust and gravel.

On my way home from The Sundowner, I pull over and open my screw-top red wine. I desperately need a drink after that debacle. After a couple of large gulps, I shove the bottle between the passenger seat and console and head for home.

The moon seems a strange colour tonight, I think as I drive along. Wait. Something isn't right here. I'm lost! How is that even possible? Just past the marina, the road curves left and I should be at the gates to my house. But I'm in the middle of nowhere.

I have never seen this road before. Even the trees are different. The wind stirs tangles of dead trees; they sway back and forth like a forest of dancing skeletons. The road is now a single lane and brown; scrawny branches attack from both sides.

After turning off the radio, I slow to a crawl and squint at the trees and bushes that flank the car. The undergrowth is sparse but as black as oil. It oozes onto the roadway, which has turned to dirt. Red dirt. I can feel the tires becoming less responsive, like I'm travelling in glue. This is nuts! I have to get out of here, but I can't because there's no more road.

I'm facing a rock wall covered with vines and black, syrupy material streaking down in crazy overlapping zigzags to pool at the base of the rock. There's no way out other than to put the car in reverse and step on the gas. Looking over my shoulder and about to boot it, I hit the brakes instead. There's an identical wall behind me now.

Thrusting the door open, I fall back as the car smashes into another rock wall. I scream and cry and shove at the door as hard as I can, but the walls keep moving in. Barely able to pull my ankle from getting trapped outside, I squeeze it in and lock the door as if that could stop what's happening.

My phone! I claw through my bag and pull out my phone, and in the fading light I dial Josh's number. It goes to voice mail. Adrienne! Nothing! There's no cell service. Tears flood my face as I try to catch my breath. I watch as my hood and trunk pop in unison. I'm about to be crushed alive.

Moving to the centre of the car, I close my eyes, duck my head and jam tight fists into my ears to escape the sound that hammers down on all four sides of the car. There's no use; it's impossible to shut out the ear-splitting scream of chunks of steel clanging and screeching as metal rips apart. As the car encloses around me, the pressure is too much to bear as I hear my ribs snap and the bones in my right arm break like crushed glass. I taste the hot blood that gushes out of my head. The stabbing, burning pain is excruciating. Everything goes black.

It's the sound of my own screaming that wakes me. I'm still in the car. I never left the garage. But there's a half a bottle of screw-top wine wedged between the passenger seat and the console and no bag of takeout in sight.

Reginald

CHAPTER FIFTY-FOUR

LEAH, RAVENS' WOOD, PRESENT DAY: THE FAMILY FILES

The next morning, the sun is a dim, watery yellow. I only know this because I slept with the drapes wide open. I fell asleep fully clothed, and now I'm a wrinkled mess. I check my phone and discover Josh left a nice voice mail welcoming me back to Vancouver—with no mention of my bizarre behaviour at the pub. It's clear yesterday's visit to The Sundowner never happened.

Aunt Shirley's office must contain some answers to all of this madness. I just have to figure out how to piece all the clues together. What drove her to build this monstrosity of a house? Why here? What does the imagery in the painting mean? What drew Aunt Shirley to her death? I start by making a flowchart of everything that has occurred since the first time I knew there was an Aunt Shirley.

I'm not sure at what point I realize I'm still sitting at her desk, and one look outside tells me it won't be long before dark. Papers lie strewn around the office. I hope there's something meaningful in my ramblings. The answers have to be here in the house, and I won't leave until I find out who—or what—was responsible for the heart attack that killed her.

Aunt Shirley's computer all charged up, it's a pretty safe bet what the password is; first attempt and I'm in, using *Leah*. Most emails are related to her work. One file is labelled "Building of Ravens' Wood", which I'll check out later. Clicking on her photos, I'm not surprised to see pictures of me. I take a moment to scroll through some memorable times on Pender and me as a truly gawky teenager.

There's a separate file marked "Family", which intrigues me. Clicking the file open, the blood drains from my face as I look into the eyes of a madman. When I see the photo labelled "Great-Uncle Reginald", my hands start to shake. He's leering into the lens, his thin lips curled up, bloodshot charcoal eyes wide and threatening. He has lightening-like scars, criss-crossing from one side of his scalp to the other. His sharp chin points to the camera, as if to threaten the very life of the person on the other side.

I can't look any longer and close his dreadful image. Shirley's entire family is here, all clearly labelled; her handsome but troubled-looking father Robert, her mother Anne, appearing pale, eyes half shut, her mouth rising slightly, looking more like a scowl than a smile.

Faded photos of her grandmother Bridget and grandfather Thomas are there as well as deeply diminished images labelled "William and Helen Everett". Not much remains of the photographs, but I can tell how handsome William must have been, even with the sneer. Helen is stunningly beautiful; the black and white make her ebony hair, dark eyes and fair complexion stand out. Her eyes are sad, her head tipped heavily to one side as if the weight of raising it was too much for her to bear.

I guess I shouldn't be surprised to see Mom there. How wonderful to see her through Shirley's eyes. She looks so young and full of life; the devilish glint in her eyes suggests she was also looking for a little trouble.

***

Watching the day fade from Aunt Shirley's office, I slump down on the desk. Even though I know much more than I did before, nothing makes sense. None of it. There is a presence here, but how is it connected to the statue? As tempted as I am to pack up once again and head for the city, I feel I owe it to myself and my future to sort this out. Josh texted earlier to say he and Adrienne have cooked up a plan for tonight. I only hope it works and that nobody dies.

CHAPTER FIFTY-FIVE

LEAH, JOSH & ADRIENNE, RAVENS' WOOD, PRESENT DAY: THE SÉANCE

The candles are lit, the drapes are drawn and the slightly cloying smell of incense fills the air. There are three of us, and we form a perfect triangle in the living room. That is important—the ancient Egyptians understood the power of the triangle, and Adrienne does too.

As I expected, she's head to toe in black. Her dress floats like a dark cloud around her body, flowing down to puddle at her feet. The tips of her black patent ballet shoes peek out like two boats in a harbour. Her lips and fingernails are dark red, and a black scrunchie holds back her hair.

I feel both silly and terrified at what might go down here tonight. Josh looks paler than usual as he picks away at his cuticles. The fire casts shadows on the wall, and the atmosphere is one of wait and see.

Adrienne raises one hand as if to calm us. That's not happening; I'm shaking from head to toe.

"We are here to summon forth the troubled spirits who walk the halls of this house. Come forward! Let us help you leave this place." Adrienne has somehow picked up a British accent along the way. I immediately picture Maggie Smith and stifle a nervous giggle. That's what happens to me when I'm scared; I find humour in all the wrong places.

The fire hisses softly. Candles flicker. Incense sends spirals of scented smoke skyward. Silence.

Then, something—but not *scritch, scritch*. Someone or something is knocking on a door. But it doesn't sound right. The sound is not within the house; it's from somewhere far away, just within hearing distance. Josh's eyes are wide, his posture straight. Adrienne's hand has stilled, her head cocked to listen.

The knocking continues, but now I hear a different texture of sound. Someone is crying, pleading: "Open the door! For god's sake, open the door!"

The cries grow louder and become shrieks.

We all jump to our feet in a state of panic. It sounds like a sledgehammer is slamming against every wall in the house. Picture frames are rattling, falling to the floor. I run to catch the candles as they pitch toward the carpet. The ground is shaking now, and I hear the sound of breaking glass.

"Enough!" Josh bellows, raising his fist in the air.

The noise doesn't stop. The voice that was pleading, praying, is now laughing. It's an ugly laugh that shrieks, then tumbles to a low growling chuckle. Adrienne looks terrified as she lifts both arms skyward and screams out words that have no meaning, at least to me. I put my head down and place both trembling hands over my ears.

In the end, there's no actual damage done to the house, only a shattered ornament. Josh re-hangs the paintings, Adrienne cleans up the candles and the incense and I pour liberal portions of wine.

Josh looks haggard, huddled down in his dark-brown leather chair, a glass of wine clenched in his fist. Adrienne has returned to her chair and is fussing her dark, cloudy shroud into place.

"What did you say?" I ask. "What made it stop screaming and laughing?"

Adrienne turns her head ever so slightly. "It was Ancient Egyptian. I told it to leave or I would set Osiris himself after it."

CHAPTER FIFTY-SIX

LEAH & JOSH, RAVENS' WOOD,
PRESENT DAY: THE LOVERS

J osh and I say goodnight to Adrienne, close the door, pull the drapes and go to bed. At first, we just hang on to each other. I feel safe and loved for the first time in so long. Josh's long, lean body fits perfectly with my smaller form, and we blend like slowly melting butter.

We awake to find the world covered in a new, soft, white blanket. It's snowed at least five inches during the night, and the result is at once stark and comforting. Every once in a while, we hear the soft whoosh as a pile of snow too large for a branch tumbles to the ground below.

We choose not to speak. My hand twists his soft hair around and around; his chin nuzzles mine. His kisses are soft, as his hand sculpts the curves of my body.

***

"Eggs over easy?" I ask, cracking two free-range eggs into a pan. Josh nods with a smile and slips two pieces of bread into the toaster. Coffee smells like heaven this morning. I pour freshly-squeezed orange juice into two glasses, slice some tomatoes and put them on a plate.

The house seems satisfied, or perhaps it's just me, hoping Josh doesn't see the contented look on my face. Either way, I have a feeling this won't last.

Sliding the eggs onto his plate, I glance up to see Josh looking at me, his head tipped to one side.

Reginald

"What?" I ask. I have to wait for a response as the eggs and toast disappear in a flash.

Josh picks up his mug and sits back in his chair.

"I'm just wondering," he says, "where do we go from here?"

This is a loaded question. Does he mean now that we've slept together, or now that a maniac ancient Egyptian spirit has haunted us, or now that we have a trapped spirit in a statue in the attic or something else?

"I mean, how can we help her? She needs to find peace."

"As I see it," I say, lounging back in my chair, "we have two, maybe three priorities: one, get rid of the evil King Tut who thinks he owns the place; two, free Ruby's spirit from the statue and three, get the hell out of here and find a warm beach somewhere!"

CHAPTER FIFTY-SEVEN

RAVENS' WOOD, PRESENT DAY:
AUNT SHIRLEY'S JOURNAL #1

T o my darling Leah:

If you have found these entries, it means I have passed on. I write because I want you to know a little more about me and how I came to be in your life.

I grew up on a small plantation in Louisiana called Ravens' Pond. It was close to New Orleans, but I was home schooled, so I didn't get there often.

It was always so hot and humid there! We had flying bugs the size of bats, so the windows were often closed but the shades were open. I got used to the sound of bus-sized bugs colliding with my screen, always grateful there were no holes in the netting.

We didn't have any curtains, so morning dawned early in our house. I'd fly out of bed, shiver and soap up in a cold shower, throw a dress over my head and hurry down the stairs for breakfast.

On my way there, I always made time for a quick glimpse at our pond. There was something so peaceful about that small body of water. Even with all the little bugs scooting around.

Those were joyful and precious times, Leah. Ma mère wasn't always well. Today, we'd understand she suffered from depression, but in those days, Dad would say, "Mère can't read with you today, Shirley. She's having one of her dark days."

Back then, I thought we lived in a haunted house. I never could sense my aunt Ruby's spirit, though. Mom used to say she probably died in water, so she was clean, and didn't feel the need to stay around. That made sense to me at the time, I guess.

My dad had a terrible time when his little sister died. He couldn't forgive himself, and obviously it wasn't his fault. They never found her body, so there was never any real closure.

Eventually they drained the pond; all they found was her soaking-wet, beloved little stuffed doggie, Pixie. I couldn't understand that. Mom said there were tributaries from the river that ran close to our pond and perhaps the water had claimed her. It was all so sad. It wasn't Dad's fault. It was terrible luck and bad timing.

Someone made a statue of Ruby. They placed her on a high bank above the lake, her sad, stony eyes searching for something just out of sight. I stayed away from that statue; there was something not right about it.

I grew up in a house filled with ancient Egyptian antiquities. There were always rumours about suspicious things that happened in Ravens' Pond and the strange neighbours. Talk of orgies and Egyptian demons made it a creepy place so I spent as much time as I could outside.

After Ruby died, Great-Uncle Reginald spent most of his time in one of two places: the downstairs Egyptian tomb, or the small outdoor shed we called the dollhouse. The shed had once been a shipping container full of Egyptian Shabti funerary dolls. But Ruby had claimed ownership of it and spent countless hours in there, playing with her own miniature dollhouse.

A few months after her daughter's death, Grandmother Bridget was admitted to a psychiatric hospital; I guess the pain of losing Ruby was too much to bear. She hanged herself two months later.

Shortly after that, my grandfather, Sir Thomas Allrand, suffered from a terrible stroke. He never fully recovered.

Once Grandfather passed, my parents moved out of the plantation and settled in a small town in Oregon called The Dalles. Our cottage was a lot smaller than Ravens' Pond, but it was quaint and cozy with a nice big yard out back, surrounded by trees that smelled like heaven itself when the sun shone.

I thought we could rediscover ourselves as a family there, but it was not to be. Dad slipped slowly into an endless vat of drink and depression that ended with his suicide—another hanging, this time on one of the beautiful cedar trees that graced our backyard.

My mom, Anne Tremblay, was Acadian French. Not long after Dad's death, she packed up everything we owned and sent it to New Brunswick. She would follow our possessions within days, to live with her mother and family back in Canada.

Grief had stripped my mother of all other emotions, and it was with a stiff hand on my back that she put me on a plane to New York City, where I would live with distant cousin and go to school. Mom visited every few months and flew me back to New Brunswick for family holidays, but I always felt like an orphan.

The only thing that kept me sane during those early black days in Oregon was the week-long summer camp my mom sent me to when we first moved to The Dalles. It was there I met my best and lifelong friend, your mother.

What a day it was when I met Laurena Miller! The sun was shining, and the noise that I initially attributed to birds was coming from boys and girls as they bolted from their parents' cars, chattering and screaming all the way.

A large wooden fence encircled the property with an arched gateway and a sign that announced welcome to hoc, which stood for Happy Oregon Campers. By the time I turned around to wave goodbye to my mom, she was a dusty blur on the horizon.

There was already a big lineup when we got to the camp, with boys on one side, girls on the other. The wind picked up, so I used my free hand to hold down my skirt. In front of me stood a girl dressed in blue poplin, her pretty dark hair curled to her bra line. Her hand shielded her face against the sun as I tilted my head to the side to catch a glimpse of her.

Suddenly, she whipped her head around to check me out, which earned me a mouthful of her hair. The softest, darkest eyes tilted up as we both laughed. "I'm so sorry," I said, pulling strands of hair out of my mouth.

"No, silly! I'm sorry! I shouldn't have turned so quickly!" She laughed. "I'm Laurena," she said, and reached out her right hand.

As my hand curled into hers, I had the strangest feeling we had already met. It passed quickly. I withdrew my hand and replied, "I'm Shirley."

The week went by so fast. We were up before the sun, fighting for space at the breakfast tables, then sprinting as fast as we could to the lake. We peeled off our clothes as we ran; it was a daily race to see who would make it into the water first. Laurena beat me every time. The lake was ice cold, so we didn't spend much time in the water but languished for hours curled up in towels on the shore. It was on these mornings I got to know the young woman who would become my lifelong best friend.

Laurena was as fascinated about my dark origins as I was of her magical island upbringing. Pender Island sounded like heaven on earth with its forests, surrounding ocean, rivers and quirky people who lived there. Laurena's family made cedar rooftop shakes. She told me all about their sweet home that sat proudly on a grassy hill, framed at the rear by a forest filled with deer and gazing out at the sea in front of the bright-blue cottage.

I could almost smell the salt and feel the coarse sand between my toes. Laurena's soft voice described the seabirds catching a puff of wind, riding it up, their lonely cry a lullaby of the sea. I longed to go back with her to Pender Island. At each sunset, the dread of returning home to watch my father continue his spiral into darkness, and the terrible sadness that filled my mother's eyes, grew until I could no longer eat nor sleep.

The sky was a dull grey on the last day of camp, and the sadness of leaving muted the children's voices. Dad picked me up, which surprised me. He even managed a slight smile as he stored my satchel in the back seat. Saying goodbye to Laurena was the hardest thing I'd ever done. We trembled as we hugged, too emotional to speak as our tears mingled together into a single flow of sadness. We promised to write, then turned away, unable to endure the pain of our separation.

Laurena's parents were waiting at the gate. I winced as I saw them embrace, having never experienced that kind of love.

We wrote letters for decades after, and the connection between your mother and me became my lifeline.

I'm so sorry you and I didn't get the chance to meet in person, but in my heart you were the daughter I never had. I have always been so proud of you, sweetheart. Have a happy and wonderful life.

Love,
Aunt Shirley

CHAPTER FIFTY-EIGHT

LEAH, JOSH & ADRIENNE, RAVENS' WOOD, PRESENT DAY: THE PRIEST

Even after reading Aunt Shirley's journal, I feel there are still so many missing pieces of the puzzle. Yes, it all starts with the statue, but first we have to understand how to protect her. We know we're dealing with evil powers—ancient Egyptian curses, murderous relatives and an innocent spirit trapped in plaster, longing to be free. We know who the spirit belongs to: Ruby. It's the only answer that makes sense.

Adrienne, Josh and I discuss it, and we all know the solution won't be simple. We also agree a Roman Catholic priest would probably not have the chops to take down an evil spirit all on his own, but maybe he could at least help Ruby communicate.

Adrienne's cousin is a priest working on the northeast side of Vancouver Island; we expect him to arrive tomorrow afternoon. Josh is at home catching up on his huge backlog of work while I prepare the guest room and spend more time poring through Aunt Shirley's desk and computer in search of clues about this demon. The snow continues to fall, creating a false sense of security that we can't afford to embrace.

***

Father Kelly arrives just before 4 p.m. Josh texts me from the ferry dock, so I'm standing at the door, watching for them. As the car approaches, a breath of icy air kisses the back of my neck and I shiver. I manage a smile and walk down to greet the priest.

Father Kelly isn't at all what I expected. He looks more like a baseball coach than a priest. No collar, no black robe, just a guy in loose-cut jeans and a bomber jacket. The vapour from our breath clouds together in the frigid air as we greet one another. Josh has pulled a single beaten-up brown leather bag from the back seat and is already making his way to the guest suite.

"Welcome, Father Kelly," I say, tilting my head up to meet his eyes. He's at least six foot two.

"A pleasure to meet you, Leah," he says. "Adrienne thinks so highly of you, and I am sorry for your troubles."

I nod and hook my arm in his, leading him up to the front of the house. I think it might be good for him to see it from the perspective I had when I first knew something was terribly wrong here.

Father Kelly has a youthful face and a receding hairline. It's hard to peg his age. Releasing my arm, he walks toward the centre of the property. The snow has stopped falling, but there's enough on the ground to make walking a little hazardous. As he stops and turns, I watch as his eyes take in the house from one side to the other; with his hands in his pockets, his body sways ever so slightly. The house is quiet; white puffs of snow blow up in random spiral shapes.

Turning his head toward the far side of the property, he makes his way to the walkway leading to the dollhouse. The path is nearly one big, white strip of snow. Father Kelly takes his time, gazing upwards at the windows on the second and third floors of the house. Memories of my recent windowcide event have me bringing up the rear at the farthest edge of the snow. He halts as the dollhouse comes into view.

If it weren't for the red earth oozing toward us, the dollhouse would look quaint and serene. The stream of polluted earth has encroached even farther; its width has also swelled and is now almost halfway across the backyard at the edge of the house. The soil is like a cauldron of fire, snowflakes hissing into it as they fall.

Looking over his shoulder, Father Kelly inclines his head in the dollhouse's direction. I nod in approval. He needs to go in. He needs to feel the evil.

Today, however, isn't the day. The door to the dollhouse is unyielding to the dozens of times Father Kelly attempts to wrench it open. It's sealed shut, but not by human hands. The windows are black as though we have painted them with pitch. I dig a rock out of the strip of garden next to the house and hurl it at the side window. It bounces back with even greater vengeance, somehow missing Father Kelly—but not by much.

***

After Father Kelly settles into the green bedroom, we share a simple meal of cold chicken, salad and crusty buns. Abstaining from the wine Josh and I share, our guest sips quietly from an after-dinner cup of chai tea. We talk the entire time, bringing him up to date on what has occurred here since my arrival.

He listens quietly until we've told him all we can. Then, placing the teacup down, he stands rather quickly and says, "Let's get started."

I had prepared the attic before Father Kelly's arrival. Somewhat surprisingly, the statue did not move or try to communicate right away, and for that, I'm grateful. Best to ease our way into this strange situation. I swept the floors, changed the lightbulbs, and pulled the curtains open to let in the opaque winter light. The shadows on the floor were like soft charcoal renditions of stacked boxes, an old bicycle, boxes and our spirit trapped in plaster.

Now, Father Kelly is slowly unpacking the gym bag he hauled up the stairs, softly whistling as he unloads candles, books, a wooden crucifix and an enormous bottle of water. I assume it's holy water ready to hurl at our crazy demon; I barely hold back a snicker when he opens it and chugs back a good portion.

Josh smiles as he takes a step forward to hold my hand.

"I'm ready to begin," says Father Kelly. "I'll need your help. Leah, as Ruby seems to want to communicate with you, I'd like you on the floor beside her. Josh, if anything goes south, I want you to take what I leave in the gym bag and step back into the shadows. You'll know what to do."

With everything that has happened, I expect to be more frightened of what might unfold here. And yet, as I step softly toward the statue, I can't sense her presence.

A loud creak behind us on the staircase has us all whipping around, nerves on edge in anticipation. An audible sigh escapes each of us in unison as Adrienne steps into the attic.

"What?" she whispers. "Did you think I would miss this?"

And then the world turns upside down.

It starts with the cold. There is no heating in the attic, so I had plugged in space heaters in each of the four corners of the room. The frigid air appears all at once.

"Father Kelly," I whisper, "I can see your breath."

He's down on his knees, inspecting the base of the statue, his breath coming in thick, white waves that lick the rough, unfinished marble and the blood-red chunks of soil at its base.

He stands up awkwardly, knees cracking as he straightens.

"That's so strange," he says. "I guess the heaters blew a fuse."

Josh and I set out in opposite directions to attend to the faulty heaters. As I bend down to inspect the one closest to me, I hear Josh gasp, "This one is fried!"

Turning, I see him standing in the back shadows, hoisting up the cable, its ends ravaged, bright copper wires twisting out like worms. It doesn't take us long to discover all four heaters have suffered the same fate.

"Must have been some kind of power surge," whispers Adrienne.

The cold starts from the floor, creeping up from the wood into the bottom of our shoes, snaking up calves, chilling its way up the torso until it reaches the head. It isn't a bitter or damp cold, nor is it dry or frosty. It's the cold of those frozen climbers on lost expeditions, their bodies now ice sculptures, melded together with the ground they died upon.

My hands are shaking, and I'm not sure I can move.

"Maybe I'll go downstairs to fix the fuse," I chatter.

Easier said than done: when I attempt to take a step forward, I discover my feet are frozen to the floor. One glance around the room confirms we're all stuck.

At first, when the noise begins, I think it's the sound of our teeth chattering in unison. But this is a noise I've heard many times before: *SCRITCH, SCRITCH, SCRITCH*. It's coming from the statue. The sound grows louder and louder until I think we will all shatter into grotesque icicles.

Someone screams. It's Father Kelly. His hands, resembling frozen twigs, try their best to cover his ears. His face is a grimace of agony. Then he whimpers—softly at first, staring down as if the cold is starting at his frozen feet, rising through his body and exiting his mouth with a powerful burst of a strangled yodel. His head shakes as he bellows, and the din is so loud I can barely stand it, trying in vain to raise my frozen arms.

Then, there's a sudden and shocking silence. The scratching noise is replaced with the soft cry of a child—a sound I'm familiar with. Tears run down my cheeks, and as I raise my hand to wipe them, I realize I'm no longer frozen. As if in a dream, I stumble across the floor to Father Kelly. Now thawed, he's shaking and shuffling slowly to the statue. He drops to his knees, wraps his arms around her and weeps.

***

We somehow find ourselves back down the stairs and in Aunt Shirley's office. With our knees drawn and throws wrapped tightly around us, the four of us stare wide-eyed into the blazing fire. Four shaking hands hold tumblers of cognac. Father Kelly is the first to leave the room, mumbling a good night as he exits. With her trembling hand on the banister, Adrienne shuffles her way up the stairs to another guest room; she had texted Jim earlier to say she was staying overnight.

Josh and I talk softly, reliving every moment leading up to the freezing. I toss the heaters into the garage, so there will be no warmth available for our second try. When the fire finally dies to sputtering embers, we make our way to bed.

We hold on to each other tightly that night, both of us fearful of what might happen to the other should we loosen our hold. My hand rests on Josh's chest while he sleeps, and his breathing is the only sound I'm aware of in this eerily quiet house. But every once in a while, in my feverish dreamless sleep, I can hear a soft chuckle ... and it chills my spine.

***

Following a quick breakfast of coffee and muffins, we're back in the attic, prepared for the worst.

Father Kelly is silent this morning and makes no attempt at light conversation. With Adrienne assisting, he's all business, laying out a sizable white satin cloth, featuring a large red cross, on the floor between him and the statue. Digging into the front pouch of his bag, he withdraws what I know to be holy water.

He straps ten vials into some kind of vintage cloth material— pulled from a poor dead saint's wardrobe, no doubt. Drawing one vial free, he walks around the white cloth and drips water on the statue, starting at her head until holy water drips down the entire length and width of her, making several small puddles as it trickles down toward the floor.

That part of the ceremony complete, Father Kelly motions

us all to come closer. We form a semicircle at his sides, facing forward in stony, tense silence, waiting for him to speak. I can feel Adrienne's entire body shaking next to mine.

"We are here today to speak to the spirit of the murdered child Ruby, encased within this statue. Ruby, we know you have been trying so hard to reach us, to make us listen, to help release your innocent spirit from this marble cage and set you free. Are you here, Ruby?"

Josh clenches his jaw and flicks his eyes around the room, on the lookout for anything suspicious. My fingernails are digging little ditches into my palms. After the freezing cold of yesterday's haunting, it seems ironic that sweat is dripping down my back. The silence is more than palpable; it's threatening.

After what feels like an eternity, Ruby's statue moves forward ever so slightly. As prepared as we all are to see this occur, it's still enough to make every hair stand up at attention. This is no natural event. This is the spirit of a young child trying to break free from the evil force that binds her.

We move forward as one, guided by an unseen hand to join our spirits with hers. And that's when the uninvited appears.

By this time, Father Kelly has his bible in hand and is reciting scripture in a loud, authoritative voice. The words are meaningless to me. Another sound appears. This time it creeps in slowly, like the chant of Gregorian monks. As it grows, the statue vibrates. For a dreadful moment, I think she will shatter before our eyes.

Is the light dimming? The walls are changing colour. Nondescript beige becomes dark red. I watch in horror as a crimson substance runs down onto the floors. Thick and lumpy, it oozes in a flood around the base of the statue, rising upward to encase her. Then, there's silence as the blood-like liquid hardens around her, like a second skin.

Later, Josh and I stand quietly in the driveway, watching the tail lights of Adrienne's car disappear in the fading light, as she drives Father Kelly back to the ferry. We are on our own once again.

None of us can find fault in Father Kelly leaving. We knew we were up against something powerful and supernatural. A mere priest couldn't combat this kind of otherworldly force, but we had to try. A sense of defeat wraps itself around us, a mantle of deep, painful despair.

CHAPTER FIFTY-NINE

REGINALD, RAVENS' WOOD, THE PAST: THE DEMON'S PLAN

D ecades ago, when the townspeople of Ravens' Pond finally drove Reginald away, there was only one place for him to go. He headed north to his family's property in Canada; five acres in an untamed area called Einer's Bay, on the west coast of British Columbia.

Reginald arrived by rail and air and caught his breath when he saw the incredible beauty of the land. There were rich, dark-green forests and massive, towering mountains. Reginald watched in fascination as immense waves crashed all the way up the coast.

Once his float plane from Vancouver landed, Reginald grabbed his well-worn, black leather suitcase and hustled his way up to the major road. It was June and the streets were dusty, making it hard for him to see let alone follow the map he held as he made his way out of the small marina and to his destination.

He stopped after about ten minutes to glug back some cool water from his thermos, then dipped in his pocket square for a quick and refreshing face wash. He adjusted his green hat and pulled it down so the scars wouldn't show. The gators had marked him good.

In another ten minutes he saw the plot of land off to the left side of the road. There wasn't much traffic, so he took his time as he approached. There was a crumbling fence to the left side of a gravel driveway. There, the land gradually flattened out, and Reginald decided it was a suitable vantage point from which to scope out the property.

He dropped his suitcase to the ground, sat down on it and

rolled his dirty black pants up over his ripped and patched black sneakers. He took a deep breath and smiled, showing cracked and blackened teeth. On that day, Reginald's deep-set eyes—once charcoal—were completely bloodshot, with a dirty sallow rim.

He was happy with what he saw before him. Reginald believed he could build his own Ravens' Pond there. He brought his lips back into what should have been a smile but registered as a grimace and let out a deep cackle. There was no water for a pond, but there were plenty of trees; Ravens' Wood was a fine name for his Northern plantation.

He continued walking toward his family's land, whistling something nondescript and out of tune along the way. Not far above Reginald's head, the branches seemed alive as they bounced up and down. Small black heads poked through the boughs from time to time, their croaks growing louder as he made his way to the small shack at the back of the lot.

When he finally arrived, he turned to see the entire five acres blanketed with ravens. Their gurgling and squawking was almost deafening. Reginald bowed to his audience of corvids, smiled, then made his way to the front door of his new lair.

***

Years later, Reginald had Rufus and four other workmen travel up from Louisiana. Their job was to take Einer's original shed apart, widen the shaft beside it and slide the entire thing down beneath ground level so no one could see it. But because of the age of the thing, it was falling apart fast. One wall had already partially collapsed. Once the four men were done, the rest of the Louisiana crew joined them and built the plantation-style mansion.

In this way, he'd always have his eye on Shirley. He could come and go from the shed, and she'd never know he'd been there. He had a telescope that was so powerful he could watch her brush her teeth, among other things.

Reginald realized he too was falling apart, much like that old shed. He had to move fast to claim his ultimate prize: immortality, with Ruby as his queen. His powers were fading, his rage diminishing. He was running out of time and he didn't have Shirley's heart, which meant he had to have Leah's. From the second she showed up as the one to inherit Ravens' Wood, Reginald knew he had finally located his daughter.

Before her death, Shirley had played her cards well, taking few vacations, always travelling alone on some kind of boring nature or historical adventure. She had always been either at Ravens' Wood or New York City except for those excursions. In search of her when she was away, Reginald's legion of spies had come up empty, time and time again. But Reginald was nothing, if not patient. And now that Leah was here ....

***

Because Ammit put a spell on Shirley's house to test Reginald's moral compass, he has no easy access to Leah. He ponders whether he should send his servant Rufus back in with something so terrifying Leah will bolt and he can take her to the lair to finish the job. It's essential that Leah's heart is still beating when he cuts it out of her chest. Thinking back to the little spell he managed while the priest was in the house, he cracks open his mouth in a smile that reveals his rotten black teeth and tongue.

Reginald gets up from the bench and begins to pace. The silver cooler is pushed up toward the back wall of the shack, waiting for him to place the heart in the ice. He closes his eyes as he pictures the series of events.

First, he will grab Leah and knock her out with chloroform. Once she's out, he will carry her over his shoulder to the shack, where his operating theatre is all set up. He sees himself laying her down on the table, ripping her blouse open and using a black felt pen on her bare skin so he can make a quick and clean cut.

The rest is easy; cut the heart out, place it in the cooler and take it to the cold river behind the shed, where he'll attach the chain and lower the waterproof container into the icy waters.

"Rufus can clean up the other mess," he chortles to himself.

Reginald's hatred for his own flesh and blood is complicated. As his soul shifted from human to demon, he lost the soft edges of life, love, laughter and hope. Whatever remains of the wailing baby with the charcoal eyes is minuscule.

Sliding up to what's left of a shattered mirror, Reginald checks his look. The darkened glass reflects back a face with withered, dark-red skin—and yet he only sees the soft, unblemished flesh of his youth. His once-charcoal eyes, now dark red, fill with tears and become pools of bloody water. He starts to laugh; a soft titter, but it builds to a loud wail that shakes the walls of the lair.

Years ago, Reginald found a beat-up guitar tossed in a dumpster. He grabs his instrument from where it's been propped up against the wall and starts to strum. He loathes Leah for the life she lives and the life she denies him. He has endless imaginary conversations and arguments with her. Now, he lifts his hideous face, straightens his back and sings the sonnet he's written for his daughter.

While the sound he makes sounds like a thousand cats being killed, his enormous ego only hears perfection.

> *Oh, daughter, how I need to find you soon*
> *You took my life from me; now you betray*
> *Your blood will flow beneath a gibbous moon*
> *It is too late to run, no need to pray*
>
> *My knife will cut your heart, your blood will shine*
> *Once-happy eyes will now begin to dim*

You'll beg for mercy but will be declined
I'll keep your blood and fill it to the rim

Drink your thick blood, which I cannot resist
I'm fading fast, no time to stop and rest
Once human, now demonic, mortal shade
Afterlife a dream no more, I'll fail the test

Sorry, Mommy, I failed you as a son
Ammit is evil—I can see that now
Not done, she'll never say I really won
She hurt me bad, but still we had our fun

Come to me, Leah, let me find peace
Just one clean cut and you will be deceased

Reginald sighs, returns his broken guitar to the wall and falls headfirst on the beaten-up, stained and malodorous mattress. It reeks of bodily fluids, sweat, rot and a special stench only the true demon can give off.

CHAPTER SIXTY

JIM, EINER'S BAY, PRESENT DAY: ADRIENNE'S BREAKDOWN

J im arrives home to the sound of wind chimes. Angling his head as he steps out of his shoes, he smiles. Adrienne is meditating. He's sorely tempted to sneak up and scare the bejesus out of her, and even the thought of her reaction (she scares easily) has him clamping both hands over his mouth and crossing his legs. He has to pee.

Once that's attended to, he walks softly up their wooden steps and pauses just outside her office door. A retired therapist, Adrienne has found her zone with meditation—thanks to lessons from Giselle, the local shaman and one of the Guardians. Now she's delving into the psychic world.

Jim gives the door three soft taps once he's sure she's completed her session. He waits until the sound of the sea mingled with wind chimes is turned off and enters the room. He stops dead in his tracks; his wife stands like a statue in the middle of the room, expressionless as tears drip down her cheeks.

"Adrienne, what's happened?" he says, rushing to her side. Jim can feel the colour drain out of his face as he reaches for her. Grabbing him in a crushing hug, she begins great gasping sobs. He thinks it's best to let her get it all out. He's never seen her so upset.

Once the tears have stopped, Jim takes Adrienne by the hand, leads her to the kitchen and puts on the kettle. Clutching a tissue in her hand, she's making an obvious effort to control her breathing.

He pours two cups of rooibos tea and sits back to let Adrienne tell her story.

CHAPTER SIXTY-ONE

WILLIE, EINER'S BAY, PRESENT DAY: THE GUARDIANS

Willie flips over the closed sign, opens the door, then slides the key into the lock of his store. He's a tall man of substance, with broad shoulders and a slight beer belly from too many nights in The Sundowner. His most prominent features are a thick, grey ponytail, long enough to tickle the back of his neck, and a gap in the middle of his front teeth.

Stepping up into his red pickup truck, he straps himself in, turns the key in the ignition and makes his way home—a five-minute drive just north of Einer's Bay. Few houses to see along the way, as trees screen most of them.

Willie's house sits even farther back than most, with a long driveway carving its way through a lush forest to a sturdy log cabin with a spacious back deck overlooking a peaceful pond. He casts a glance at the snowy mound beside his house that slopes down to back of his cabin.

Groceries put away and a pot of stew on the stove, Willie reclines in his favourite chair, staring outside as the day darkens, turning the lake to a shadowy, misty grey. Sighing, he picks up his cellphone and makes a call.

"Patty, we have a problem," he says. "Get the group together and come over in two hours."

***

Patty tosses her phone onto the sofa and walks to the window. She looks out at the boats bobbing in the marina below and shakes her head, wondering how she even got here. Closing her eyes, she rewinds her memory until she gets to the last thing she remembers before getting off the cruise ship.

She'd worked hard on her look that night. Skin-tight sleeveless red dress, gold high heels with matching purse, her hair worn up. Sparkling gold earrings completed the look.

Pearce had barely taken notice of her when she walked into the ballroom; he tilted his head down in deep concentration as he spoke with one of the servers. Patty stood back to observe. He was such a good-looking guy, but his secret weapon with women was his sense of humour.

Even as she watched, the young waitress threw her head back, her long, straight hair rising up like a wave. Patty hated her. She hated all of them. They saw Pearce's wedding band but couldn't give a crap. They think this guy must have money; look at the expensive clothes he wears and breathe in that sexy, spicy cologne.

Trying to shake off the memory, Patty opens her eyes, pulls out a can of cola from the fridge and makes her way to her deck. Leaning over the rail, she takes a big drink and is shocked to feel hot tears running down her cheeks.

"Stop it!" she cries.

One of the dock workers looks up in alarm; Patty waves to let him know all is okay. She closes her eyes again and returns to her memory of the cruise ship.

That little popsy with the long, black hair wasn't present in their cabin that night to witness the madness. Shitfaced after countless bottles of champagne Pearce could ill afford, he yanked Patty by the hair, ripped her red silk dress in half, threw her face down on the bed and took her from behind. When it was over, he zipped his fly, checked his look in the mirror and walked out.

Patty didn't hesitate; pulling her backpack from under the bed, she climbed into jeans, put on her hoodie, jammed her feet into runners and took off. It cost her a pretty penny to bribe one of the ship's crew to take her to Einer's Bay in the dark of night, but it was all worthwhile.

Patty had planned her exit well. Her youngest brother, Sam, owned a camping outfitter store in Oklahoma. She had arranged for Sam to travel to Einer's Bay a month before the cruise and set up a campsite for her to live in until her evil husband stopped looking for her. Not that he was interested in locating the great love of his life, just the five million dollars Patty had moved out of their joint account, which was only reasonable because the money belonged to her.

A month after her disappearance at sea, Patty changed her name, opened up the hair salon and began her new life.

CHAPTER SIXTY-TWO

THE SIX GUARDIANS OF EINER'S BAY, PRESENT DAY: THE MEETING

As the sun makes a final wink before descending into night, the six that comprise the Guardians are present and accounted for: Willie, Patty, Adrienne, Josh, his father Jack and Giselle, a shaman from the Hawaiian Islands.

Their shared mood is one of anxiety, with a generous serving of dread on the side. Jack and Josh have their heads down in what looks to be a serious conversation; something is upsetting Adrienne, and Giselle is in her usual semi-meditative state, making the rounds, checking on everyone's energy.

Willie clears his throat and addresses the group.

"We all know what we're up against here. It's coming at us too soon, but there it is."

Adrienne sinks in her chair, drumming her nails on the arms of it, which she usually does when she's nervous or uptight.

"You have no clue what we're up against," she says, her lips taut. "If you had been there, you'd know the evil in that room seeps into your bones. I'm not sure I'll ever feel the same after what I experienced." With that, she rests her bloodshot eyes on Josh, who nods once in agreement.

Patty's expression is harder to read. She normally looks happy and confident. Today, the corners of her lips curl down; her normally bright eyes are heavy lidded. The tapping of her foot is no doubt annoying to the rest of the group, but it's what's stopping her from leaving.

Normally the optimist in the group, Patty is also not one to mess with. She handles the scalps of every citizen in town, so her connection to the residents is widespread and powerful. People mistake her sweet personality at their peril; she's a true badass who can be found at the gun range several times a week.

Her long, blond hair is in a tightly-braided bun at the back of her neck, accentuating her pointy chin. Wisps of hair frame Patty's face, helping to soften the wrinkles that are becoming increasingly more prominent. In her fifties, she dresses like someone in their early thirties, and she wears her wardrobe with authority. Today she sports ripped black jeans, a low-cut red sweater and dangling unicorn earrings.

Leaning forward, elbow on knee, Patty says, "The way I see it, we have no option but to move in and move in fast."

When it comes to dealing with dangerous situations, Jack is the most experienced in the group. Having spent time in Vancouver's Gang Crime Unit, he has street smarts a mile long. With his large cowboy-booted foot up on the fireplace hearth, he's tall, lean and muscled.

He's had to walk a fine line with this situation; it's not like he can easily call on his former undercover cop pals to come on over and help him take down a demon, but he's come close. Pulling his reading glasses out of his pocket, he pretends to clean them using the corner of his blue flannel shirt while he watches his team members.

Looking around at this group of oddballs who somehow came together for the town, Jack smiles and shakes his head when he thinks of some dust-ups they've already come together on. The town of Einer's Bay has no clue. Demons present an unfamiliar challenge, but then so do thieves, human traffickers and drug dealers.

Giselle is their spiritual centre. She moved from Maui to Einer's Bay just over seven years ago. At a diminutive five-foot four, carrying a little more weight than she's comfortable with, she surprises most people when they find out what she does for a living. Sitting cross-legged in front of the window, looking out at the lake, she tents her hands as she listens. Most people also never guess she's had a career as a soldier. Giselle appears to be calm, but then she always does. She frowns a lot when she's nervous, and she's frowning now.

Pocketing his glasses, Jack clears his throat and says, "Let's look at the facts we've learned to date." Counting on his hand, he pulls on one finger at a time. "One, Shirley's death was some kind of a supernatural event. Two, Leah's arrival has stirred things up again. Three, we believe we've identified the spirit in the statue as Ruby. Four, from what we learned from Shirley, we know the demon to be Reginald. Five, we know his power comes from the Egyptian underworld. Six, we know he has run out of lives and cannot enter the underworld until he can get his hands on Ruby. He needs Ruby for her pure spirit and the papyrus with his name written on it."

Jack turns to face the group, one hand fully open, the second in a peace sign.

"Seven, if we don't find an answer to meet and defeat his power, Leah will be dead within days."

***

The meeting now concluded, Willie says goodbye to his fellow Guardians, then closes and locks the door. Smiling, he recalls how shocked he was when he first moved here and learned people never locked their doors. Things have changed since then, and not necessarily for the better. Gathering up dirty coffee mugs, he walks into the kitchen, flexing his elbow to turn on the light. He fills the sink with warm water and soap, sighs and rests his elbows on the kitchen counter. Reaching around to his back pocket, he pulls out a package of cigarettes. Straightening his back, he lifts one out, slides it under his nose for a good long sniff, then slowly, almost seductively, pushes it between two lips.

Pulling in a deep breath of unlit fresh tobacco, Willie's eyes close in pleasure. This trying to quit smoking is brutal. He thinks about the last time he saw Shirley. She'd come into the store, and in her usual way drew instant attention. He always knew when she was in the shop. First, there was a rush of air from the door that brought with it a subtle hint of Chanel perfume. Willie loved to watch as she stopped, her eyes sweeping the store for people she knew, stopping at the face of a friend.

There was something so complex about her expression, thought Willie, pulling another deep breath of his unlit cigarette. How her smile would break open and the sun would start shining—but that beam of light shone just shy of her eyes.

What a terrible loss, thinks Willie as he opens his eyes and looks up at a framed photograph on the wall to his right. Staring intently as if it's the first time he's seen it, he scoops up a handful of soap bubbles and hurls them at the picture. The bubbles burst, cascading down the wall.

The photograph is of Willie, dressed in chef's whites, his trademark dark-blue clogs peeking out from the hem of his pants; the smile on his face could light up a town, but it's obvious from the slightly ragged edge on one side that the photo has been cut in half. He's posing outside of a restaurant, one hand gesturing to a stainless-steel sign etched with the words WILLIE AND LUC.

Willie shakes his head, grabs a dishcloth and wipes the picture frame dry. Now isn't the best time to get nostalgic; there's too much at stake, and he doesn't have much time.

Advanced lung cancer the doctor had said.

"Well," Willie says out loud. "No big surprise there."

He'd known something was wrong for about a year. He first noticed it when he and Josh went fishing. Their favourite spots are up river, which means a big hike up a steep trail while hauling a canoe. Josh is young and can easily sprint up, never even breaking a sweat. But it is getting harder and harder for Willie.

He hid it well for a while, but when their usual three stops to reach the river became thirty—well, he couldn't keep it from Josh any longer.

Willie has a rage building inside of him at the stupidity of it all. In the restaurant business since leaving high school, he'd been exposed to second-hand smoke his entire adult life. He remembers the time he lit his first cigarette. It was after school, and he was sitting on a log in the thick forest by the school. He had his arm around Kimmy Fletcher; he thought he was in love with her long, wavy blonde hair, big, green eyes, perfect teeth and gorgeous athletic body. But this was before he finally figured out he was gay.

Their relationship ended amicability a few months later, but the smoking had become a habit that could cost Willie his life.

Willie had another theory regarding his disease—that the stress of his relationship with Luc was also a factor. Willie believed in the power of the strong connection between mind, body, spirit. If anyone of these were damaged, the other two would soon fail.

Reginald

CHAPTER SIXTY-THREE

WILLIE, EINER'S BAY, PRESENT DAY: THE MEMORIES OF LUC

Willie thinks back to when he first met Luc, who was fresh out of cooking school in San Francisco. They were at a birthday party for a fellow chef when Luc approached Willie to enquire about his tie. Willie had a thing for ties. Some of them were expensive Italian and French, while others were more whimsical. That night's tie was Mickey Mouse depicted in many activities on the tie including hiking, skiing, swimming and fishing. In each activity, he also sported a white chef's hat.

"Is it the hat, or the mouse you're crazy about?" asked Luc in a European accent of some kind.

Willie pulled up his tie and gave it a once-over.

"You know, I think it's the mouse!" he laughed.

They saw a lot of each other over the next few weeks—going to movies, enjoying the local restaurants, watching the San Francisco Giants play and taking long walks.

A year after they met, Luc invited Willie over for a special dinner. It was their anniversary as a couple and time to celebrate. Luc had outdone himself, preparing a spectacular Coq Au Vin. The first serving was a delicious cold mint soup, then the main course. Dessert was tiramisu and a glass of Marsala.

"That was amazing!" chuckled Willie as he rubbed his full belly. "I hope you don't expect me to outdo that!"

Luc paused a moment, then pulled a white envelope from behind his back. It had bold black words that read WILLIE & LUC. Willie's eyebrows shot up in surprise.

"What is this about, Luc?" he asked.

"Open it up!" laughed Luc. Willie struggled a little getting it open, but when he did, he pulled out a large piece of white paper.

Pulling his glasses from his front pocket he did a quick glance before handing it back to Luc.

"Again. What is this about? It would appear some kind of legal document you want me to sign pertaining to a lease on a restaurant in the Bay area," he said, tilting his head, his eyebrows pinched.

Luc sighed and sat down on the footstool in front of Willie. As he spoke, his eyes filled with tears.

Placing his hands on Willie's he said, "This is what you and I have been dreaming about all of our lives. To have our own kitchen. To prepare food we will be proud of. Think of it!"

Willie pulled his hands from underneath Luc's and stood.

"This is crazy Luc! I don't have any money!" he said. "At least not that kind!"

Willie's body language had gone from relaxed to tense. His palms were clenched, his mouth tight. The silence was finally broken by Luc.

"Yes, Willie, I know. But I do."

Like so many ventures in life, this one started with the best of intentions. The restaurant opened to rave reviews, and reservations were increasingly hard to get. Willie and Luc worked from sunup to sundown, seven days a week, and it was starting to show in Willie as the older of the couple.

Things finally began to slow down on this particular Friday night. Luc grabbed Willie by the hand and showed him the door.

"Willie, I need you to get some rest. Don't come in tomorrow—I've already got it covered," Luc said with a smile.

"Who?" asked Willie, arms crossed across his chest, one foot tapping.

"Connor," he said. Willie stared at his partner for a moment before tearing off his white chef's coat, bagging his blue clogs and, with a quick tug of the door, storming down the street.

Reginald

The restaurant closed to its patrons at midnight on Saturdays, giving the clean-up crew time to get prepared for the next day. Willie waited until 1:30 a.m. before returning to the restaurant. While he was expecting it, the horrible, sick picture of betrayal had him on his knees and throwing up all over the street in front of "WILLIE & LUC."

Of course there was a highly dramatic scene with Luc charging out, one hand trying to do up his belt buckle, the other to open the door. Connor was right behind him, his hair all over the place, his facial expression one of despair and victory.

***

Luc bought Willie out of the business, and they parted bitterly. Luc and Connor ran the restaurant for another year until it folded; Connor decided he didn't like the food industry, broke up with Luc and moved to Oregon. Luc moved to Mexico, fell in love and opened a taco bar.

Willie decided to head back home to Canada. He rented a room in Victoria for a few months, scanning the papers and Internet for either a grocery store or small restaurant to purchase. He finally found one on the mainland, in the town of Einer's Bay, and it sounded perfect. The whole idea of getting away from it all appealed to him, so he packed his things and moved to Einer's Bay. He was able to leave the pain behind, but he was in for more than he bargained in the quiet little town he was escaping to.

CHAPTER SIXTY-FOUR

JACK, EINER'S BAY, PRESENT DAY: THE SPIDER

The day after the meeting at Willie's, Jack's mind is running in all kinds of directions as he makes his way home from shopping. Chuckling to himself, he figures his mind has been spinning since Shirley's arrival. Tonight, the Guardians are going to meet with Leah at The Sundowner. But Jack is feeling way too anxious to enjoy a beer at the pub right now. Instead, he's driving home from shopping, going for a run in the forest and meeting up with them after. The light is fading, but Jack knows his property well.

Pulling into the garage, he shuts the gate behind him. Jack is passionate about running. He keeps his gear in the garage so he can hit the trails as soon as possible. He decides on long pants tonight; he can feel a winter chill in the air. After he changes and does a few quick calf stretches, Jack closes the garage door and begins his run.

There's a skiff of snow on the ground as his trainers bite hard into the gravel. The skies are darkening, and Jack can already feel the tension draining from his body. He thinks about the meeting;

based on what Josh has already told him, he can sure understand why his son has formed such a quick attraction to Leah. From the way he described her quiet confidence, she sounds different from the young women his son has dated over the years.

Although artistic and soft-spoken, Josh has a fiery temper and usually gravitates to similar personalities. Leah sounds more like Josh's mom, an astute businesswoman, madly in love with the arts.

Jack crosses over to the side of the woods with a creek that runs downhill to the ocean. He'll need a long drink of that crystal-clear, icy mountain water by the time he gets there. Jack slows. He hears something moving, and it's close to him. He's got bear spray in his back pocket, but this doesn't sound like a bear. It sounds like something with more than four big legs as it thrashes through the trees in his direction.

Jack picks up his stride; the water is close, and maybe he can escape whatever is hunting him. Quickly, he turns to see what kind of animal is in pursuit. This, he immediately regrets—it's a giant spider. Jack is tall at six-foot-four, but this thing is mammoth, with at least six thick legs covered in wiry, black hair, sharp, iron-shaped feet and a substantial middle riddled with big bumps that sway as it runs. The head is large with what looks like a red-and-black hairy hat sitting atop large black oval eyes and a red mouth, its corners turned up to reveal a mouthful of jagged teeth.

Jack runs faster as the monster is gaining on him. Catching a toe on a root, he almost goes down. The spider makes a five-foot jump in the air, landing just behind Jack, its pointed teeth snapping as it closes in on its prey. It's closer now and emits a putrid smell, like something that crawled out of the morgue. He knows whatever this monster is, it will be on him soon.

The forest ground rises to the right on one side and leads to a jump-off point—Jack and Josh used to have a blast diving off those rocks. If only he can make it. The spider spits and jumps again, only now its prey is within reach.

Jack screams as the beast bites down hard on his right ankle. With little time to lose, he pulls the bear spray out of his back pocket and blasts the spider in the eyes. It howls in pain but keeps running in Jack's direction, all the way to the top of the mountain, where he is waiting. After more quick blasts of the spray, he grabs hold of two of the spider's thick, muscled legs and spins the creature down into the rapids below.

***

Showered, bandaged and ointment applied, Jack is about to get into his car and head to The Sundowner when Giselle calls him about some kind of beast trying to hack its way into her yurt. He knows it can't be the spider because with any luck that thing is dead. He slams his car in reverse and heads for Giselle's place, a quick four-minute blast down another gravel road. The demon is having a busy night.

CHAPTER SIXTY-FIVE

THE GUARDIANS, EINER'S BAY, PRESENT DAY: THE GUARDIANS' PLAN

The Guardians of Einer's Bay know the clock is ticking; they have little choice but to activate their plan. So much depends on Giselle; her knowledge of shamanism, magic and Egyptology will make their mission either a success or a deadly failure.

Giselle's yurt is in the middle of a forest which is part of Jack's fifty acres of wilderness. Complete with solar panels, running water and electricity, her amber-coloured, round home lacks for nothing. It sits in a small clearing close to a rushing creek, so fresh water is never a problem.

Having been shunted from foster home to foster home in her youth, Giselle feels living in this yurt is a dream come true. Throughout the years of living with people who weren't her parents, she'd longed to have control of her own space. While those years toughened her up and made her the woman she is, she is eternally grateful for the precious and private space of the yurt. That the yurt is also circular is a bonus.

As a shaman, Giselle understands the power of the circle. From the standing stones, to the beehive tombs in ancient Greece, to the circle of life, humankind's affinity for the power of the circle is ancient.

The medicine wheel is a powerful symbol representing the spiritual, mental, physical and emotional aspects of life. One only has to gaze up to the trees to see the round nests of baby birds and eggs about to hatch. Life itself is a circle from childhood to adulthood and back to childhood. It's significant in many cultures, including the Huna spiritualism that Giselle practices.

The yurt is her circle of peace, healing and magic. It could also become a place for enormous power, strong enough to protect against and perhaps destroy evil. Giselle is no fool: she knows this battle will test every ounce of her ability.

Seated directly over the centre of the circle, she bends her head down, placing her forehead on the middle of a medicine wheel that, while still imbued with power, is showing its age; it still shimmers for those who have the sight.

Giselle secures all windows and doors before she prepares to meditate. She makes sure the front door is closed tightly and locked; crystal chimes strung across the top come together in a soothing melody. Her favourite path to mindfulness is to visualize walking through her spiritual garden. Pulling the soft cotton sheet and wool blanket to her chin, she closes her eyes and sinks into a deep state of being. It's time for her to walk.

The sand is warm and golden. Her feet are unadorned, suntanned and clean. As she moves forward, she shifts her focus upward to the warm sun bathing her. Colours spring from every direction, the scent of gardenia is overpowering ... sweet, seductive, soothing.

All at once, a violent bang spoils the walk. What is happening to her garden?

Giselle jolts up in shock, realizing the crashing is being wreaked upon the side of her yurt. She's on her feet in seconds, grabbing a big black flashlight as both light source and weapon. Crouching down, she sees a large, black shape moving toward the back of the yurt. A bear! There are large black bears here, yes, but usually they're only interested in food. But there's no food outside.

She hears a hissing sound. It's not a bear. And now there's scratching! Shining her flashlight, she's horrified to see an enormous claw trying to poke its way through the side of the yurt. It's something wild but not animal, and definitely not human. It lets out a scream.

Giselle scrambles for her cellphone and hits Jack's number.

"Giselle?" he says. "What's going on?"

She hears the concern in his voice.

"What the hell is that noise? Giselle!"

She's on the floor, sliding slowly under the bed. There's a rifle underneath it.

"Jack," she whispers. "It's a beast. Some kind of monster. Look!" she says through clenched teeth while turning the phone away from her.

"Oh my god, Giselle! Shoot it!"

The beam of the flashlight reveals a beast that's almost as tall as the yurt. Its giant head twists to one side as it pushes into the side of the yurt. Its claw is the size of a steak knife. It pokes and pokes, causing a small hole to grow with every assault, through thick layers of wool and canvas.

"Get away from here!" Giselle screams. "I have a loaded rifle and I'm about to blast you back to hell!"

The creature pauses at this, backing away slowly. Silhouette fading, the low throaty grumble seems to grow louder. Then it stops.

Giselle holds her breath, slipping out from under her bed, rifle up and ready.

Silence. Maybe it left.

Breathing heavily, Giselle shuffles forward, leaning to hear or see if that thing is still there.

Quiet. It's gone.

Giselle detects the sound of a car. Jack—he's here! All at once, a chill runs through her body. What if that thing goes for Jack? She plucks her sweater off the chair, drives her feet into gumboots and yanks open the door, legs in a wide stance, ready for battle.

Suddenly, it's quiet. But there's something ... a smell. Like a dead animal left to rot in the forest. Giselle knows that stench all too well, living on the edge of a forest where animal carcasses have become a common site.

Headlights are bouncing up and down, speeding toward her. Giselle brings the rifle to her side and runs as fast as her boots can carry her. She flings herself onto the hood of the car, somehow hoisting her body and the rifle into the car and slamming the door shut.

"What was that thing?" says Jack, his pale expression one of horror and disbelief.

There's no time for an answer—the creature is back. Jack's headlights reveal a monster of a man striding toward them as if they're trespassers on his estate, his long legs thrusting forward. Giselle thinks for a moment he's wearing shiny, black boots, but that could be his skin. Jack slams the car in reverse and stomps on the pedal.

The beast is now running toward the car, giant arms pumping up and down like oil drills. Claws slash the air as the creature's face enters the beam of the headlights. The head is the size of a lion! Hair as black as pitch swings back and forth across its body.

Giselle winces, cramming her head as hard as she can into the headrest. A scream is building in her belly; she can't keep it in much longer.

There's something in its hand. What is it? She wonders. Oh, dear god, it looks like a baby animal! A puppy or a kitten or—

WHACK. It hits the windshield and bounces off into the brush to her side of the car.

"Jack!" she screams. "It's not giving up! It killed something and threw it at the car!"

Jack hits the brakes. The creature keeps coming. They can both hear the horrid, ragged breath as it steams toward them. Jack grabs the gun, opens the door and leaves the relative safety of the car. Giselle, screaming Jack's name, gets out on the other side. The monster is almost at the car when Jack fires his gun. The ragged breathing has stopped, so Jack assumes he killed it. Giselle is looking his way and shaking her head.

"He's gone, Jack. He just disappeared the second you shot him."

CHAPTER SIXTY-SIX

PATTY, EINER'S BAY, PRESENT DAY: THE HAIRY HELL

P atty is almost ready to close up shop for the night. It's abnormally busy for the middle of the week: first there was the stagette from Vancouver, followed by the cruise ship passengers, both of which have kept local businesses humming.

Why would someone need their hair done to view whales and bears? Patty wonders. It only makes sense when you know the money it takes to have your fanny on that cruise. She knows the scenario all too well, having bolted from one of those pricey cruises herself, abandoning a complicated life with a dickhead of a husband, for a fresh start in this quirky little place.

The salon staff are at home after a long day, so she pours herself half a coffee cup of scotch, lights a cigarette and sits in her aging, creaking, pinching desk chair. Last night's meeting with the Guardians was a lot to absorb. It takes a significant leap of faith to believe that anything that evil, that powerful, could live in this once-peaceful haven. Patty doesn't blame Shirley; she loved her and feels devastated by her death. And she's royally pissed—Patty doesn't handle loss well.

Normally Patty enjoys her wind-down time at the salon, making sure everything is in its place for the morning. If there's one thing she's learned over twenty years of being in the hairstyling business, it's if she doesn't put things back where they should be at the end of the day, the beginning of the next day will be chaos. Every stylist has their own tools, and knowing their exact location is paramount to the salon's success. But Patty could find no enjoyment there tonight. Only fear of the demon.

With one last glance, Patty nods, removes her smock and retrieves her purse from the back office. And that's when she hears the noise.

It's nothing at first, like a butterfly wing brushing against glass. She sniffs, cocking her head to one side. It's definitely getting louder.

In the sink on the left, there's movement where there shouldn't be. The bowl is empty and polished clean by Patty herself. Inching her way over, she's shocked to see the basin full of hair. An inch of dark-black hair covers the entire sink, clogging the drain and standing at attention on the chrome faucet.

To her horror, the hair moves. Along with the motion comes a sound. Soft hissing at first, then evolving into that of a moth captured in a glass—only hundreds of them. Patty steps back in disbelief as the pieces of hair join, forming a swarm of fluttering insects. All at once, they're on her, flying into her open and screaming mouth. She chokes on them, swallows them, clawing pitifully to dislodge the mass. They fill up in her hair until it feels like someone is yanking her backward. She struggles to breathe as they tunnel their way up her nostrils, on a march to her brain.

Staggering backwards, Patty's only thought is to drown them somehow. Blinded by the ones sucking the moisture from her eyes, she stumbles, fumbling her way to the largest sink in the salon. With shaking hands, she turns both faucets on full, pushes the plug in and waits until the water is half up the side of the sink. She plunges her head in once, twice, three times, spitting the little hairy, biting bodies out. Snorting as hard as she can, she feels the space growing inside her nostrils. Scooping out the dead bodies with her fingers, she plunges her head into the water again and again.

After cleaning up herself and the mess created in the salon, Patty finds a few bodies still clinging to clippers and scissors. She quickly gathers them up, rinses them in the sink, makes sure they're bug free and dumps them in the sterilizer jar with the others. She pulls back her soaking-wet hair, twisting it into a bun as best she can with her shaking hands. A quick glance in the mirror tells her a great deal: she is frightened to her core.

Patty picks up her purse, jacket and keys. Wait. There's something written on the outside of the glass door. Her hand goes automatically to her mouth as she gasps in disbelief. Someone has etched closed for good into the glass. Whatever or whoever did it must have used a diamond drill. The letters are deep and thick. Rivulets of blood—syrupy, clotted blood—ooze out of each letter. As she watches in horror, the clots turn into hair insects and fly into her face, becoming a swarm around her head as she screams and runs for the protection of her car.

CHAPTER SIXTY-SEVEN

LEAH, RAVENS' WOOD, PRESENT DAY: THE DEMON IN THE ATTIC

Days later, the attic is unchanged. The walls, floor and Ruby's statue remain covered in a bloody skin-like substance. I pull my black hair behind my shoulders and shuffle my feet toward her, breathing out her name with every step.

"Ruby. I'm here. Can you hear me?" I whisper.

Her silence fills me with dismay. Kneeling at her side, I place both hands on the arms of the statue, and they sink deeply into the gory mush that covers her. I gag on the stench and recoil in revulsion. It is living tissue that ensconces her.

"You bastard!" I scream, turning to face an invisible enemy. "Let her go!"

Suddenly, he appears in front of me—he's levitating. He of the small head, red eyes and long, limp penis that swings to the floor below like a skin pendulum. He's coming toward me, giggling like a drunken sailor.

Screaming, I lunge toward him, hands up, nails ready to tear his ugly red face to shreds. He evaporates as I fall hard to the floor.

When I open my eyes, the attic looks normal again. The blood, the skin tissue and gore have disappeared. I don't know what's real anymore.

***

I change my clothes three times, finally settling with the first pair of jeans I tried on and a black sweater. My hands shake as I try to fix my makeup.

Did that just happen? Did I really see that grotesque monster floating toward me? Were the blood and gore even real? What if it's all in my head?

Staring myself down in the mirror, I concentrate on breathing. On top of dealing with what just went down in my attic, I'm a little nervous about meeting the Guardians. What if they think I'm making all this up? They're kind people who knew Aunt Shirley, and they want to help. I just don't want to disappoint them. Sighing, I wonder if they would still want to get involved if they had seen that creature in the attic with their own eyes. What the hell is he?

Adrienne is picking me up in ten minutes. We're meeting the Guardians at The Sundowner for a drink.

She pulls up just as I lock up the side door, and I get in the car. As we pull away, Adrienne describes each member of the group and a bit about their background. I can't help but look back over my shoulder and shudder as the house fades away.

***

Josh heads down to The Sundowner so he'll be there well before the others arrive. He needs a drink and some time to think. Things are moving so quickly with Leah. His feelings for her are real and they're growing. Pushing his sleeves up, he signals to the server and orders a gin and tonic. Checking his cell for messages, he notices his father has called. No voice mail, so Jack must have found an answer for whatever he was looking for.

The server approaches with a big smile, sets the drink on the table and heads off; it's a busy night at The Sundowner. Josh takes a big swig, leans back in his chair and sighs. This whole demon thing is totally stressing him out. As the alcohol burns its way down his throat, the buzz of the bar fades away and Josh sinks into a memory of his childhood.

They were on vacation in Maui. Josh was a rambunctious

twelve-year-old. It was supposed to be a fun family getaway, but it started off wrong.

As soon as they got on the plane, Josh picked up that something wasn't right. His mom was hammering back the Bloody Marys, and his dad was silent, his face tense, arms crossed, head pressed against the window. Josh had his headphones on, listening to what his mother referred to as "that dreaded dubstepper thing." Five minutes into the flight and she was frantically signalling him to turn it down. He turned up the music and shrugged his shoulders with a grin.

***

They checked into a one-bedroom suite at the Napili Hibiscus for seven nights, and Josh had the sofa bed. His dad's mood hadn't changed since they arrived, and he was now slamming cupboard doors as he unpacked. His mom was on the deck with a glass of white wine, one hand stroking her blonde hair back while the other made return trips of the wine to her lips.

"Dad?" Josh questioned in a soft voice. "Can I go check out the place?"

His dad was staring at his mother out on the deck, his face flushed.

"Yes, Josh, but be back in half an hour. Here's your card."

Josh grabbed it and ran out of the room, his destination the beach he had only glimpsed out of the hotel window. Feet flying down the stairs, he kept running past the people at the pool who were holding out for the last rays of sun and the final happy hour cocktail.

Josh remembers how blown away he was by the feel of warm sand beneath his feet. The turquoise waves were small, but as he slowly walked forward, he felt a powerful undertow. Josh was an excellent swimmer, but he'd have to be careful. As he dipped down into the warm sea, he heard glass breaking, then yelling. Wrenching his head around, it shocked him to see it was coming from their hotel room!

They were both on the balcony, his father screaming at his mom. She had her back to the water and was yelling back at him; Josh could hear her sobs between the shouting. Josh turned and sprinted, sand flying behind him as he ran. Blasting up the three flights of stairs, his hand fumbled to find the hotel card. The yelling continued as he stood shaking outside their room. He raised his right hand to knock, to give them a chance to stop before he entered the room. Three taps. Nothing. Just more screaming.

Tears ran down his cheeks as he tried again. Four harder taps. Nothing. Then more breaking glass. Josh inserted the card and pushed in, terrified of what he might see.

His mother was on the floor, blood flowing from her right foot, and his father was in the bathroom, rummaging around for something. His mom cried softly as she finally realized Josh was in the room. He fell to his knees and grabbed her hand.

His father rushed into the room, and with a quick glance at his son, held a towel to his wife's foot to stop the bleeding. The broken wine glass shards glowed in the setting sun as they trailed from the deck to the living room; it's bloody stem somehow upright, beside his mother's bleeding foot.

"Another G and T, Josh?" asks the server, as Josh jerks back to the present and gives a curt nod. His hands trembling, Josh drains the last drops of his first drink.

It was such a mess, he thinks, shaking his head. Nothing was the same after that trip to the tropics. His mother had been having an affair for six months, his dad found out; they divorced and Josh just had to deal with it.

Well, he didn't deal with it, and it still festered in his gut like a parasite. That is the home of his anger, and while he's seen therapists and learned to meditate, that pain, fear and suppressed rage over the end of his childhood was never far away. That is, until Leah entered his life. For the first time since he was a terrified twelve-year-old watching his life fall apart, he has hope.

***

As we approach The Sundowner, I notice a short woman wearing black tights and a dark-purple sweater who I assume is Giselle, and she's comforting a blonde woman—must be Patty—who seems to be upset about something. They turn as Adrienne and I approach, and they move as one to hug me. I know they were all important to Shirley, and their warmth seems genuine.

Josh and his dad, Jack, who arrived shortly after Josh did, have put aside a private table for us to talk, and introductions are made.

But something drastic has happened to Patty. Her hands shake, her wine spills and her blond hair is a mess, half stuffed into a scrunchie; the other half is limp, wet and trailing around her face and neck. Between gulps of her wine, she blows her nose with a vengeance and tries hard to cover up whatever is in her tissues.

Giselle, on the other hand, seems relatively composed, but there's something bubbling under the surface. Her pretty features are tight with tension, hands twisting something beneath the tabletop. It didn't surprise me when Adrienne told me she's the head Guardian. Between her military background and knowledge of shamanism and spiritualism, she must make a perfect combination of toughness and intuition.

The unlit cigarette in Willie's mouth bounces up and down with every word.

"Leah, we're all very sorry you have to deal with any of this. We all loved Shirley and swore an oath to protect you should something happen to her."

Jack, wearing a black tracksuit, places his large, weathered hand on Willie's arm and says, "We're here to protect you, and we will find a way to kill that demon."

I squirm a little in my seat and say, "I'm not so sure you can do that—in fact I'm not so sure why you would."

Everyone sits up a little straighter at that comment.

Adrienne smiles, takes my hand, and says, "Sweetie, we loved Shirley so much. When she wasn't storming around, accusing us of cheating at pickleball, she'd be talking non-stop about you and how kind you are, how smart you are and how incredibly special you were to her. We'll try to destroy this evil with everything we've got, even if it means we die trying."

***

After the meeting breaks up, everyone takes off in different directions. Josh and Jack have their heads down and are engaged in what looks like a serious conversation. I nudge my way in.

"Excuse me," I say, "I don't want to interrupt, but I'd like to speak with you, Jack, if you have a moment."

Jack smiles. "Sure, would love to. I just have to see a man about a horse, and I'll be right back."

Josh's jaw drops at that one. Laughing, I say, "An oldie but a goodie."

We sit back down at the table we've just vacated and moments later, Jack reappears. Josh's eyes focus somewhere below Jack's waist. His dad gets the hint and zips up his fly. As he finishes, his face breaks into this most adorable grin, his complexion slightly flushed. I see a glimpse of the mischievous little boy Jack once was, so different from the tough guy he is today.

"Thanks, son," he says to Josh, then takes a seat. Rolling up the sleeves of his black hoodie Jack gets down to business, looks at me, and asks, "What's up?"

Exhaling, I don't know where to start, but I keep it as simple as possible.

"I think someone is poisoning me. I stayed in Shirley's old bedroom last night. The window in her old room was wide open, and I stood for a time, my hands on the windowsill, just enjoying the birds chirping and the peace. I took a big drink of the water on my nightstand and lay down on the bed, staring up at the painted cherubs on the ceiling." I pull my chair right up to the edge of the table and continue. "This will sound psychotic, but those little cherubs came to life."

Jack puts his hand up to stop me. "Wait," he says, "how is that possible?"

I check the room to make sure no one else can hear my whacked-out story.

"Well, Jack, clearly it isn't. Someone or something spiked my water or painted the ceiling with some kind of hallucinogenic goop; some of it got in my eyes. I then apparently grabbed a bottle of wine, jumped into the car, drove to The Sundowner where I met Josh and his ex."

Jack's head whips to look at his son. "Didn't happen," Josh softly responds, without making eye contact with Jack.

"I got lost driving home," I continue, "ending up at the dead end of a forest that tried to crush me and my car. When I came to, I was still in the garage with the bottle of wine. And so I believe someone drugged me."

Josh fires back in his chair, hands raking his hair back in exasperation yelling, "Jesus Christ, Leah!" His face deepens to a dark berry as his father reaches across the table to grab his arm and pull him forward.

The next step is a faceoff as Jack's intensity wins over his son's anger. I watch as Josh's skin tone returns to normal and he's breathing calmly once again. My hand reaches up to stroke his curls, and he sighs and takes a deep breath.

They watch as I carefully pull out my glass of water, tightly wrapped inside a plastic wine bag.

"I'm wondering if you could have this tested for me, Jack. My theory is somebody dosed me with something nasty, sending me down a rabbit hole."

Jack kindly offers to take it to his friend who is still working in the drug squad in Vancouver; he thinks he'll have an answer for me in a couple of days. I'm not sure what good it'll do, but at least I'll know to keep my windows locked.

CHAPTER SIXTY-EIGHT

GUARDIANS, EINER'S BAY, PRESENT DAY: ANOTHER MEETING

The group leaves The Sundowner, and Josh drives Leah home in the pouring rain. He does a quick walkthrough of the house when they arrive, making sure everything is safe before heading to Jack's. Josh gives Leah a quick kiss as he leaves, and she closes the door. Once he's heard the bolt slide shut, he hurries to his car; the others are expecting him.

***

Willie and Adrienne both head home, while Josh, Jack, Giselle and Patty meet for the second time that day. They have chosen Jack's house as a meeting place, as it's best suited to accommodate several guests. All three guests have retired for the night, exhausted by the terrible stories they shared and the sullen presence they can't seem to shake. It walks closely behind each of them, its foul breath on the back of their necks, a bony finger flexed and ready to poke a shoulder. They'll reconvene after they get some sleep.

***

Jack waits until all the lights are off in the guest rooms before he walks back downstairs to his study. He smiles as he enters his man cave; he covets the peace he finds here. Once the green library banker's light is on, he makes his way to the bar cart, pours himself a healthy portion of smoky scotch, then drops into a dark-green leather visitor's chair.

Stretching his long legs up on the desk, he pulls out a cigar, lights it and takes a drag of the spicy earthy taste. Wait—there's a green-faced monster in the window! Jack's shoulders fall as he shakes his head, knowing how wound up he must be to have his own reflection frighten him.

To Jack's mind, two things went well today: he killed that god-awful spider creature, and he validated his gut feeling about Leah. She seems to be a very special woman. Intelligent, a good listener, genuine, and she clearly tries her best to make the world believe that she doesn't carry around a gigantic backpack of pain. She must fool most people, he speculates, but not him. This drugging situation troubles him. He plucks at the skin around his fingernails—something he does when he's unsettled.

Jack thinks back to his time with the police force. Instinct backed by solid intel was everything. Their enemies might have changed over the years, but the same tactics applied, whether it was the Russians or the Hell's Angels. These criminals connected through drugs, prostitution, weapons, sex trafficking and the non-stop trail of bloodshed unleashed against their competition or themselves. With demons running loose in Einer's Bay, Jack almost longed for the simplicity of gang wars. Almost.

Vancouver has changed so much since his time on the police force. The city is much bigger. Bigger isn't always a good thing. Jack tops off his scotch, reflecting on his last visit. The never-ending construction and hopelessly snarled traffic. Fifty-plus storey high-rises sprung up throughout the downtown core. The city was an angry one. Sirens were non-stop, car horns blaring as frustrated drivers tried to weave their way out of the chaos.

Scrunching his shoulders to loosen the tension, Jack reflects on the city Vancouver used to be. Stunningly scenic—as it still is today—the bad guys, drugs, prostitution and gun violence seemed to take place in the shadows. That's where Jack lived in those days. Undercover with a scraggly beard, tattoos and jeans that revealed the crack of his butt, he wasn't much to look at. But he fit in just fine with the dangerous thugs he loved to take down.

Now, walk down many streets downtown and you'll see homeless people lying on sidewalks, ambulances, sirens screaming on their way to another drug overdose and increasingly, people with mental illness becoming violent. Young families who once cherished their seaside communities are leaving for the suburbs; a trade-off of safety for a long commute.

CHAPTER SIXTY-NINE

ADRIENNE, EINER'S BAY, PRESENT DAY: THE CHILI WITH TOAST

A drienne opens the front door of her two-level cottage, kicking off her boots and shaking the rain from her umbrella.

"Jim?" she calls out, walking in stocking feet, closing the door behind with one heel. She carries the many bags of groceries she'd bought just prior to picking up Leah tonight. She shakes her head in frustration. "Jim! I need help!"

The only response is the sound of the football game playing loudly on the TV upstairs and the stomps from the floor above that seem to signal both touchdowns and flags.

Resigned to the fact that she is on her own, she lets her raincoat fall to the linoleum floor and carefully unloads her cloth bags of groceries for tonight's dinner: chili with toast.

Adrienne loves to cook—chopping onions, mincing garlic, unwrapping ground beef, slicing green peppers and opening up cans of tomato sauce. Having purchased only one can, she's confident she has more. Opening the cupboard, she sees rows of tomato soup, but where there'd be a row for tomato sauce there's nothing.

"Damn," she sighs, then yells, "JIM!"

More thuds upstairs; the volume rises.

"Fine," she snaps, and walks the few feet over to the cellar door. The grandchild of a Depression-era grandmother, Adrienne always has lots of extra cans of food and bottles of water on hand in case the big one—an earthquake or other disaster—ever comes.

She flicks the light switch at the top of the stairs, but the bulb snaps and dies, leaving her to make her way in the dark. The small window on the other side of the cellar does little to light her way, but she knows where to find the sauce.

Reaching up on her tiptoes, Adrienne slides the nearest can to the edge of the shelf.

Wait. There's a red light visible behind the rows of tins. What could that be?

Carefully stepping on the edge of the lowest shelf to get a better look, she pops her head up. She can't see the red light anymore. How strange is that? She tilts her head sideways to think this through as her eyes scan the other shelves.

"Everything is normal," she whispers to herself. But now she sees red lights again, only they're larger. Not only are they bigger, they're moving toward her.

Adrienne shrieks and falls backwards to the floor. Hitting her head hard on the cement, she screams loudly for her husband. She pulls back in horror and disbelief as the monster—its slick, red, hairless human form sheathed in some kind of translucent casing— snakes down the shelving, cat-like red eyes glowing. There's a small rodent hanging from its mouth; the creature slurps it up and swallows it.

Adrienne shrieks and throws herself up and onto the stairs, screaming, "JIM!" all the way. Sobbing, she slams and locks the cellar door behind her.

And now, what's happening on her stove? She must have cranked up the heat before she left, but she has no memory of doing that. Red sauce bubbles over, cascading in thick streams down the front of the oven.

Grabbing her oven mitt, she lifts the top. Hundreds of baby rats squirm their way out of the hot pot, slide down the oven to hit the floor, then scurry to the crack under the cellar door.

Adrienne screeches one more time for her husband just as the front door swings open.

"What in the name of all things holy are you yelling about!"

Jim yells. He holds a case of beer in one hand, a bag of snacks in the other and his wet umbrella is dripping all over the floor. They both cock their heads in unison as someone or something stomps and cranks up the volume for the game upstairs.

CHAPTER SEVENTY

LEAH, RAVENS' WOOD, PRESENT DAY: THE MURDER

I 'm jolted out of a deep sleep. Dawn has barely arrived and shadows are only just appearing. I have found the answer in my dreams: Aunt Shirley's journals! There must be another one somewhere.

My first thought is the dollhouse. Armed with a hammer, saw and a mug of hot coffee, I make my way quietly to the structure. There's still snow on the ground, but it looks different today. Somebody has been here since I brought Father Kelly.

The shoe prints—no, footprints—are large. I see claw shapes at the end of each toe. Could be a bear, I think with a gulp, bringing my hammer up a little higher. Something else has changed. The footprints are leading away from the dollhouse. They seem to fade back into the snow around the rear of the house.

Where there once was snow at the doorway to the dollhouse, there's now dark blood-coloured earth. I choke on the stench, drain the remains of my coffee into the strange soil and watch in horror as it froths and boils on contact.

***

Morning dawns bright and early at Jack's house, and he's not in the least surprised to see everyone already up and drinking coffee. His housekeeper has arrived early, putting on the coffee and laying out trays of muffins and croissants.

"Well," says Giselle, nibbling a cheese croissant, "I think we all know what has to happen."

The others nod in agreement, except for Josh, who shoots to his feet, face flushed with frustration.

"How do you figure that, Giselle? We have no clue what Reginald needs from Ruby or Leah." He grabs for his phone that's now vibrating on the coffee table. "Leah? What's going on?"

The others hold their breath while he listens. Her news can't be good.

"Okay," says Josh, then disconnecting the call and stuffing the phone into his back pocket. "Leah thinks there's a second journal and she knows where it might be, but she can't get to it."

At this, every one of them lean backwards in their chairs. Only one of them has the courage to voice the obvious.

"It's in the dollhouse," says Patty, standing and placing her hands on her hips, her face etched with certainty.

***

Josh calls Willie and Adrienne and asks them to meet the rest of the Guardians at Ravens' Wood; they will explain what's going on once they're all together. Jack opens his car with his fob; Giselle slides into the front, with Patty and Josh in the back. It's a quiet ride, filled with worry and fear.

All Jack can think about is that horror who attacked them at the yurt; he can't get rid of the image of the big black creature running at them faster than any human could. How can they possibly defeat something that could manifest any kind of monstrous physical form it desires? Jack has a sick feeling as he tries to relax his stranglehold on the steering wheel.

Patty's trying her best to take control of the fear that simmers inside her, like those wicked insects. She's still picking those disgusting dead hair bugs out of her nose. She knows she won't survive another similar encounter. She'd rather blow her brains out.

Jack parks at the top of Leah's driveway and they all get out in anticipation of Willie and Adrienne's arrival.

***

Willie's eyes are wide, his hands holding the wheel so tightly his fingers are chalk white.

Adrienne looks over at him. "Willie, don't throttle the poor thing! We need it to get us to Leah's house."

Willie keeps staring ahead, giving her a slight side glance and nod.

Adrienne is doing her best to forget the rats. Jim is still cleaning up, and while they searched for hours, they couldn't find the mystery football fan or the red-eyed creature. Thankfully, it looks like the rats left too.

All at once, Willie slams on the brakes.

"What the hell, Willie!" she cries. "Why did you do that? There's nothing on the road!"

But she's dead wrong about that.

There is something on the road—or rather, was. Now it's on the back of the pickup truck. Willie and Adrienne turn in unison to face whatever has hitched a ride.

It's Reginald. Or, better described, Reginald the demon, his hideous, long talons poking furiously at the glass, seeking a place to slide one in. He stares at them, his head upside down, through the rear window. So repulsive is his appearance that both Willie and Adrienne can't help but look away.

His dark, enflamed eyes continue to stare, his long tongue wiping across the glass. He's laughing loudly, dripping saliva down in little black puddles streaming down his face and showing off the rotted stumps of his teeth.

"Get off my truck, you piece of shit!" screams Willie, pressing the gas pedal with everything he has.

"For god's sake, Willie! Boot it!" yells Adrienne.

"Adrienne? Can you see it? Is it off the truck?" yells Willie, looking furiously at the rear-view mirror.

As Adrienne turns to check, the pickup truck slams headfirst into a gigantic boulder that did not exist seconds before. There's a horrible screeching, wrenching noise. Metal tears apart, tires blow up, glass shatters as if hit by a thousand baseball bats.

The bedlam goes on for what seems like hours; then suddenly, it stops. Adrienne's head is bloody and bruised from the airbag. Her knees are jammed under the console, but other than that, she's alive.

"Willie?" she whispers, terrified the demon lurks right outside her door. "You okay?"

She barely has the strength to turn her head. What she sees will haunt her for the rest of her life.

Willie is dead. The airbag didn't deploy. He went part way through the windshield, his torso smashed into the steering wheel. His head is right through the shattered glass. His once-whimsical ponytail hangs like a bloody rag.

Having just pulled up to the house and hearing the crash, Jack and Josh run back to the gate as fast as they can, with Patty and Giselle hot on their tails. Rounding the corner just outside the entrance to the estate, they step into a nightmarish scene. Smoke is billowing out of Willie's destroyed pickup, which is mashed into a huge boulder.

"Oh my god, Dad!" cries Josh. "What the hell happened here?"

But his father is already in motion, sprinting toward the truck, looking into the cab of Willie's vehicle, using his coat as a shield to yank open the searing hot passenger door. He pulls Adrienne out of the truck, into his arms, and screams at his son to run. Jack shakes his head as Josh hesitates in desperation, hoping against hope that his close friend could have survived. Josh spins on his right heel and heads back to the gates.

The explosion happens within seconds. A large fireball shoots up from the wreckage, landing just short of the group and mashing Willie's remains into a bizarre blend of metal, fabric, flesh and blood.

***

The police have come and gone, taking statements from all involved. They examine the crash site, photographing the fireball and towing away the pickup. It's all just one horrid blur.

The ambulance carries Adrienne to the local medical clinic. Jim calls to say that the doctor sedated her; thankfully she has no broken bones although her bruising is severe. The cuts on her face will heal in time, but the memory of her friend's horrible death will stay with her forever.

Everyone is in a state of shock.

***

What happened is inexplicable to the rational mind. Time seems to stand still after the accident. Josh is shaking and crying, and I can't seem to calm him down. He's in shock, losing his buddy in such a violent way. Josh was constantly in the grocery store as Willie continued to make changes; he only trusted one guy to do the work—and that was Josh.

When they weren't tearing down or building up, they were fishing. Josh will feel so lost without his friend's wisdom and endless support. Willie loved Josh like his own son.

Jack nods and gives me a brave smile as he wraps his own sweater over his son's shoulders and gets him settled in his passenger seat. Patty has left for her little cottage near the marina, but she has to drive past Willie's house; that will be hard. It's just Giselle and me now, and I'm thankful for her peaceful presence.

I need to get away from all of this. Pulling my sweatshirt off a peg near the back door, I decide to take a chance and go for a walk. Even a demon has to take a rest between murdering people, don't they? I can only hope.

I zip my sweatshirt up high and the gravel crunches beneath my feet. I stop and take a deep breath. The air is cold and cleansing. I end up at the gate, and I see there are still pieces of the wreckage littered across the street. I'm drawn to it, and I resist my inner voice, which tells me to stop and go back where it's safe. But Willie isn't safe, I tell myself. Tears stream down my face as I survey the scene before me. I can still smell burning rubber and see the vicious skid marks on the pavement that end at a rock that had inexplicably appeared. Dropping to the ground, I whisper words I hope Willie can hear:

"You're dead because of me," I sob. "I should never have come here." I stop to catch my breath. "I'm cursed. And my curse has cost you your life." My voice cracks as I choke on my tears.

"You didn't think twice to try to save me." My throat feels swollen and my breath hitches as I try to get the words out. "I can never replace your friendship with Josh but I promise I'll try my best to always have his back ... as you did." Snot runs down my face. I find what's left of a tissue in my jacket pocket and wipe. It's getting dark, which means I'm now in grave danger if that monster is still around.

My fast walk quickly turns into a jog as I head back to the house. There's somebody behind me. I can hear him breathing deep, raspy breaths that catch then rattle. He's getting closer, and I start screaming for help.

Giselle crashes out of the front door and runs toward me, shotgun in hand.

"Get out of the way!" she yells, so I cut hard to the right. Glancing over my shoulder at Giselle, I can see she's lowered the gun. She shrugs her shoulders. There's no one behind me.

I have reached a few conclusions in the past forty-eight hours. Reginald—despite all odds—is still alive in a physical sense. All remaining answers are in the dollhouse. He has enormous power over that place. I need the help of someone with strong spiritual understanding and power to unlock that door. Out of all the Guardians, Giselle, I believe, is the one to do it.

As I walk up the long driveway to the plantation-style house, it's like I'm truly seeing it for the first time. The sides of the house, no longer cream-coloured and welcoming, have rivulets of rust running down them, puddling on the ground below. Even the once-glorious trees now look barren and rotting.

CHAPTER SEVENTY-ONE

LEAH & THE GUARDIANS, RAVENS' WOOD, PRESENT DAY: THE IMMOVABLE DOOR

After a restless night, I'm dressed and ready for battle at six the following morning. The Guardians arrive at about the same time.

I greet them with a nod and lead them around the back of the house. Giselle is already standing in front of the dollhouse. She's dressed in skin-tight blue jeans, with her fuchsia-streaked black hair wrenched up on the top of her head. She holds a shotgun—clearly she's ready for a fight.

"What's the plan?" asks Jack as we approach. Patty flanks Jack to the left, Josh to the right. Adrienne and I hold hands as we bring up the rear. Adrienne's heavily bruised face is drawn, her eyes flashing.

"We need to open the goddamn door!" shouts Patty, clutching a large axe in her right arm.

Pushing Giselle to one side, Patty raises the hatchet with both hands. With a warrior cry that has every bird abandoning the forest in a great cloud of feathers, she brings the axe down on the door. But it makes not a dent.

She uses a different weapon but gets the same result. After two hours of hammering, sawing, explosives, shotgun blasts and every swear word in the book, the dollhouse still stands impenetrable.

At a loss, we consider our options. Then, I have an idea: alternative access to the dollhouse might be a tunnel behind the wine cellar in the basement. With nothing to lose, we make our way there.

After considerable effort to move the cooler and the metal

panel behind it, we're relieved to see the dark mouth of a shaft. I feel the blood rush to my head when I see the claw marks around the edges. *Scritch, scritch. Scritch, scritch.*

The passageway, if you can call it that, is tight and small. We are down on our hands and knees, crawling in the thick blackness. The earth beneath us is that horrible rust-stained dirt, which has no doubt oozed its way here from the dollhouse.

My heart is beating so hard I think I'll pass out. I'm trying to judge the distance, but we're moving so slowly I can't grasp how much farther we have to go. I'm more than slightly claustrophobic, and I try to turn down the voice in my head that screams to turn around, turn around before it's too late. But it is, of course, too late.

After what seems like hours, we reach the floor underneath the dollhouse. There's a small panel that will allow us access. Jack stops and turns to face us, with a finger to his lips.

"Shhhhhhh," he whispers, as if anyone of us has any inclination to speak or make a sound. With that he turns back, rising to his knees and placing his hands on either side of the panel; it doesn't take much effort to lift it. Jack shoves it to the side and pulls himself up. The rest of us wait in tense silence, breathing softly. Seconds later, his head pops back down.

"All clear."

It's a tight squeeze to get all of us into the space.

Even though the stench from the soil is overwhelming, we take a minute to explore. Located directly behind the entrance door is a small-scale dollhouse. It's cracked and rotting, so it takes a moment to see the contents of each compact room. Patty leans in first; after a few seconds, she draws back, catching her breath and turning away. My turn.

There are four miniature effigies. It's easy to determine their identities: Shirley's grandmother, Bridget, is hanging on a nail by a shredded piece of cloth; her father, Robert, is dangling from a single rotting twig; Shirley's figure is lying on her back just outside the front door of the dollhouse, dressed in a white nightgown, her face in rictus. And Ruby—there's just a diminutive version, all white except for the bloody stroke of red paint that begins at her tiny wrist and runs over the table and down to the floor we're standing on.

Josh has ripped away the stained canvas cover on what first appeared to be a high table to reveal a wooden lid. Josh and Patty lift the lid and shove it to one side. We all move in closer to see what's in the box. Packed in some kind of hardened mud and what looks like straw is an ancient Egyptian funeral mask.

Gleaming back at us in shining gold, lapis blue, and carnelian, the death mask of the god Anubis looks to be authentic. We carefully remove the mask and place it gently on the floor.

***

Two hours of careful combing later, we have found nothing of interest. There are no signs of life in the coffin, and the dollhouse is empty, except for the sinister miniature death scenes.

Josh is hurling cuss words like crazy; every muscle in his body has tightened to the point where he looks like he's made of rock. I wave my arm up and down to calm him, but I don't think he even sees me through his rage.

Adrienne leans back.

"Shit, how can there be nothing here?" she says, kicking the wall hard with her heel. Jack and Josh have turned away from the empty box, staring outside at the dreary winter day while Jack places a muscular arm around his son's shoulder.

Patty continues to poke around, her manicured hands plucking away at the hard mud and straw.

"There *has* to be something here!" she screams.

Without instruction, without hesitation, we set upon the packing, determined to unearth something of value from it. It is all for naught; there's nothing but an old and rotting wooden base full of mud. I feel like all the blood is slowly draining out of me, and I cover my face as tears stream down.

My mind flashes back to the beginning of this nightmare. Scenes fly through my brain, reminding me of the incredible loyalty and courage these virtual strangers have shown to Shirley and me.

I feel my sadness ebbing away, replaced with a tidal wave of anger. I see all the fear and pain, the horror of Willie's death. Without thought, I turn to Patty, wrench her axe from her hand and bring it down with all of my strength onto the hardened mud below.

Stabbing it again and again, the mud is flying, filling the air with chunks and dust. I'm not sure who pulls me back, but it's Giselle who surges forward like an avenging Valkyrie, plunging her hand into the gaping hole I've made and emerging with something from it. She uses her hand to dust off what appears to be another journal and passes it to me, her eyes filling with tears.

CHAPTER SEVENTY-TWO

LEAH, RAVENS' WOOD, PRESENT DAY: AUNT SHIRLEY'S FINAL JOURNAL

L eah, if you find this, please know that I did my best to shield you from the terrible truth.

I was always an optimistic child. Even with everything that happened, I constantly sought a bright light in the dark. Once I understood why my mother sent me away—she was terminally ill—I found some peace in that. I tried to not judge her. She did her best.

Great-Uncle Reginald is your father. I have held those words in my head and mouth for so long. The truth is too terrible to speak. He raped me when I was twenty-five. I fell into the care of kind people who took me in and held my hand when I gave birth to the most beautiful child on earth. Leah, I conceived you in terrible violence and incest, but somehow you emerged into this world a perfect angel.

To give you to my best friend was the only answer. And so I handed you off to my family's trusted maid, god bless her soul. She bundled you up, packed her suitcase and jumped on a train to a place she'd never heard of. Your new mother met her at the train station in Vancouver and took you home to Pender Island as her daughter.

Your adoptive parents accepted you with open arms, and they raised you in a place of peace, tranquillity and protection. I thought I could rest. But it was not to be. Reginald tore up every strip of Louisiana to find you. While looking for you, he discovered me.

I made a deal with the devil that day. In return for leaving you alone and stop trying to locate you, I would ensure his evil, cursed longevity by building a replica of Ravens' Pond here in British Columbia.

Once Reginald's neighbours in Louisiana realized they had an Egyptian demon living in their midst, they hatched a plan to kill him. People of different races, classes and creeds put any disputes aside and came together as one, with shotguns, pitchforks and buckets of burning pitch in hand. They should have come better prepared.

While they almost burned Ravens' Pond to the ground, Reginald was one step ahead. He exhumed one slave from the plantation cemetery and placed his desiccated corpse in the sarcophagus. They thought they had succeeded but Reginald had already gone to ground.

After giving birth to you, my precious angel, I returned to New York City and opened my first practise as a psychologist. I lived a good life, and I never married. I watched you grow into the beautiful woman you are. Your mother sent me countless photographs, videos and report cards, and kept me up to speed on who you were dating.

We decided it would be best for you not to know the truth; what good would that do? My priority was, and always has been, your safety. I knew how closely Reginald was watching me, and like the evil monster he is, he would have tracked you and taken your life. So while we never had the chance to go for a walk together, or hug, or wrap an understanding arm around a shoulder, always know I didn't need to meet you in person to love you more than life itself.

I have and always will love you, my beautiful daughter.
Maman

***

I ask to read this last journal alone. As I read, the tears splash down like raindrops in the mud. I don't care if the black ink runs; I tattoo the words in my mind and soul for eternity.

I had put two and two together a while ago. There had to be a stronger connection between Shirley and me—something that exceeded one week of friendship formed at summer camp with the woman I had thought was my mother.

The truth is, Shirley is my mother. But that I share any genes with the monster stalking me—possibly within the walls of my own home—leaves me paralyzed with terror.

CHAPTER SEVENTY-THREE

GUARDIANS, EINER'S BAY, PRESENT DAY: REGINALD'S END GAME

The remaining members of the Guardians of Einer's Bay gather at Jack's, trying to make sense of it all. While they know more than they did when they first started this cause, their greatest challenge is no closer to being solved. What can they do to dispense of, kill, exorcise or destroy Reginald?

Having figured out what and who Reginald is—Leah's father through rape and incest, Shirley's great-uncle, monstrous Egyptian demon who has somehow tapped into a fountain of youth—the Guardians have yet to determine his end game. Until they understand that, they're powerless.

Jack attacks the chalkboard with savagery, tension emanating through his body in almost visible waves. The balance of the group sits randomly about the living room, shoulders fallen and faces pale. Giselle stands up slowly and walks around the perimeter of the group. Head bowed, she twists the dark-pink strands of her hair with her right index finger.

"It's all about the heart!" she says, circling around to face the group. "Don't you see? It's the only thing that makes sense. We've learned from ancient Egyptian mythology that the pathway to immortality is the weighing of the human heart of a moral person who has done many good deeds."

Patty rises to face the group, her cheeks flushed in anger.

"Well, we know that sick and evil bastard won't get past the gate with what he has ticking in his chest, which means he needs another one."

Josh walks over to Jack. He gently removes the piece of chalk from his father's hand.

"Let's see what we do know. We realize he dug a tunnel from the dollhouse to the main house. We assume that the scritching Leah has heard since day one was him digging or clawing his way through the tunnel. We see he has some kind of power over Ruby's statue, yet not enough to break it open. What or who has the power to keep him from getting what he wants, and what else is in that statue?"

CHAPTER SEVENTY-FOUR

GISELLE, EINER'S BAY, PRESENT DAY: THE CRICKETS

J ack drops Giselle off at her yurt with grave misgivings. It's only when she accepts a walkie-talkie with back-up batteries that he agrees to let her return. While Jack has taken care of the damage to the yurt and strategically placed weapons throughout the dwelling, Jack thinks the creature might not have much of a fighting chance; Giselle's the toughest soldier he's ever met.

Giselle lifts her hand, gives a soft wave to Jack and watches as his headlights vanish over the last bump in the road back to town. She shakes as an icy chill runs through her body. Looking skyward to a starless, inky black night, she sighs and steps back into the yurt, slamming home the deadbolt, securing the lock.

She drops to the floor and whips off a hundred perfect push-ups; now, she feels restored.

Time to get serious, she thinks.

Giselle spends the next half hour designing her circle on a sizable piece of parchment. When it's done, she stands back to make sure she has missed nothing.

Pulling her hair back into the yellow scrunchie she had on her wrist, she walks slowly over to her cabinet of curiosities. She's thought long and hard about her medicine wheel. She's far more accustomed to healing than sending screaming demons back to the hell they crawled out of, and she hopes she's up to the challenge.

The cabinet itself is a wonder. Constructed of the finest of Hawaiian acacia koa wood, it stands six feet tall and four feet wide, with countless deep drawers with brass pulls. Giselle manages a one-sided grin at the thought that the word *koa* also means brave, bold, fearless and warrior. She must be all fours to get this particular job done.

Her wheel's design is a hybrid of traditions—some ancient, some current. The top of her circle is the Upper World or Valhalla. This is where the dead warriors hold court, overseen by the powerful Odin. The rest of the top of the wheel is a playground for the gods and goddesses and deities of the sky.

The centre of her wheel is the Middle World realm of Land and Sea Deities, Elves and Air Spirits, Human Beings and Trolls. The Underworld of the Dead is Mist, Ice and Cold Energy, sharing space with Fire Giants, Primordial Flame, Dwarves, Dark Elves and Demons.

The Lower World is perhaps the most impressive of all as it's home to the Dragon, Death Goddess and Ancestors. It is here, in the Lower World, where Giselle believes she has her best shot at breaking Reginald.

Pulling a large tray out from underneath the cabinet, she compiles the elements of her circle. Starting with the outer rim, she chooses large chunks of amethysts interspersed with sizable pieces of lapis lazuli.

After closing one drawer, she carefully opens another. She pauses, turning her head to the door and shuttered windows on either side. Something has made a noise. Swallowing hard, she strains to listen, but the only sounds she can hear are the crickets, which is a good thing because when they stop ....

The crickets stop.

In seconds, Giselle pulls the gun out of the back of her jeans. Crouching low to the ground, she does a quick scan all around her yurt. The crickets remain silent. Giselle holds her ground, barely breathing.

CHAPTER SEVENTY-FIVE

PATTY & ADRIENNE, EINER'S BAY, PRESENT DAY: THE WOEFUL TIMES

"You're dead wrong on this, Adrienne! I don't think the girl should know that terrible truth," Patty fumes as she makes tight circles in the middle of Adrienne's cream-coloured living room carpet as they wait for Giselle to complete her circle. Josh and Jack are at The Sundowner, dealing with their anger by drinking.

Adrienne has one hand on the back of her wooden kitchen chair, the other on the light blue windowpane looking out at the backyard. The wind is up, and the leaves are doing a fine dance of their own. She winces in pain, recalling a fun summer picnic with Shirley and the Guardians held there, by the little creek that bubbles its way through the yard. They had gathered for no particular reason other than to celebrate each other.

Before Shirley came to town, Adrienne and Patty barely said hello. Usually there was only a smile and a nod while shopping at Willie's or passing in the street. Einer's Bay was that kind of small town. People minded their own business; Shirley changed all that.

It was Giselle who first noticed something unusual about her. Even before she built the plantation-style house, Shirley always seemed to be looking over her shoulder; she was always watchful for some reason. Soon, she and Giselle formed a nice little friendship circle that included Patty and Adrienne. But whether they were playing games, going for walks on the beach or meeting for drinks at The Sundowner, Shirley always had her guard up.

Adrienne's expression grows serious as she recalls one night at the bar, when Shirley had just arrived home from New York.

"She came flying in the door like the hounds of hell were nipping at her heels. Dressed uncharacteristically casual in dark-green jeans and an untucked white T-shirt, she seemed out of breath and kept looking over her shoulder.

"Her eyes had darted around the pub, searching for something or someone. She seemed to relax once she spotted us; one could see the tension ebbing out of her body. She ordered a glass of wine from the bar, took one long drink, then pulled up a chair to join us. Adrienne had placed her hand on Shirley's shoulder and asked her if everything was ok. Shirley just nodded her head and raised her shoulders and said something about it being all in her imagination. They never found out exactly what had frightened her so badly."

Continuing to tune out Patty's ongoing rant, Adrienne returns to that perfect picnic memory when they were all together, when the sun was hot and the beer was ice cold, the laughter was loud and silly and Willie and Shirley were still alive.

CHAPTER SEVENTY-SIX

JACK & JOSH, EINER'S BAY, PRESENT DAY: THE EX

Over at The Sundowner, Jack isn't happy with his son. As far as he is concerned, Josh is way too much like his mother—stubborn as hell. They stare at each other across a battlefield of uneaten fries smothered in ketchup, half-eaten burgers—their middles cold and blood-red—two empty beer glasses and a half-empty pitcher. It's not an appetizing scene. Josh reaches for another fry and upends his beer, sending half a pint of hoppy-smelling brew down the side of the table. Josh swears and jumps up quickly to avoid a sousing.

His anger grows, and his strong language causes the other diners to put their forks down to see what's happening.

"Josh! For god's sake," yells Jack. He grabs Josh by the arm, forcing him to stand quietly while the server wipes off the chair. "What the hell is going on?"

Josh apologizes to the server, grabs a cloth and does his best to help clean up the mess before returning to his still-damp seat.

"I don't know what's going on with me, Dad," he sighs. "Everything seems to piss me off these days."

Jack is slow to respond, taking another bite out of his now cold burger, followed by a big slug of beer.

"Does this have something to do with Leah?" asks Jack.

Josh turns away as he feels a warm flush on his face.

"Yes, it is to do with Leah, and yes it has to do with Finola and yes it has to do with what an idiot I am."

Jack smiles, then pulls his chair in closer so he can hear better over the din.

"Well, you won't get any argument out of me on that, son," he says, gently reaching for his son's forearm. "Josh, you screwed up. All of that romantic art in that starry-eyed city, and there she was: drop-dead gorgeous with long red hair to her waist and bright green eyes that could swallow a man alive. Christ, man, how did you leave her?"

"She was all that and more, Dad. She was an incredible sculptor who could wrestle a lump of clay into the most delicate of creatures. Fairies, elves, dragons, horses that were all so lifelike. Pure magic," says Josh.

"Well, something wasn't magical Josh, or you'd still be in Edinburgh. What really went down?"

Josh lays his head back on the vinyl headrest and closes his eyes. He runs the whole movie in his head, top to bottom, and when it's over, he visualizes the last piece of film flickering on and on for what seems an eternity.

Jack waits quietly.

"Dad, she just left me. She said I had no magic in my soul. Like I was cardboard. She packed up and took off the next day, leaving the divorce papers on the bedside table."

Josh brings his arm up out of his lap, quickly refilling his father's glass and his own. They sit quietly, sipping their beers. Jack breaks the silence.

"Josh, I know how hard it was for you to deal with your mom and I divorcing."

Josh nods, his head bowed.

"When it was all said and done—we both know it was the right thing. Staying together would have just prolonged the inevitable and caused you further pain," Jack says, reaching for his son's hand.

"I know, Dad. I just feel like such a fool. Going to school in Edinburgh was like a dream come true, and I know how much it cost you and Mom to make that happen. And then I blew it," he says, his lips quivering.

"All the more reason you've got to let this go, Josh. You got off lightly! Can you imagine staying together with such a dreadful person?"

Sniffing, Josh straightens his posture, smiles at his dad and says, "You know I can still whip your ass at hockey, right?"

Jack leans in, just inches away from Josh and says, "Bring it on son, bring it on!"

Their new waitress approaches the table with extreme caution. This isn't her first rodeo with the explosive father and son known somewhat affectionately as "J & J."

"All done here, gentlemen?" she asks, reaching for the tray holding the abandoned fries. A quick nod from Josh is all it takes for her to scoop up the plates, leaving the men on their own with the remaining beer.

Packing up to leave, Jack leans over to Josh.

"Hey, one of my old crew from the drug squad came up with a new one today. Wanna hear it? It's a killer joke!"

Josh places both hands over his ears as they make their way to the parking lot. Some things are just too painful to hear, and his father's jokes fall right into that category. Time to get back to demon hunting.

CHAPTER SEVENTY-SEVEN

GISELLE, EINER'S BAY, PRESENT DAY: THE GUNS & AMMO

And just like that, the crickets resume their chorus. Giselle continues to take shallow, quiet breaths, not moving a muscle. Must have been a deer, she thinks, slowly lowering her gun.

Five tense minutes later, she shoves the locked gun back into her waistband.

As she checks her place to make sure she hasn't forgotten anything for her ceremony, the crickets stop again. She freezes. Crickets normally resume their noise once the danger moves on. Not this time. Tilting her head to one side, Giselle can barely make out a faint noise; it sounds like someone is sweeping the forest floor. As it grows louder, Giselle stands up, quickly pulling her gun, spinning to face the door. Where there was previously a thin band of moonlight, there's now utter darkness, but there's movement.

Suddenly, the door bursts open. The first wave catches Giselle by surprise and clearly, they're not normal crickets! Their little metal bodies clang along as one as they swarm toward her. By the second wave, she has spun around, yanked open the closet door and pulled out a flamethrower. Using the flamethrower like a leaf blower, she crouches down in the entranceway and takes them out.

***

Having dispensed with every monster cricket left standing, Giselle finally arrives at the estate in her bright red KIA. The rest of the Guardians are already inside by the time she parks her car. A few brief taps on her horn and all hands are on deck to shepherd the precious and dangerous cargo.

She has marked every carton with its contents. Josh's eyes grow large as he grabs a box with white cartons marked *polonium*, *arsenic* and *beryllium*. What on earth is Giselle planning to do, he wonders. Blow them all to kingdom come?

***

As soon as I see Josh, I almost lose it. He looks like a scared little boy, holding onto a cardboard box as if it's about to blow up in his face. Little did I know. One quick worried glance in my direction and he's carefully and slowly moving up the staircase. I know his destination.

By the time I reach the attic, the Guardians are all in place, forming a tight semicircle around Giselle and her strange boxes.

Giselle looks different somehow. Her posture is ramrod straight and her black-and-pink hair is in a tight knot, slicked back with gel to keep it in place.

Jack approaches Giselle, and after she gives him a brief nod, he bends down to check out the contents of the boxes.

Giselle steps backward out of the circle, turning so she can face us all. Arms behind her back, legs firmly planted in a wide stance, her normally placid features are taut with tension.

"Leah, I don't know how to explain what's about to happen. I guess I should expect none of you to understand," she says, her eyes scanning each of their faces. "I won't lie to you: I've never done anything like this before. As you know, prior to coming to live here in Einer's Bay, I was a practising shaman on the island of Maui and before that, a part of specialized forces in the army," she says, scanning the group. "Nothing, and I mean n o t h i n g could have prepared me for what we are about to do."

The others are silent, each processing this information about someone they thought could do anything. I take this opportunity to rise, grab a thermos and pass around cups of water.

All at once, Josh flings his empty cup at the wall.

"This has to end. NOW!" he yells. Everyone moves back a step as if he had thrown a bucket of water at them. Josh paces back and forth across the attic, stopping only to stare at the statue.

Adrienne walks over and pulls him in close. Josh pushes back at first, then crumbles into her arms for a moment before pulling back again. Clearing his throat, he faces me. This won't be good news.

"Leah. There is something we need to say, and I'm telling you, baby, you're not going to like it."

My mind is flying in a hundred different directions, wondering how much worse the news actually can get before I jump out the attic window, a tight squeeze though it might be.

Jack nods, and the words spill out of his son's mouth like a flood of black flies.

"Leah, remember what I told you at The Sundowner on our first date? I said that Shirley died of a heart attack. I also said that Reginald somehow got her out of the house. But what I didn't tell you is that his plan was to cut her heart out of her chest while it was still beating. Shirley passed before he could do that and took away one of his requirements for eternal life—her still beating heart."

I guess some part of me suspected this, which explains why I'm not fainting. I am, however, going to vomit into my cup.

Josh is quick on his feet as I let go. Adrienne gathers me up, her kind, warm, brown eyes giving me sympathy and strength. The mental image of Shirley lying dead in excruciating pain while that fiend stood over her with a knife is seared forever in my mind. I am also suddenly aware that I'm in even more danger than I thought.

***

Patty, Adrienne and Jack spend an hour preparing the attic for the ceremony. They cover the floor in black cloth; Giselle stands over her creation.

Laid between the statue and the medicine wheel sits an over-sized version of the ancient Egyptian Book of the Dead, held open by a ceremonial knife that's encrusted with precious stones. Giselle holds up the book in her right hand, the glinting blade in her left.

She clears her throat to get everyone's attention.

"I'll read you a small part from the Egyptian Book of the Dead, which I admit sounds kind of scary, but it is more like a road map to a second chance at life." Noting a high level of confusion in the room, she begins again: "A high official discovered an important shrine from the First Dynasty."

Eyes grow wide with interest as the Guardians inch closer.

Giselle carries on: "Found high in the foundations of this important shrine was The Papyrus of Ani—very fine paper with writing on it."

Giselle stretches out her legs, then tucks them back under her. She continues: "It was the son of King Cheops, who found the papyrus and then gave it to his father. King Cheops exhibited it as a 'most wonderful' thing, for it would make a man victorious upon earth and in the Other World. It would ensure him a safe and free passage through the Under World; it would allow him to enter and exit at any time and to take whatever form he pleased. It would make his soul flourish and would prevent him from dying the second death. For the deceased to receive the full benefit of this text it had to be recited by a man who was ceremonially pure."

Giselle sits back on her heels, wiping her brow with a white cloth. Her voice lowers.

"But not everyone could enter. You had to earn your way by being a good person, collecting countless charitable deeds as you lived your life. The culmination of all these deeds ensured a light heart. If your heart was heavy, your chances of getting into the afterlife were slim.

"The Goddess Ma'at weighed your heart upon your death. If it was as light as her divine feather, she granted you access to the Land of Two Fields and the freedom for your soul to come and go. However, if your heart was heavy with all the terrible things you had done in your life, she sealed you in your tomb for all eternity, or fed your heart to her personal demon, Ammit."

Patty and Adrienne exchange looks of concern and confusion. Where is all this going? Patty reaches for Adrienne's hand, squeezing it hard enough to make her wince.

Giselle clears her throat and continues.

"In addition to passing the test that weighs your heart, you must possess a perfectly preserved body and have your name written on parchment by someone who vouches for your pristine life."

Giselle relaxes her arms, turning slowly to lock eyes with the others, one by one.

"The ancient Egyptians believed in a soul that split into two parts after you died. *Ba* flew out as the sun rose to keep watch over your living family. *Ka* soared every morning to the Land of Two Fields to enjoy your well-earned afterlife. Ba and Ka returned every night to your tomb, and the cycle would repeat itself every day."

CHAPTER SEVENTY-EIGHT

LEAH, RAVENS' WOOD, PRESENT DAY: THE REAL DAD

My head is spinning with ancient Egyptian mythology, and despite the obvious risks of being outside and alone, I'm in desperate need of fresh air. It's still cold out, so I grab my winter jacket on my way out the front door. Pausing, I turn back. The staircase I once thought was beautiful now looks dull, dark and dangerous. The chandelier is filthy, the carpets frayed and stained.

There's still snow on the ground, although most of it has melted. It's a slushy walk to the other side of the house, opposite the dollhouse. I picture a giant fireball igniting that cursed little shack, blowing it off the face of the earth with that creature from Hades locked inside.

I've found the ability to separate myself from him; he isn't my father. My dad was a gentle soul from Pender Island. He taught me how to ride a bike, skip stones, build a campfire, belch and punch like a guy. Tears blur in my eyes when I think of his death—torn from this world by a drunk driver on his way to the ferry and back to his family. After he died, we were never the same. How could we be? We'd already lost Danny. I watched as Mom faded from this world, and soon she was gone as well.

The quiet out here is startling after the pandemonium inside. Nothing makes sense to me. Why doesn't Reginald just walk in the front door and kill me? There has to be a reason. Something prevents him. In that lies our power over him. We just have to figure it out.

Turning back, I hear what sounds like a huge gust of wind.

When I scan the trees, I see movement but the trees aren't swaying in the wind like they usually would.

All the branches are moving up and down, and as I walk closer to them, I can't believe my eyes! They seem to be bouncing on their own. Inching closer, I see there's something standing on each bough. Enormous deep brown eyes pop open, as large black wings rise, then fall as the branches drop by several feet. I back away slowly, turn, and run like hell for the house.

CHAPTER SEVENTY-NINE

REGINALD'S UNDERGROUND HIDEOUT, RAVENS' WOOD, PRESENT DAY: THE DEMON'S LAIR

T he sound of running water is omnipresent at the lair; a busy creek is frothing several yards from Reginald's dark and damp cave. He paces back and forth with such violence that the forest floor has sunk by several feet. His large, red, bare heels thump down a little deeper with every step.

Reginald's rage is palpable; he's almost out of time. His head shakes back and forth as he marches, black spittle frothing from his mouth. His hands shaking with anger, he stops and roars, a horrible, raw cry that rips through his hideout. His frustration overwhelms him.

His years on this earth are legion, and he's growing weary. All he can think about is rebirth. A chance to fly free from the cold chains that keep him earthbound. He dreams of walking along the sunlit river with his mother, her soft hand on his shoulder as they laugh and talk about friends and life.

Reginald stops, bracing himself for what he knows is about to occur; it happens every time he dares dream of a life he could never have. Raising his fists, he shoves them into his sockets, but he knows nothing can stop it from happening. Blood seeps out of both eyes as the memories begin to flood his mind.

The scenes come in flashes. His father, throwing a dinner knife at him across the dinner table. The pain when the butt of the knife smashes into his cheek. The horror reflected in the eyes of the servants who scurry out of the room. They know what's coming next. His sister Bridget drops her eyes; she understands what will happen to her if she dare interfere.

Flash. His father's face pinched in disgust as he yanks Reginald out of the dining room chair and drags him to his bedroom. Door slams. No food. No light. No love.

Flash. The obscenity of it all. The merciless man who sold his son for a bad gambling debt. Reginald feels every scar, every kick, every slap, every second he paid the price for being the one who lived. Slowly, he lowers his hands to his side and takes a deep breath to focus. Everything is on the line.

His next moves must be swift and deadly. While those idiots stare at a chalkboard inside the house, he plans every one of their terrifying and painful demises.

He'll have Ba once he cuts out Leah's heart, but he can't set Ka free until he has possession of the contents of the statue—and that is seemingly next to impossible. Now, however, he has Ammit, and she has the magic to open the house and the portal if he can convince her to. But where the hell is Rufus?

CHAPTER EIGHTY

GUARDIANS, RAVENS' WOOD, PRESENT DAY: THE CEREMONY

Giselle has laid out her plans for Reginald. Now the Guardians understand what Reginald needs to attain immortality, and how important the medicine wheel is to getting the job done.

The house has somehow transformed; it looks like a ship dragged up from the bottom of the ocean. Walls are cracked, light fixtures broken, sofa cushions stained, curtains shredded. And it stinks like the bottom of a dry fish tank.

The kitchen is marginally better, although all the appliances have mysteriously rusted overnight. There's no sound other than the occasional clearing of a throat. Jack surveys his friends; they're all hunched over, trying their best to choke down hunks of stale bread and moldy, stinky cheese. The pall of hopelessness hangs over them like the bright chef's kitchen light once did.

***

Giselle stands between the statue and her medicine wheel; the others drop to their knees, forming a semicircle around it. The light outside is gradually fading and it will be soon be dark. After what seems like an hour, but is seconds, Giselle speaks:

"Reginald still needs a human heart to weigh, and we have every reason to believe the heart he's after belongs to his own daughter." She pauses and says, "I'm, sorry, Leah. He missed his chance with Shirley, so there's no other option.

"Because it's the heart of a kind person with a multitude of good deeds, he believes he can fool Ma'at. I believe that the papyrus he has in his possession is the powerful Papyrus of Ani, stolen by his father. If it is, it is even more powerful. Presumably, the papyrus with his name written on it lies within the statue; he lacks two more things."

"I know what those two things are," says Josh. "It's having a perfectly preserved body, and that certainly doesn't apply to Reginald. I believe he found the one person he could kill, embalm and keep hidden until his time was right; Ruby. And it's someone who can speak highly of his character. I think everyone in this attic would agree that person doesn't exist."

"Oh, but you're wrong, Josh," Jack replies. "There is one man."

Jack names the one human who knows of Reginald's past. As William's right arm, sidekick and the keeper of all of the Everett family's secrets, Louis passed that knowledge down to his great-grandson, who knows where all the bodies are.

"It's Rufus," says Jack. "The head contractor on the building of Ravens' Wood. Loyal defender of William Everett and his demon son, Reginald."

***

The light is dimming slowly in the attic. The group stands together as one unit as Giselle begins her ceremony.

CHAPTER EIGHTY-ONE

RUFUS, RAVENS' WOOD, PRESENT DAY: THE TUNNEL

Rufus—all six feet eight inches and 320 pounds of him—is stuck in the tunnel—the wrong tunnel, in fact. What began as a heroic journey to set Reginald free from this awful world, is, at the moment, a complete disaster. He's unable to stand up in the slimy, disgusting shaft.

Reginald's instructions were clear: the tunnel is short, straight and leads to a full-sized red wooden door. After creeping in through the basement door that he himself had built, he made an easy trip to the wine cellar.

He's okay for the first few feet, right until he encounters what appears to be a second passageway. Smaller and less worn than the first, Rufus writes it off as a failed first effort and keeps going. Which brings him to his current predicament.

Having to scramble in on his knees, he's currently wedged in a sharp turn to the right. Scraping up his size-14 feet in a runner's stance, he attempts to propel himself around the stubborn, putrid corner. Head and shoulders are free enough on the other side to see the tunnel coming to an abrupt halt outside of a small black door; this is not good.

***

Reginald is furious; he can only assume they've caught Rufus in the act. His only recourse is to rush through the tunnel to the attic and kill them all. He'll end them at the precise moment his life on earth is due to expire; even demons have best-before dates.

CHAPTER EIGHTY-TWO

LEAH & THE GUARDIANS, RAVENS' WOOD, PRESENT DAY: THE MEDICINE WHEEL

The medicine wheel ceremony is almost complete. The portal will open and the deities will enter, one by one. Guardians now line the walls, allowing space for their ethereal houseguests.

Adrienne's eyes are wide with fear. She looks from face to face for some kind of reassurance; she finds none.

To say the heathen cosmology medicine wheel is a disaster is like saying the *Titanic* hit an ice cube. By the time the dust has settled, there's just one entity standing. The Valkyries ripped the heads off the Light Elves and Air Spirits; a large and particularly smelly troll trampled the Dark Elves into powder and the Fire Giants incinerated the Sky Gods into a small pile of smoking ash.

Giselle pulls herself away from the tight ball of shaking jelly formerly known as the Guardians of Einer's Bay and makes her way to her collection of the world's most deadly poisons. She has to have them at the ready should she be unsuccessful in sending Reginald back to hell through the wheel. One way or the other, he'll be dead soon.

CHAPTER EIGHTY-THREE

LEAH, RAVENS' WOOD, PRESENT DAY: THE APPEARANCE OF HELEN

I have to pry my fingers off the stair banister. It's all I can do not to run screaming into the night. I'm still trying to process it all when Giselle pulls away from the group. There's a dark-haired woman standing in the middle of the medicine wheel. My body ripples in a waterfall of goosebumps.

I recognize her at once, from the family photos on Shirley's computer; Helen is as beautiful in death as she was in life. Raven-black hair curves around her skull like an ocean wave at midnight. Her eyes are dark caramel, the whites gleaming in contrast. She's a dead ringer for the immortal Egyptian beauty Queen Nefertiti.

"Helen," I whisper. "How is it possible?"

As she turns to face me, I'm startled by how much I resemble my great-great-grandmother. She smiles, walks toward me, pushes my hair over my shoulders and draws me in.

"Leah," she says softly. "I finally get to meet you in person. I've been watching you grow since the day you were born."

I pull back to examine the shape of her face, her heavy-lidded eyes, inky black hair, the tiny cleft in her chin; it's like I'm looking in a mirror.

Giselle steps forward, saying, "Helen, you must be of Hellaheim, the realm of Death Goddess and Ancestors."

Helen nods slowly. Straightening her back and levelling her gaze, she demands, "Why have you summoned me to this place?"

As the Guardians stand in awe before her, a loud crashing sound rocks the foundation of the house.

CHAPTER EIGHTY-FOUR

LEAH, THE GUARDIANS, ET AL, RAVENS' WOOD, PRESENT DAY: THE BATTLE

Rufus finally squeezes himself out of the tunnel, up the back stairs and runs hard to the lair at the end of the lawn. There, he finds Reginald in a terrifying rage and in the company of a beast the likes of which Rufus has never seen. Screams ripping from his throat, Rufus falls back and turns to the tunnel. He has to know: What the hell did he just see?

The creature towers over Reginald. Appearing to be part hippo, part cat and part crocodile, it bends down inches from Rufus. As the demon opens its mouth to smile, small fish tumble out of its maw; they flop around on the floor as Rufus looks on, eyes wide, muscles tense.

"Ammit," says Reginald, "you need to let me in the house. I'm out of time."

Ammit tilts her slimy green head, her jagged lip pulled up in a hideous smile.

"My dear boy, I've already reversed the spell," she croaks. "See, Reggie? I told you I'd never leave you. Go."

Reginald bolts out of the shed to the house. Rufus, right on his heels, glances upward to see a sky darkened by hundreds of ravens.

They burst through the wine cellar, pounding up the stairs, Rufus barely keeping up with the demon.

Jack and Josh run down the attic stairs, charging straight into whatever trouble is coming their way.

"The cellar!" screams Josh, overtaking his father, grabbing the oak staircase banister by one hand and vaulting to the floor below.

They didn't have to go any farther than that. The furious rush of red-fleshed demon comes at them with such speed, they have absolutely no chance to defend themselves. Reginald picks up Josh, smashes him to the floor, lifts him again and tosses him backward over his shoulder into the waiting arms of Rufus.

Jack screams his son's name, then uses his head as a battering ram against the stomach of the beast.

Reginald grabs Jack by the hair, pulling him straight up until his feet are dangling in midair. Jack's screams ping against the walls as Reginald releases him, kicking his head as he falls hard to the floor.

The remaining Guardians thunder down the staircase, fearful of what they might see.

With Jack and Josh both unconscious on the floor, Adrienne, Patty and Giselle are left alone to fight a demon and the largest man they have ever seen. Rufus's skin is shiny and black as oil, his biceps bulging and thighs like tree trunks; he must be nearly seven feet tall.

Rufus doesn't look angry—not like Reginald, who has finally stopped screaming. But the gurgling growl emerging from his throat is even worse than the screams.

Patty pulls the rifle from behind her back, choosing Reginald's henchman as her target. Giselle drops to one knee, her gun aiming straight at the middle of Reginald's forehead. Rufus rolls his eyes when he sees what Giselle and Patty are up to while Reginald crooks his finger, inviting them to come closer.

I find and use a hammer to break apart the sculpture. Removing the fragments of marble one by one, we gently detach the perfectly preserved body of the child Ruby from her prison and carry her to the middle of the attic. It's heart-wrenching to gaze upon her mummified face.

Reginald has applied makeup, painted on dark-brown eyebrows and affixed a black-haired wig to Ruby's head. He has stitched her lips into a one-sided grin and stained them with dark-red paint. Helen draws back in horror as she realizes who her son chose as his inspiration, right down to the tiny cleft in her chin. There is no stopping her from re-wrapping the child in the ripped papyrus, picking her up and walking straight into the demon's lair. She has to end this.

***

Josh stays down on the floor, pretending to be unconscious. His head hurts like hell. Blood is coursing down the back of his throat; it takes every ounce of his self-control not to choke. He has to make Rufus and Reginald think he's no longer a threat.

His head lies near the side of the staircase and his feet are splayed out, right beside Reginald's left foot. He has one chance to take him down. He kicks out, bringing his right foot in a hard motion that sweeps Reginald to the floor. Josh carries on the assault, punching, kicking, biting the beast.

At once, Rufus is on Josh, grabbing him around the waist and squeezing until Josh almost passes out. And he would have if Patty hadn't shot Rufus in the bicep.

Rufus screams in agony, pulling Josh with him to the floor, eyeball to eyeball, each trying to choke the other one to death. Hot blood spurting from the wound in Rufus's arm makes it slippery and Josh pulls away and gets on his feet; he plants one foot on the gunshot wound and Rufus passes out from the pain.

While Josh is busy taking care of Rufus, Reginald has wrenched away both weapons and holds all three women in a tight grip. Josh sees them struggling to breathe.

"Let them go, you asshole!" he yells, moving toward his enemy.

This only makes Reginald angrier, and the women pay for it, choking, crying, trying desperately to wrestle out of his python grip.

As Helen and I approach, I can't believe what I'm seeing. How can that tall red creature with claws for hands be human? It's simply not possible. The worn black leather boots look like they came from the Civil War. His entire body is desiccated.

"Stop it now!" I cry, feeling a sense of out-of-control rage I didn't know existed in me.

Reginald whips around to challenge me, dropping all three women to the floor. They grab one another and pull themselves up the staircase, forming a wall of defence around me.

"You!" he hisses. "Ammit thought she could control my destiny—and that, by locking me out of this house, it would somehow save you. I'm coming for you now, daughter. All I require of you is your heart," he rumbled. At that, Reginald pulls a small but lethal-looking knife and makes his way toward me.

I'm paralyzed by fear as I watch my death approach. I don't have a weapon to defend myself with, and there's no point in running. He'll catch me and hack out my heart. His eyes are filled with a hatred I have never known. I almost want this to end so there will be no more death. Looking down at my feet, I try to will them to run, but they remain fixed in place.

"Once I have your heart, I will also have Rufus, who will attest for me. I will have my name written on sacred papyrus, wrapped around the embalmed corpse of my niece, Ruby, who I will pass off as myself. I will be able to cross over the river and be free."

At this he pauses, shifting to face me full on. A wicked smile cracks across his face as he utters, "Finally ... and I will take the spirit of Ruby with me as my queen."

"Oh, no you won't."

Reginald freezes. Everyone draws back in shock at the sight of the enormous creature that has suddenly appeared. Reginald's face twists sideways at the monster, his shoulders raised.

"I am Ammit, and I have only one boss. Her name is Ma'at, and she protects Order, Truth and Justice," she says and appears to grow in size as her shoulders hammer back, her strange yellow eyes flashing.

Giselle crumples to her knees in a bow toward the demon.

"Ma'at assigned me to keep watch over William and then Reginald," says Ammit. "But it was always the boy that worried her the most. You cannot blame yourself, Helen."

Helen raises her arms as she steps out in front of Ammit. She's cradling the lifeless, embalmed body of Ruby, swathed in what appears to be a sizable piece of papyrus. I can just make out part of the demon's name, scrawled in black ink across the paper. It's ripped in half, exposing the perfectly preserved body of Ruby, but destroying what was left of Reginald's name.

Reginald's head shakes violently from side to side as he tries to comprehend what's before him.

While Helen moves down the staircase to greet the son she died giving birth to, she cradles the child.

"Here, my son," she whispers. "This is what you want, right?"

"Did you not think there would be a price for your evil, Reggie boy?" Ammit roars so loudly that the walls shake. "You are a thief, a torturer, a murderer and a rapist! Look at her, Reggie!" Ammit rages on, her long, lean arm pointing directly to my face. "She deserved a life of happiness, didn't she? Didn't she earn the chance to know her birth mother? Isn't it ironic that by denying Leah a lifetime with Shirley, you cursed her with the same fate you suffered? But you—*you* are not worthy of anything but death! Ma'at denies you!"

Reginald is puddled at Ammit's knees, sobbing and begging for his afterlife. Pulling himself back up to his feet, he places both of his hands on his face and rakes off chunks of skin with his claws. Great tears drain from his now-yellowed eyes, pooling at his neck and flowing down each dreadful ribbon of skin to the carpet below. He croaks one word: "Mother?"

"Son," sobs Helen, with the bloodless body of her grand-daughter in her arms. "I never had the chance to know you. The gods exchanged my life for yours, and that was our fate." She steps closer to Reginald. "I was denied a life with you, to help you understand the difference between right and wrong." Tears flow down her cheeks. "If only I had survived, Reginald. I could have saved you from yourself."

Reginald pauses, then extends an index finger forward to plant a ripped claw just under his mother's chin.

"Momma," he wheezes. "You're the reason I became a demon. I wanted the life I lost when you died. Father was a monster to me! You would never have let that happen," he chokes on his tears. "Ammit taught me what I needed to do to become a demon and claim my afterlife; she promised me I'd get back all that was ripped away from me."

Helen is now an arm's length away from her son. With the mummified child held tightly between them, she steps in toward Reginald, bringing them together in a strange embrace. Helen looks over her shoulder and gives me a tragic smile, then nods to Ammit. The demon steps forward and lifts her arms up, claws raking the air between her and the trio of Helen, Ruby and Regi-nald. The smell of burning flesh is strong as dark-red flames arc from Ammit. Rather than stepping back and away from the lethal flames—Reginald wraps his mother in a tight hug—one that will be their first, and their last.

When the three figures are fused as one smoking pile of ash, the strange fire disappears. An awful silence fills the room as we try to comprehend what we have just witnessed. After a few minutes, I step forward and fold the area carpet over the charred remains. I look over my shoulder to see what's happening with Rufus, but he is gone; Ammit has disappeared as well.

Josh, Jack, Giselle, Adrienne, Patty and I each take hold of the carpet, carrying it down the stairs to the backyard. Exhausted, we fall on our knees and form an impromptu circle. The only sounds are our deep breaths and sobs.

CHAPTER EIGHTY-FIVE

LEAH, RAVENS' WOOD, PRESENT DAY: THE FALLOUT

I drive Josh and Jack to the hospital, where the doctor stitches them up and releases them. Adrienne, Patty and Giselle return to their homes. Reginald is gone, forever.

***

A few days later, I'm sitting on the back lawn of Ravens' Wood, bundled up in a warm sweater. The day is still chilly while winter creeps quietly away; spring will bring a sense of cleansing to the world, but not yet. I breathe in the cool air, hoping for a hint of a change in seasons, but I'm left disappointed.

I'll tear down the walls of this evil house, eventually. We'll destroy the tunnels, lair and dollhouse.

Until then, I have accepted Adrienne's offer to stay in her cottage. Perhaps there I can clear my mind and decide on my future. Josh has been keeping his distance to give me some time to think.

***

I moved back into the house three weeks ago. It holds no further menace to me. Josh and I clean up most of the damage and make it livable for the time I need before I have it destroyed. I close all but one bedroom and lock off the basement and attic. I need more time to go through Shirley's things to get them packed up and ready to ship to Vancouver.

Strangely enough, I'm content here. Josh comes and goes.

We are getting to know each other better. We're different people than we were before. Softer. Kinder. Quieter. We embrace the soft sounds of early morning. Nighttime falls peacefully, not at all what we're accustomed to.

I finally tell Josh about Mike. Big tears spill down his face as I describe the small rescue terrier who saved my life and my sanity. "Little Mike" was a feisty warrior with a heart of gold and a loyalty that could not be measured. Whether it was his cold, wet, blackberry nose tickling my neck, or him charging freshly groomed into a mud pit, he was my sweet trickster. They say that losing a precious animal can be as painful as losing a close relative, and I have to say that's true. He no longer visits me as he did for several months after he passed away, but I've moved his brown cushion to the bedroom chair, where I know he still watches over me.

***

Josh and Jack built a small and simple wooden box; Adrienne, Patty, and Giselle worked their magic, sewing the effigy of Ruby a soft flannel bed to lie upon and an equally cozy blanket to cradle her in. The last addition to the coffin was Ruby's stuffed dog, Pixie, recovered at the bottom of Ravens' Pond years ago, after Ruby had gone missing. I had found Pixie carefully wrapped up in the wooden box we found in Shirley's safe. The little black-and-white dog almost looks brand new. Shirley must have had Pixie restored. Now he will snuggle in beside the spirit of the little girl who'd adored him during her life and will embrace him forever.

CHAPTER EIGHTY-SIX

RAVENS' WOOD, PRESENT DAY: RUBY'S FUNERAL

The day of Ruby's service dawns; the air is still, and the only sounds are the birds as they chirp in harmony to the day's arrival in soft blue and gold.

I'd spent hours searching for just the right place, and eventually I found a small creek bubbling along the perimeter of the property. Surrounded by tall cedar trees, there's a small flat spot. If Ruby were alive, lying on her back, her face up to the sun, she could dangle her hand in the cool water. I knew I had found her last place to rest.

Josh had taken on the responsibility of carving an effigy of Ruby and had created a loving, diminutive version of her statue, wrested from fragrant cedar and blessed by Giselle and Father Kelly.

Before I found this spot, Josh and I had many discussions about where Ruby should rest. The most obvious choice was beside Shirley in Einer's Bay Memorial Cemetery, located just above the marina. But my decision is final: she will be in the land that rightfully belongs to her.

We schedule the ceremony for 2 p.m.. The single row of white chairs looks terribly out of place against the trees. I keep it simple with a single podium, where Father Kelly will say a few words.

Josh and I walk in together, arm in arm.

Father Kelly looks haggard; no surprise after what we've put him through. His hands are shaking as he shuffles papers in front of him. We asked him to merely give a simple blessing, and he was greatly relieved at this.

I sit in the last seat beside Josh, who looks over and smiles, his eyes both loving and sad. This will all be over soon. We can move on with our lives.

Father Kelly clears his voice, then speaks.

"We gather here today to mourn the loss of a young girl," he says, his voice quivering. "We know little about her, only that she came from a place far from here. We understand she was beautiful and kind and that she mattered very much to her family. Her time on this earth ended long ago, but now we must release her to the heaven she belongs in." When he concludes, he lifts his hands to the sky.

On his cue, the Guardians stand and walk toward the small cedar box, heads bowed in sorrow for the loss of the little girl named Ruby, who'd had her life snatched away by unfathomable evil.

***

The week following Ruby's funeral is full of decisions on what to take and what to give away. I'll go back to Vancouver; this place can never be home to me, not after the terrible things that have transpired here.

I finally have some answers to the questions that haunted me. The scritching? That was Reginald literally clawing his way through the tunnels. He had no access through normal human ways, like doors or windows; Ammit took care of that with her spell. Her spell also prevented anyone from moving the statue out of the house; she knew what he'd do with Ruby's corpse.

After Reginald raped her, Shirley arranged for the removal of the statue from Ravens' Pond. It was well hidden in a friend's backyard for many years before Shirley had it moved up to Einer's Bay. She'd do anything to make sure that evil monster would never touch Ruby again.

We have no idea where the dollhouse was hidden for all those years, although Josh speculated it might have been used as an occasional home for the beast.

On that terrible day when Josh discovered my bedroom drenched in blood, acting on his master's instructions, Rufus killed a deer and covered me with its fresh, warm blood. Reginald had been waiting for me to bolt out of the house and was lurking outside, ready to grab me. But he was held back from entering the house because of Ammit's spell. It would ensure he could only attain his way to the afterlife if he didn't have her help.

I now know the man in the painting and the forest is the ghost of Shirley's father; my grandfather.

One question remains: Why did Shirley leave the protection of her home on the night of her murder when she knew she'd be in terrible danger?

Everything else I could link to Reginald's demon powers: the illusion of that crazy drive I took to nowhere; the giant raven that hit my car; Willie's death; the trickery the town had closed. All of it, in a weird and twisted way, now makes sense.

Jack got back to me about the drugging. It was LSD in my glass of water; once again, Rufus.

Ammit's spell was intended to keep Reginald from accessing the house. Ma'at had been clear: there could be no deception with the weighing of the heart. Reginald thought he could cheat by using Rufus to do his dirty work.

I'll never know how Shirley's second journal ended up in the sarcophagus, but that kind of magic would be simple for a demon like Ammit.

CHAPTER EIGHTY-SEVEN

LEAH & THE GUARDIANS, RAVENS' WOOD, PRESENT DAY: A MEMORIAL DAY

The Guardians of Einer's Bay come together one last time, now in memory of our much-loved and brave friend Willie. Rather than a service, we know he'd much prefer to have a few beers, shuck oysters and celebrate his life with those who became his dearest friends. His fellow Guardians place pictures of him all over my house, his big smiling face reminding us of the wonderful friend we lost and the impact he had on all of our lives. Jack even brings along Willie's hockey stick; they'd played in a beer league together every Wednesday.

Later that day, Giselle holds a healing circle for both Ruby and Willie in the exact centre of the back lawn. Other visitors come under their own power—ravens, large and as dark as the night itself. They circle and make short, shrill calls throughout the ceremony and fly off together at the end, their dark, feathered wings silhouetted against the moon, like hands waving soft goodbyes.

Ravens' Wood will be ground to dust eventually. For tonight, I want one last chance to thank the remarkable, brave people I met here, for literally saving my life and my sanity. For now, this house deserves one night of light and happiness—with no demons in sight.

Embracing my newly discovered ancestral background, I'd hired a band to play some scorching hot Cajun tunes, and the caterers are up to their armpits in prawns and jambalaya. Even the ordinarily cool weather cooperates, and while it isn't humid and sultry, nobody needs a jacket or sweater.

The moon is full, which I think appropriate, although I swear

I see Reginald in it. I guess I will never again see the image of the man in the moon without being reminded of his evil red face. Josh sits across from me, head bowed in a deep discussion with his father.

We have had many lengthy conversations about what's to come, and I believe we're at peace with it. Maybe some time apart will help us decide if what we have is real or a manifestation of the unfolding drama that brought us together.

Jim has his arm around Adrienne, but she has her back to me, so I can't see her face, and I'm not sure what she's thinking. It all hurts too much. We've had many wonderful hugs and consumed much wine this week. While we acknowledge the fact we're just a float plane ride away, we know the truth of the matter: we may never see each other again.

I can't resist a quick tap on the top of Jim's new cowboy hat.

"Hey!" he growls.

I know he's all bark and no bite, so I can't resist a tease:

"Have any of that yummy chili over at your place, Jim? Or is that ratatouille?"

Now he's on his feet and swatting at me, but I can outrun him, laughing all the way.

It's different now with the Guardians. They are all at peace. Giselle has resumed her life as a popular shaman (takes me three weeks to get in for a reading), and unless I'm mistaken, she and Jack have something going on between them.

Patty is the kind of person capable of dusting herself off and getting back on the horse. It's like nothing ever happened, and I envy that skill—but I do catch her dabbing her eyes from time to time. I'll miss Patty, but I have a feeling I'll be seeing her in Vancouver soon.

***

The caterers and entertainment left an hour ago. After many tearful hugs, the Guardians have also gone home. Josh is the last to leave. I'm biting my tongue as hard as I can stand it. I don't want to break down in front of him.

When I open my mouth to speak, what comes out is the sound of a cat getting its tail stepped on, so I stop.

Josh snorts. Placing his powerful hands on my shoulders, he says, "If you think I'm letting you go, you're nuttier than Reginald." He grins, eyes twinkling with tears.

Instead of mewling, I decide it's probably best just to kiss him. So, I do.

EPILOGUE

EINER & WILLIAM, OLD WINTER PALACE HOTEL, LUXOR, THE PAST: THE GODDAMN DEED

Einer Magnusson peered through thick clouds of smoke in search of a certain pair of eyes. He didn't have to look hard. Those soulless, cruel orbs found his. Hoodless crocodile eyes that didn't as much look at you as pin you, like a helpless moth, onto the wall.

Einer cleared his throat and glanced away. The crowd of poker players was slowly staggering out of the dining room of the Old Winter Palace Hotel . There was nothing there to entice them; the staff had already hauled away the half-eaten plates of food. The lingering smell of cooked lamb and cigarette smoke nauseated him.

And then there were just the two of them. William Everett sat ramrod straight across the polished teak table, with his hands folded beneath it. He took a deep breath and felt remarkably calm for someone determined to kill another human being. Einer, on the other hand, was sweating profusely; the circles under his armpits were almost to his waistline.

"Mr. Magnusson," William hissed as he brought his hands up to the table. "I do believe you owe me something."

"Mr. Everett, while it is always a pleasure to outbid you at antiquity auctions, I believe this is the first time I have lost anything of value to you," replied Einer. "Perhaps we can solve this like gentlemen. I have several statues that will more than compensate for my little dirty patch of wilderness you seem to crave."

Other than the slightest shift of his left index finger, William didn't move. He did not appear to breathe or blink. He just observed.

This went on for at least five minutes, and when he finally spoke, it was with such venom and volume that Einer almost fell off of his chair.

"You miserable little shit! You lost the bet fair and square!"

William shot to his feet, his body rigid, shaking his right fist right under Einer's nose.

Einer slowly removed a napkin from his breast pocket to wipe William's spittle from his face. With shaking hands, he withdrew a scroll of paper from the inside pocket of his jacket.

"Here!" he growled. "Take the goddamn deed, and may you find the special place in hell you deserve."

Einer tossed the scroll across the table and threw the chair back and onto the floor with a crash. He reached the door to the dining room when he felt a sudden, incredible pain in his back. Screaming, he reached around to try to pull out the knife. He knew he was a dead man. And seconds later, his short fat elf body crumpled to the floor as his bowels and bladder emptied in unison.

WILLIAM, EGYPT, THE PAST: LOUIS'S DISAPPEARANCE

William had to solve the mystery of Louis's recent disappearance. On his first trip through the portal, he'd walked the property in Einer's Bay searching for his loyal manservant. But there had been no trace of Louis.

Returning home to Ravens' Pond and having combed every piece of Louisiana in search of him, William had come up empty. The answer had to lie in the portal, so he returned to Egypt. The last thing he did before heading out was to command the ravens to head north to Einer's Bay. It was there that William would cross over into the afterlife and he would need them as Guardians. He'd stood in silence as the wave of black bodies flew, their wingbeats loud and aggressive as they mimicked his name.

***

Now, settled near the Great Pyramids in Giza's Mena House Hotel, William waited until the stars were aligned, filled a backpack with tools and provisions, stood on the podium and shook in anticipation. What would he discover? He knew he was taking a monumental risk. If the alignments were off by even a number, he could find himself at the bottom of the sea.

William stepped once again onto the platform at Abu Ghurab. A bolt of lightning streaked across the night sky. William shut his eyes, trying to block out the terrible burning sensation he had on his first trip through the portal so many years ago. Now—like then—just prior to losing consciousness, he saw the sky above split by lightening. Once again, he landed beside the large boulder.

When he had assembled his gear, he made his way to the shack and looked for anything Louis might have dropped along the way. He didn't have to go far. The first thing that caught his attention was Louis's destroyed rucksack, located right at the base of an enormous tree. The rucksack was empty.

As he stood up, something grabbed his hair, hard. It was all he could do to pull his hair out of whatever had snaked around it, but he managed. He ran back ten feet and turned to see what kind of creature had assaulted him.

William dropped to his knees, his mouth open, drool leaking from his lips.

"Jesus Christ," he mumbled softly.

Louis was in the tree. Actually, Louis had become the tree. His legs twisted like dark-brown vines; William could discern no distinction between one leg or the other. His torso seemed massive; little birds landed then launched from it or perched on a polished ebony shoulder to rest. Louis's face had merged into the tree, and while he wouldn't bet on it, William would swear he was smiling.

At last, the mystery of his loyal friend and manservant had been solved. His head bowed in sadness, William did something he'd never done before in his entire life; he prayed. He prayed Louis was at peace.

William sighed and gathered up the rucksack, stuffing all the contents from his own inside so he only had the one to carry. He took another moment to close his eyes and recall the remarkable adventures they'd shared. Then he replaced his hat and made his way to the old shack.

Soon, he stumbled into Einer's shed and into a jumble of cartons of all shapes and sizes. The horrible way Einer had lived shocked William. The flooring was of mud with random slats of wood. There were many ripped boxes of statues and artwork, and precious cargo was strewn all over the shack.

Not wanting to risk sitting on a box filled with fragile and valuable artifacts, William found a relatively dry piece of mud on which to sit. He needed to think. Why would someone like Einer risk the destruction of everything he had, only to see it sink slowly into quicksand? William shoved his hair back in annoyance. Now that he had settled, he noticed the sound of running water. Had it started to rain? With his gun in his right hand, William made his way back out of the shed.

The noise seemed to come from the rocky ledge he'd seen at the back of the property. The sound of rushing water was growing much louder now, and he'd be able to see it soon. It was no doubt a creek fed by the melting snow on the tops of these massive mountains.

William found a spot that was closest to Einer's shack, and there it was: a large rock formation providing access and protection to the side of the hut. Carefully making his way around the back of the rock, it shocked him to see a circular shaft. It looked to be a natural formation, until he got close enough to see the man-made metal lid on the top of it. After several tries, William finally managed to pull the lid far enough away to inspect the shaft more closely and gain access.

He took a moment to strap his carbide lamp around his forehead. Scrambling into the shaft on his belly, he saw it went down more than twenty feet. There looked to be a small cave off to one side, and when he directed his light in that direction, he was awarded with the glint of gold. This must be Einer's hiding place for some of his treasure, he thought.

William stood on the small platform and made his way down the chute. Iron rings cut in half and welded into place acted as footholds. The channel was narrow; it could fit only one person.

All at once he slipped, losing his grip on the rope. It was wickedly cold down the chute, and the foothold was like ice. If there were any footings missing on his way down, he would be in trouble. Two more steps down and William paused to direct his lamp below.

Something was coming up at him.

What the hell is that thing? he thought. Its pointy, green face was snapping as it writhed quickly toward him. William inhaled putrid fishy breath and saw the flash of bright yellow eyes before he felt needle-sharp teeth sink into his right arm. As he was pulled down into her jagged crocodile teeth, Ammit spit out the last words that William would ever hear:

"That is for what you did to your own son, you sick bastard!"

CINDY, RAVENS' WOOD, ONE YEAR AFTER THE DEMOLITION OF THE HOUSE: THE RAVENS

Cindy zips up her gumboots, shrugs on her yellow slicker, grabs her oversized bag and leaves the house. Locking up, she looks at the sky, shielding her eyes from the bright mid-morning light. Her phone rings.

"Of course, it's at the bottom of my bloody purse," she growls through clenched teeth. "Hello?" she yells when she retrieves it. "What is it?"

The person on the other end of the line takes a moment to clear their throat before speaking.

"Yes, hello, it's Doug again. Just don't want to, um, bother you, but are you able to go check out Ravens' Wood this morning? We have an agent from out of town who wants to walk around the property."

Cindy pulls back her arm, fully intending to lob the damn phone into the forest. Let some squirrel take it apart, she thinks. Taking a deep breath, she brings the phone back to her ear.

"What exactly is the point, Doug? Every day I go by that hell swamp, I'm convinced something terrible will happen. Just like what went down when they tried to destroy that monstrosity of a house."

"Cindy, this is what I pay you to do. Now, get over there and check out the scene. We've got serious buyers coming up from Seattle, and I know Leah and Josh want this gone." At that, he hangs up.

Cindy mumbles under her breath, something about guys with small hands, and what a stupid waste of time this is, and how scared she is of that weird plot of land.

It's a brisk ten-minute walk to what's left of Leah's Southern plantation-style mansion. Workers have hauled away every scrap of wood. All that remains is nasty red earth and those weird chunks of black plastic.

Cindy fishes her sunglasses out of the bottom of her bag; the sun is glaring, and she can already see the inky black reflection of those weird chunks. Are they metal? Why didn't the damn excavators remove them?

She slows her approach, taking off her glasses, her eyes squinting in disbelief. The chunks appear to have grown in size and are fluttering like dark-black tents. The earth is now scarlet, and as she draws near, she sees the soil is moving, like it's filled with giant worms.

Cindy opens her mouth to scream but stops short. The tents are rising. As if a giant hand plucks them up one by one, their flaps turn into wings. She drops her bag and runs as the entire field of birds breaks into waves of attack.

She screams and runs as fast as she can until she trips. As Cindy goes down, her face is the first thing that hits the ground. Damp earth fills her nostrils as she tries to get on her feet. Her screeches are muffled by the ground. Trying to roll as hard as she can to her right side, her face is immediately battered by black wings. Face down again, something heavy is clawing her back. Vomit spews out of her mouth momentarily, but her instinct is to breathe, so she can't help but inhale the puke. She's choking on it, but there's no way for her to move. She has no feeling in her legs. Hot blood rushes into her ears as her entire body seems to deflate. As her life fades from this world, the slashing continues while the predators peck and claw until there's nothing left but blood and chunks of fabric.

LEAH, VANCOUVER, ONE YEAR AFTER THE DISTRUCTION OF RAVENS' WOOD: A BAD DREAM

I'm in the middle of a vivid dream. Josh is calling me, his voice becoming more and more urgent, as I don't seem to have the ability to call back. I'm walking in the forest, but it's changing beneath my feet. What started as a glorious sunlit walk through the woods is morphing with every step.

This area of the forest is rotten. Looking down, I cautiously test the log in front of me. It seems to be okay. I put my full weight on it and it explodes like a bomb of wooden fragments. I lose my balance and quickly reach out for a branch to stop my fall. It disintegrates, leaving a thick cloud of sawdust in its wake. Josh's voice is getting louder, and it's clear he's upset and growing angry.

Opening my mouth to yell back, I take my eyes off the forest ground for one second, and I'm falling into a pit of decaying, soupy, sludge. Still I can't scream.

There! Something that appears to be a solid tree branch is within my reach and should enable me to crawl out of the filth.

Trying to find purchase for my sodden feet, I heave myself up the side of the mudhole, stretching up as far as I can. I've got it! It doesn't feel like a tree branch, but as long as I can get out, I don't care. Wrist over wrist, I'm making slow but steady progress, getting almost eye level with it.

It looks like something that used to be white, but the treacly muck has discoloured it. It's not a stick, or a branch, or a pole, or anything good. As I tumble back into the quagmire, I'm screaming as loud as I can. My stick is a human bone.

I finally find my voice and scream as Josh recoils and falls into a heap beside our bed. It would seem I was having a bad dream.

***

"I said I forgive you, Leah!" Josh declares, and I know he has; I just feel awful about scaring him to death.

It's taken some time to get past the horrible things that happened in Einer's Bay. Jack monitored the teardown of the buildings and the levelling of the land to prepare for sale. Even that undertaking had been cursed, with one worker losing his life in the process.

Josh thinks once we sell the property, my dreadful dreams will stop; I can only hope. Adrienne and I are in regular touch via email and I know she misses me as much as I do her. It's too soon to go back, though.

Walking out to our deck that looks directly at the marina, I'm struck by the vibrancy of the colours: white, bright blue, dark green, vibrant red. The boats wobble back and forth against the fenders on the dock. The sun chair is nice and toasty warm as I sit, extending my bare legs and enjoying the heat of the sun.

"Leah!" yells Josh, causing me to drop the magazine I had propped up on my knees.

"What?" I say, wondering what has happened in the last five minutes to make him so anxious.

He looks stressed out. Plunking down on the other sun chair, he twists his hair and his face scrunches up, lips tight.

"What!" I say again, a little tersely.

"I just got off the phone with Doug, our realtor." By his expression, I'm thinking Doug hasn't presented a good offer on the property.

"Another low ball?" I ask, frowning.

"Way worse than that, Leah. There's something wrong with the earth. The red soil is back, and it covers the entire property now."

I stand up, facing him, prepared for more rotten news.

"Leah, there are ravens."

I step back abruptly, banging the sun chair with the inside of both knees.

"What the hell do you mean, there are ravens?" All at once, I'm back in my car staring at shredded black bird and blood.

"There are hundreds of them and they won't leave, no matter what," says Josh. "Leah, first they killed the guy on the excavator when they demolished the house and now, the other realtor is dead. We have to call the Guardians. We have to go back."

LISA, RAVEN'S WOOD, A YEAR AFTER THE HOUSE WAS DEMOLISHED: A SUPERNATURAL EVENT

Lisa can't stay away from the ground that was once under the plantation-style house called Ravens' Wood. Her parents get so pissed at her when they discover her muddy shoes outside, knowing she's been there again and always at night when they're sleeping. Tonight is no exception. Now that the property is finally clear of those horrible black birds, she's free to search the grounds for something, anything she can take to the town psychic; she's desperate to know what kind of crazy magic was going on there.

She's convinced there's something evil about that place. Slipping her Celtic protection necklace over her head, she knows it's supernatural and scary. Lisa loves horror. Something's going down tonight. She feels it in her blood.

Dressed in her pyjamas with a warm, black hoodie, she steps into black rubber boots. Gently shutting the front door, she heads out for the five-minute walk to the property. She travels lightly, taking only her keys, cellphone and a small flashlight. Tucking her red hair behind her ears, she digs for her phone. She has her best friend Mattias's number ready to go, just in case. Lisa and Mattias have been spying on Ravens' Wood since the big house was taken down. Something's not right with that property.

As Lisa approaches the west side of the land, she sees a small light dancing around the area that used to be the back of the house. Weird. She shoots Mattias a quick text to let him know about the light, then pockets the phone, making sure the volume is off.

She moves slowly now, crouching down, her senses heightened. As she gets closer, she sees what looks to be one person standing on another's shoulder because nothing could be so tall. All of a sudden, the huge thing falls to its knees. Lisa clamps a hand to her mouth to stop from screaming. It's some kind of monster!

From this distance, it's hard to make out detail, but it looks like an old woman with long grey hair and big rubber boots. She's digging around in the dirt and appears to have found what she's been looking for. As the creature brings her flashlight closer to her face, Lisa screams. Diamond-shaped yellow eyes flash around, trying to find the source of the scream.

Lisa bolts into the nearby woods as she hears the voice of the old woman screeching, "Come back, come back! I won't hurt you! We can share a bowl of hot blood!"

Lisa keeps running until she sees the lights on in her house. Her parents are going to kill her, but it's all worth it.

Ammit has carefully combed the earth beneath the carpet that cradled the charred remains of Reginald, Ruby and Helen. Finally! She has found blood in the soil.

She can bring him back.

ACKNOWLEDGEMENTS

I'd like to thank two women who possessed not only a voracious desire to read but for sharing their great love of books with me. Thanks, Mom and Granny.

I'd also like to thank my family and friends for their encouragement, even when my scenes gave them nightmares, and for forgiving me when I smiled at their retelling.

I could not have written this novel without the relentless dedication and patience of my friend and writing coach, Maria Lironi.

I'd also like to thank my beta readers: Sandra Benson, Adrienne Bauder, Clint Montgomery, Lorraine Dame, Dean Mailey, Jason and Lindsay Walsh and Vicky Songphanich. Your input was invaluable.

Thanks to my husband Dean for having to read so many versions as well as keep my wine glass full, my son Shane for listening to me babble on about the next chapter and, to my sweet granddaughter Layla for being the light when I found myself staring down the dark.

And to Zeus, my loyal Jack Russell Terrier, who sat curled at my side as I wrote and never complained. I miss you, little man.

And finally, I'd like to thank Reginald for teaching me that being a little twisted isn't such a bad thing.